Crows in the
Autumn
Sky

Crows in the
Autumn
Sky

Ted Sabine

Library of Congress Control Number:		2011913581
ISBN:	Hardcover	978-1-4653-4562-2
	Softcover	978-1-4653-4561-5
	Ebook	978-1-4653-4563-9

To order additional copies of this book, contact:
Xlibris Corporation
1-888-795-4274
www.Xlibris.com
Orders@Xlibris.com
102469

Acknowledgements

To Paula Sholly and my wife Mogie who read the rough copy of Crows in The Autumn Sky to their elementary school students over the years, insisting that Sammy crow would fly into the hearts of the reading public. For Tamara Saarinen an exstudent of Mogie's who remembers Sam fondly and wants his story told to her children. For Tanya Rux who validated Mogie, Paula and Tamara's opinions, To Loie Davies who did a final editing of the manuscript. Also to the good, and sometimes not so good, people in my past who were the clay from which most of my characters were formed. Including:

Alice

From the wrong side of the tracks
A stack of worn rubber tires in her back yard
Pink geraniums planted in an old bathtub
Next to a beaten-down picket fence.

A faded red dress
Frayed at the hem
Stringy yellow hair tied back
With red yarn

"Get her," they yelled.
She running
And crying
Scabby-kneed, long legged
Like a gangly colt
Her broken-strapped sandals clip-clopping
As she ran.

And me running after
Stepping on her panicked shadow
With a dead bullhead
Which I stuffed down the back of her neck

When I was ten they told me
She was ugly.

Now, in the seventy-fifth year of my life,
I know she was beautiful.

Finally: to Mom and Dad, Kit, Noel and Bob. And, of course, to Sam.

Introduction

It's been said that a journalist searches for truth while a fiction writer creates it. That's why Crows in The Autumn Sky is indeed a fictionalized account of my love affair with Sammy the crow. Sam and his watch-stealing ear-tugging antics really existed. So did many of the other characters, places and events, albeit in different sizes, shapes and moments. But, the vibrant truth of them exists in my memory as it drifts back sixty years. Unburdened by the need to be journalistically correct, the fluttering kite of my memory can dip and soar through the sky, yet dive back to the real world, guided by gentle pulls on a thin string. Thus, I can allow the water in such places as the frog ditch, the Zion Pond and Dead River to be far deeper and more mysterious than they may have been. The taste and aroma of sausages and hotdogs in my dad's store, Sabine Fine Foods, do not merely linger; they surge. And the characters, most of them in composite form, can hulk, stride and scamper like mythic characters out of the past, painted in colors, all fresh and new.

Truth, warm and sunny, prevails over cold, hard fact.

Chapter 1

No one feels spring better than a ten-year-old kid, especially when he's lying in bed in the morning, tasting the sharp, wet smell of skunk cabbage drifting through an open window. And then the rusty police-whistle screech of a blue jay shrills out of the big cottonwood tree in the backyard.

So there I was, eyes shut, breathing in spring. And along with the blue jay's screaming came the screechy chatter of sparrows fighting over potato peelings and bread crusts by the garbage cans out back.

Then it drifted in, clear but far away: *Gronk gronk.* The back of my neck prickled at the sound of Canadian geese honking their way north over the Illinois Dunes. Yes, you sure could tell it was spring.

I yawned, blinked my eyes open, and saw sunlight spreading all warm and buttery through the room, then shimmering around in the ten-gallon aquarium tank on an old apple crate bookshelf standing against the wall. Shiners and sunfish changed colors while scooting through jungly elodea and vallisneria plants. A couple of bullheads butted their noses against the sides and bottom of the tank. I sucked in a deep breath, shut my eyes, and started to count: *Thousand-nine, thousand ten . . .* I was a pearl diver swimming through an underwater cave, and I had to hold my breath for a minute. Otherwise, I'd drown. Hammerheads swam everywhere. Big as torpedoes. Silvery. With railroad-spike teeth.

Twenty-nine, thirty . . . An octopus snagged my leg. One of the bullheads was chasing a shiner around and around.

I whipped out my diver's knife and hacked through an arm-thick tentacle cratered all over with suction cups.

Now a moray eel. A big one, about ten feet long.

Forty-nine, fifty . . . Now I'm banging my head against the pillow. My legs are thrashing and twisting the blankets around, like cookie dough in a bowl.

Fifty-nine, sixty . . . I've made it. But the room is spinning and dark, like maybe I've gone blind from not enough oxygen. But it's just the blankets piled on top of my head. The blue jay keeps screaming outside.

A bacon-and-coffee smell. And the whole house starts trembling as Mom puts on her roller skates and rumbles back and forth while working in the kitchen downstairs.

"Holy Pete! What's next? A trampoline in the living room?" Dad is laughing at Mom about the roller skates. She's always trying to find ways to keep her thighs from getting fat.

Other sounds drift upstairs, comfortable ones a kid likes to hear while coming awake. My little brother, Carson John, is banging on his high chair with a cereal spoon.

I feel my face crinkle into a grin. It's Saturday, and after eating breakfast and taking out the garbage, I'll have the whole day to myself.

Floorboards creak as Dad goes out the back door and down the porch steps. His footsteps crunch down our driveway, then stop. *Plink . . . plink.* Pea gravel peppers my windowpane. "Heave to!" he yells.

"Teddy!" Mom hollers at me as she skates through the living room, then stops at the bottom of the stairs. "Come on. Time to shake a leg."

The blue jay shrieks and flies away as Dad fires up his old '36 Chevrolet. It sputters, grumps, and moans, then sort of lurches backward out of the drive.

Dad is on his way to the grocery store and meat market he owns. It's a plain, folksy place, not like Kroger's or A&P with meat wrapped in cellophane and people wearing uniforms and name tags and grinning at you and saying, "Good morning," even if it isn't a good morning; and they can't remember your name.

At Sabine Fine Foods, if you want a steak cut special, Dad goes inside his big walk-in meat cooler, his breath steaming from the cold air inside. With a little dip of his legs, he hoists a hind quarter of prime steer off a meat hook, lays it across one of his broad shoulders, hauls it out to the chopping block behind the counter, and whacks off a steak exactly the size you want. He weighs it, wraps it in brown paper, then ties it with a piece of string, his fingers skittering so fast you can hardly see them making the knots.

And when Dad hands you the meat package, he sort of cradles it in small delicate hands that look like they belong to a violinist instead of a butcher. And he knows your name too. Maybe he cracks a joke. But if it isn't a nice day, he won't pretend it is.

Dad's store has honest-to-goodness meat smells too, especially with beef bacon smoking in the smokehouse and rings of sausages and strands of hot dogs simmering in the gigantic black kettle in the back room. "That kettle came all the way from Africa," Dad told me and my friend Arvey one day. "It's the kind they boil missionaries in."

When the sausage and hot dogs come dripping out of the kettle, you can cut off a piece of hot, spicy meat and feel the juice swarm into your mouth with each bite. Dad gives samples to all the customers in the store: Old Man Bishop, Si Dreyer, and even Mrs. LaBelle, who slips canned goods into the pockets of her mink coat and stuffs packages of Sun Maid raisins and Lipton tea bags down the front of her dress.

"Look at that old bat." Si Dreyer squints over his glasses at Mrs. LaBelle's reflection in the meat counter display case while Dad plunks a seven-bone pot roast down on his Toledo scale. "Theodore, that old gal is stealing you blind."

Dad grins. "I know. I know."

Meanwhile, Mrs. LaBelle has started to sweat. A one-pound can of Libby's freestone peaches and two cans of Campbell's pork and beans shoved in the pocket of her mink coat make her walk with a starboard list. She is seventy years old, wears a hairpiece, and dyes what is left of her hair carrot red. When she shoplifts, she gets nervous, and squiggles of red hair dye trickle down her cheeks.

Dad nods and winks at Lydia, the cash register lady, who rings up an extra $1.75 on Mrs. LaBelle's bill.

"What the heck, Si," Dad says. "If I have her arrested for shoplifting, I lose a customer, and she goes and steals from somebody else."

Thinking about Mrs. LaBelle and her runny hair dye makes me giggle as I lie in bed. She wears elbow-length black silk gloves with the fingertips worn through. And she has a ratty old fur piece that looks like it just bailed out of a tree, landed on the back of her neck, and is hanging on for dear life with its own tail clamped between its teeth.

Finally, I crawl out from under the teddy bear quilt Grandma Hoover made for me, shivering just a bit when my bare feet spank down on the cold floorboards of our old two-storey house. My bedroom window is fogged up around the edges, and I lick the cold wetness of the windowpane.

"Ummmmm." A cool taste of April melts against my tongue. I lick my name in the fog before flinging the window all the way up.

I suck in another throat and lungful of spring air, then rummage around under my bed. My clothes are wadded and jumbled in with my butterfly net, a couple of baseball bats, and a mess of *Captain Marvel* comic books. It takes a while to get my Montgomery Ward jeans yanked right side out; but I finally get dressed, go to the window again, and crawl out on the ledge. The air sort of rushes at me again, wet and cool and so springy that I let out a Tarzan yell as I jump from the window ledge to the back porch roof. For a while, I pretend I'm a gorilla, snuffing and lumbering around with my knuckles scraping the top of the roof. Then I jump into an elm tree growing next to the porch, shinny down it, and go in the back door.

"Hey, Ma. I can hold my breath two minutes—almost."

"That's nice." Mom skates away from the refrigerator and over to the table. Carson John is jigging up and down in his high chair, and Mom almost trips over the cereal spoon he's thrown on the floor.

"Here, Tarzan. Feed your brother. Okay?" She picks up the spoon, starts to take it to the sink, then shrugs and wipes it off on her red-and-white-checked apron.

You can see Mom is really frazzled when she hands me the spoon and a bowl of Gerber's baby cereal. Her brown hair is jumbled in front of her eyes, and her apron has just come untied. She skates over some Wonderbread toast covered with Welch's grape jelly Carson John has dropped on the floor. Her roller skate wheels leave purple tracks on the blue linoleum as they clunk around and around.

Carson John. What a messy kid. Just getting near him makes a guy feel sticky all over. I like him, though. Here's a kid who hardly ever cries, and you can do funny things with him, like feed him modeling clay and bugs. But you'd think a kid who ate such gaggy stuff would eat real food. Not Carson John. As soon as Mom gave me the spoon, he clamped his mouth shut, puffed up his cheeks, and shook his head back and forth.

"C'mon. There's a bug in it. Open up." I pinched his nose shut so he couldn't breathe and would have to open his mouth. For fun, I started counting, holding my breath too. "Thousand-twenty, thousand-twenty-one . . ."

"Puffoooo." Like a whale breaking surface, Carson John opened up, so I shoveled some cereal inside.

Burrrrrrr. His lips vibrated and spattered baby food all over my face.

"Hey, wudja eat somethin' now. C'mon." Food is everywhere: chocolate custard, jelly, cereal, toast. On the floor, on the high chair, on me, on Carson John. He reminds me of the Lon Chaney horror movie my friend Arvey Hicks and I'd seen last week, the one where someone got too close to some kind of radiation machine, then turned gooey and sort of melted away.

Now it's like two wars going on at the same time. In the living room, our Philco floor model radio, which is about the size of a telephone booth, is blaring news about American Marines and the Japanese on some place called New Guinea fighting hand to hand. Carson John and I are at war too. I'm making gorilla faces at him, and he's scowling back, peeking out from between those jelly-plastered fingers of his.

Mom wasn't looking, so I pretended the spoon was a Roman catapult and snapped a gob of cereal at Carson John. I tried to hit him in the face, right between the eyes. But it blooped up in the air like a gummy mortar round and plopped on top of his head.

Good old Carson John. He giggled, unwound the cereal from his hair, and stuck it in his mouth.

"See. It's num num. Have some more."

I plastered another spoonful behind his ear.

"Hey. Be nice." Mom skated over to the table and used a wet towel to wipe off Carson John's face the way Rich Harrison down at the Deep Rock gas station cleaned the windshield of Dad's car. She made a face at the towel and swatted me with it across the back of the head. It's the kind of swat a mom will give a kid when she's trying to be mad but really can't.

Mom was always doing things like that: swatting me with towels and dishrags or roller-skating in the house or playing kick the can in the backyard. She even helped me build an ant colony once, the kind with glass on both sides, so you could see the ants tunneling through dirt. The day after we set it up, Carson John knocked it over, and the ants swarmed all over him because he had Aunt Jemima's pancake syrup smeared on his hands and face. Mom even let me keep frogs in the house until Aunt Jane sat on one and spilled coffee all over her pink-and-white dress. Most of the time, Mom was the kind of mother a kid like me was lucky to have.

One time, this kid named Gordie Brownlow kept picking on me at school. "Well, we'll see about that," Mom said, her eyes turning glittery and hard. There was a big trunk smelling like mothballs in our hall closet, and from the bottom of it, she pulled two pairs of boxing gloves. They had the words "Lake Forest College Boxing Team, 1915" stenciled on the part you hit people with. "They were your uncle Carson's," she said. "Put them on." Then all at once, we are going at it, right there in the living room—both of us dancing around, Mom snorting hair out of her eyes and almost tripping over a pair of fluffy red slippers she had on.

"Huff huff," she snorted, bonking me on the nose with a quick little punch I found out later is called a left jab. I got mad and frustrated and started crying a little bit. Then I wound up and swung at Mom with what Dad explained later was a left hook.

But Mom danced out of the way, and I clobbered one of her good table lamps instead. Most moms would have shrieked and scolded like the Wicked Witch of the West. But she just laughed and thumped me on the nose again. "'At's it." She was breathing heavy and wiping her nose with the thumb of one boxing glove. "C'mon. Try another one . . . C'mon."

My next left hook would have knocked her "rear end over teakettle," as my grandma Hoover used to say. But I got that big pillowy boxing glove snagged in the drapes and yanked them down instead, along with a bowl of goldfish and another table lamp.

Now there are three goldfish flopping around. Broken glass too. And a table lamp all busted up but still plugged in. "Watch out!" Mom yelled. "We're all going to be electrocuted!" She yanked the lamp cord out of the wall socket and scooped up Carson John who was crawling around in water and broken glass, yelling, "Ishee . . . ishee" and trying to pick the goldfish up.

Next day after school, I went up to old Gordie and looked him right in his squinty green eyes. "Hey, Gordie. Ya better stop pickin' on me 'cause my mom taught me how to fight."

Gordie blinked, then grinned. Not a nice grin. More of a nasty, pulling-wings-off-flies kind of grin. "Oh geez," he moaned. "Don't tell me yer ma taught ya how to fight. Pleeze don't hurt me. Oh, pleeeze." Then he yelled at Donnie Smith, Corky Wilson, and some other friends of his. "Hey, you guys, run fer yer lives. Teddy Sabine's ma just taught him how to fight."

They all bunched around me in a little circle, with Gordie punching my shoulder and yelling, "Puhleeze don't hurt me. Puhleeeez."

I started crying. But I was mad too, about as mad as a bumblebee mixed in with a jar full of red ants. So I cranked up the King Kong left hook that nearly demolished our house the day before. This time, no lamps or drapes, just Gordie's nose. There was this wet, squishy feeling against my fist as I knocked him right on his rump.

"Ufff." He blinked, then started wheezing as if a chunk of Cracker Jack was wedged in his throat. When he got up, I kept squashing his nose with that left jab Mom used on me the day before.

Pretty soon, it was old Gordie doing the crying, with his breath stuttering out in whimpered gasps. His nose began to look like a mashed strawberry, and blood trickled down over his upper lip. Finally, I wound up with another left hook that made a ripe watermelon thump against his ribs. "Wanna quit?" I'm jigging up and down on my toes with the untied laces of my Buster Brown shoes flapping around like mad.

"Yeah." Poor old Gordie was wheezing and all doubled up. Except for where it was leaking blood, his face was fish-belly white.

"Hey, don't quit now. Go ahead an' knock him out." My friend Arvey Hicks had just arrived. A two-pound wad of Tops Bubble Gum in his mouth made his cheeks look like they belonged to a squirrel gathering nuts.

"Nah," I said. Mom had also taught me it wasn't right to hit people when they didn't want to fight.

So Gordie and I quit fighting. But when he figured he was far enough away, he called me a dirty name and yelled, "My big brother's gonna beat ya up!"

"Oh yeah?" I was feeling like Joe Louis, especially after beating up a tough kid like Gordie who had a butch haircut and could do ten chin-ups on the monkey bars at school.

I took off after Gordie, and he lit out for home, his U.S. Keds spanking the sidewalk and the legs of his purple corduroy pants rubbing together with a swishing sandpaper sound. "Yaaa! Git yer tail on outta here, whistle britches," Arvey yelled.

Like I said earlier, most of the time, Mom was the kind of mother a kid like me was lucky to have.

Chapter 2

"Braaaaak!" All at once, it sounded like a squad of Nazi storm troopers had set up a machine gun nest on our back porch. I stopped feeding Carson John, looked through the back door windowpane, and saw Wally Hubble, the kid next door. Wally was a tall, skinny kid. Kind of gawky too, with bony elbows and shoulder blades, big ears, and a long neck about as big around as a baseball bat. This morning, he had on a German army helmet that was so big he had to tilt his head back before he could see anything except his feet.

"Braaaaak!" Old Wally could crank out war noises better than anyone. He did them while riding his bike, reading comics, or doing homework. His mom said he even made war noises sometimes in his sleep.

This morning, Wally had a homemade Tommy gun made out of wood with an old pie pan for a cartridge drum.

"Braaaaack!" His skinny body shook as he opened up on me through the back door. The German army helmet looked like a soup kettle plunked down and vibrating on top of his head.

"Dow dow dow!" I fired back at him with Carson John's cereal spoon, then got up and went to the back door.

Along with the Tommy gun, Wally had a bazooka made out of a cardboard mailing tube. On his belt hung a canteen he carried with him just about all the time. Mostly he kept it full of grape Kool-Aid, and you could see the purple ring it made around his lips each time he took a swig. Even if he was only going half a block from home, Wally lugged enough equipment along to supply a whole panzer division for a couple of weeks. "Hey, Teddy Sabine an' yer flyin' machine, can ya come out an' play?"

"Sure. Soon as I eat. Gotta empty the garbage too."

Wally grinned, showing the chipped tooth he got while pretending he was a Jap sniper, and Arvey Hicks and I blasted him with crab apples, and he fell off the top of Mrs. McFarlan's shed. "Hey, me an' my uncle Floyd are goin' crow huntin'. Can ya come along?"

Crow hunting! With real guns! Not just kid's stuff with wooden guns, crab apples, peashooters, and war shields made out of garbage can lids. Wally's uncle had been talking about a crow hunt for quite a while. "Holy cow," I said.

"I get to use Uncle Floyd's .410. And maybe I can take Sparky along an' teach him how to retrieve." Wally grinned and nodded at his little black-and-white spaniel sniffing around in the backyard.

"Whatcha think? Can ya go?" Wally was eyeing Mom while she poured bacon grease into a tin can. She'd been listening. You could bet on that. It's something all moms can do: be canning tomatoes or rinsing out diapers but still be able to hear you when you're out in the backyard rolling cigarettes out of toilet paper and ground up oak leaves or setting anthills on fire with kitchen matches and a squirt can of sewing machine oil.

"Can I, Ma? Huh?"

Mom put down her bacon grease can and gave me that dangerous, sideways look that a mom will give a kid sometimes.

"Can you what?"

I groaned. A stomachache kind of groan. "Can you what?" didn't really mean "Can you what?" It really meant that the idea of my going crow hunting was such a pile of garbage there was no sense in talking about it at all.

But I had one of those squirmy feelings a kid gets every once in a while. Like when he wants to go to a six-hour monster movie matinee or stay up late or skip school because the weather is just too fine to be cooped up for a zillion hours making squiggly letters in a penmanship workbook.

"Aw, c'mon, Ma. Can't I go?"

"Go where?"

"Aw, you know. Crow huntin' with Wally and his uncle Floyd."

"Go where with who?" Mom wadded up her dish towel and dropped it on the countertop. It was as if her voice had put on a pair of army boots and was stomping around the room.

Wally wiped his nose on the sleeve of his red-and-white mackinaw and stepped back from the open door.

I sucked in a deep breath. "Go crow huntin' with Wally and his uncle Floyd."

You can bet this was "Can you what?" stretched out as far as a ten-year-old kid could make it go.

"Go crow hunting with Wally and his uncle Floyd!"

There it was—the war whoop of an outraged mom. Out in the backyard, Sparky had just lifted his leg against one of Mom's clothesline poles. When he heard her voice, he let out a little yelp, put his leg down where he figured it belonged, and slunk on home.

"Aw, Ma. Geee."

"No. You may not go crow hunting with Wally and his uncle Floyd."

"C'mon, Ma. I ain't gonna shoot no gun. I just wanna go along and watch."

"That makes no difference. You're not going, and that's that." She scooped up Carson John and started digging gobs of cereal out of his hair.

"My uncle Floyd's real careful around guns," Wally squeaked.

Mom put Carson John back in his high chair and shoved a toy fire truck into his hands. "I know your uncle Floyd is careful around guns. It's just that—"

"And we ain't gonna stick any shells in the guns until just before we shoot."

"Well . . ." Mom picked up her cup of Maxwell House coffee, frowned over the top of it at Wally, then took another sip. She liked Wally a lot but was suspicious of him too. For example, there was the time last Halloween when he pretended he was the headless horseman and threw a jack-o'-lantern against the side of our house. Only it crashed through the dining room window instead.

"Gee, Ma. C'mon."

Mom leaned against the counter, sipping coffee and looking out the kitchen window while Wally and I sort of itched and danced around while standing in one place. "Well," she said after a while, "let me call Dad."

Wally and I started punching each other on the shoulder while Mom went in the living room, turned off the invasion of Hollandia, and picked up the phone. I was almost sure to go. "Let me call Dad" was Mom's way of changing her mind without letting on she'd changed her mind.

"Uncle Floyd's gonna let me shoot his .410," Wally said again.

I wished I had a gun to take along too. Only I pretended I didn't care about an old .410 while talking about taking my slingshot and a bag of marbles along.

Wally gave me a disgusted look, like I had mayonnaise for brains. The German army helmet wobbled like crazy as he shook his head. "Jeeeez. Ya can't use no slingshot to kill a crow."

"Can too."

"Cannot."

"Can too. There's this guy I read about in *Popular Mechanics* that kills rabbits and pheasants that way."

"That's different. He's a grown-up, and he uses big old ball bearings and special gum rubber straps and stuff like that." Wally tossed me another disgusted look and wiped his nose on his sleeve again.

Mom was back in the kitchen now. "Dad says it's okay."

"Holy cow!"

"Golleeee." Wally punched me on the shoulder again, then took off before I could punch him back. We're gonna be leavin' in about an hour," he yelled. Sparrows and blue jays scattered as he ran through our back gate.

Wow! A crow shoot! Hunting with real guns! I was so excited I could hardly eat my bacon and eggs. "Badoom . . . Badoom." Maybe we'd see a bobcat or a fox. Maybe even a wolf. "Badoom . . . Badoom."

"Stop blowing bubbles in your milk." Mom screwed her face into a worried frown as she used her dish towel to swat me on the back of the head again. Carson John had pulled his Pluto T-shirt up and was stuffing baby cereal in his belly button. She swatted him too.

Chapter 3

A couple of hours later, Wally and I and Uncle Floyd were standing in a blind set up in a grove of trees next to a field of plowed-up corn stubble. Sparky hadn't come along. After sniffing the barrel of Uncle Floyd's twelve-gauge, he crawled under Wally's back porch. Wally crawled in after him, but Sparky howled, then piddled all over Wally when he tried to haul him out. Wally called him a dumb mutt and said he was too stupid to learn about guns.

"Well," Uncle Floyd was saying, "you kids ready to shoot a couple dozen crows?"

"You bet!" Old Wally's eyes were bugged out so far you could have knocked them off with a stick. He was sort of hefting and stroking the .410 Uncle Floyd had given him to carry along.

I didn't say a word. Wally's uncle was a deputy sheriff, and I was a little scared of a guy who roared around in a cop car shooting at robbers and rumrunners and guys like that.

"Well, let's see." Uncle Floyd took off his red hunter's cap and wiped his forehead with his sleeve. He had on an olive colored jacket, the kind army guys wear. His hair was dark and curly, like a shag rug. He had big hands and long fingers that he kept running through his hair.

Anyway, Uncle Floyd reached inside a gunny sack and pulled out this ratty old stuffed owl that looked like it had only about half its feathers left. "Best crow bait in the world."

No kidding. I wanted to laugh. But I kept my trap shut while Uncle Floyd left the blind and fastened the owl on top of a fence post not far away. How an owl that ratty looking was going to fool anything as smart as a crow was more than I could figure out.

Uncle Floyd came back and clicked some shells into the twelve-gauge and the .410. "Okay. Let's be quiet and sit tight."

I stood as still as I could, but pretty soon, an itch started spidering up and down the middle of my back. Then I got a tickle in my throat and had to cough so bad it was like I was going to explode.

Anyway, I shut my eyes and put my hands over my face while pretending to be swimming underwater again. It's funny how you can hear so many different things when your eyes are shut. Like a train whistle moaning along the edge of the Illinois Dunes. Or a killdeer out in the corn stubble whimpering its worried, trembling call. Then I got to thinking what it would be like to be blind and have to use all your other senses instead of your eyes. It might be fun for a while, knowing I was in Dad's meat market because of the sausage and smoked ham smells. Or knowing it was a late spring day by smelling lilac blossoms in the backyard.

Then I clamped my hands over my ears and heard my heart thumping inside my head.

Soon I got scared about having my eyes shut too long because maybe a guy might open them and really be blind. So I opened my eyes and started looking at an old farmhouse on the other side of the field. Next to it sat a busted-up John Deere tractor and an old junky Model A. I got out my slingshot and aimed it at them, pretending to zero a bazooka in on some German tiger tanks. "Whoomp." Forgetting myself, I made a bazooka noise.

"Shh." Wally stuck a bony elbow in my ribs.

Feeling stupid, I looked down at the ground for a few minutes, then hung the slingshot around my neck and started watching Uncle Floyd's eyes slide back and forth across the field. Those eyes of his were light colored, kind of grayish green, soft, but a little scary; and they got me thinking about all the guys Wally told me Uncle Floyd had shot. Bank robbers, rumrunners, and even a whole bunch of Nazis before he got wounded in the leg and came home from the war.

Uncle Floyd had brought home all kinds of war stuff—like a Nazi flag, the helmet he'd given Wally, and even a pair of field glasses he got off a German general when the Americans landed in North Africa or Sicily. I don't remember exactly where.

Now Uncle Floyd was making a squeaking noise with his lips. I looked up and saw black dots, a dozen at least. Bigger and bigger they got, rushing over the treetops at the far end of the field.

"Get ready." Uncle Floyd stuck a long wooden whistle in his mouth. When he blew on it, you wouldn't believe how much it sounded like a crow.

Well, of course, those black dots we'd seen were crows—a whole flock of them, all strung out and beating like sixty across the field.

"Holy cow." Wally started fumbling like crazy, his fingers getting in each other's way when he tried to cock the hammer on the .410.

"Easy." Uncle Floyd helped him cock the hammer, then sucked a deep breath, and blew on that crow call so hard you could see the spit fly out.

The crows answered, *Caaaaaw caaaaaw*, shrill and stretched way out while swarming in circles above that stuffed owl. Ratty old thing. You'd hardly believe it could fool those crows. But it did. They screeched and dived from every direction at once. Meanwhile, it sounded like Uncle Floyd had that crow call stuck in my ear as he blew it for all he was worth.

All of a sudden, a big crow flapped right over the blind.

"Now."

Whump whump.

It was like someone banging on an oil drum with me inside. Two crows turned summersaults in the sky.

"I got it! I got it!" Wally aimed the .410 again, and his whole body jerked. But the trigger just clicked because he'd forgotten to reload.

I heard a gurgling sound next to me and saw Uncle Floyd laughing through the crow call while aiming his twelve-gauge pump.

Whump whump! Two more crows going limp and tumbling in midair.

Poor old Wally. He dropped a fresh shotgun shell on the ground, then stepped on it while trying to pick it up. "Aw, crud," he swore.

A blood-rushing, tingly feeling made my hands shake as I started shooting marbles at the crows that had turned into a screeching black wheel spinning overhead. I remember swearing under my breath as the marbles zinged close with each shot but didn't hit anything except the blue sky.

Old Uncle Floyd made more spit fly out of the crow call while banging away with his twelve-gauge pump. Explosions whanged and ripped through the trees while blue smoke and a gunpowdery taste hung in the air. You'd think Uncle Floyd would have been as excited as Wally and me. But he wasn't. He just kept blasting away, cawing and reloading like he was shooting at tin cans down at the Twenty-ninth Street dump.

He even stepped out of the blind, grabbed a wounded crow by the legs, swung it around and around, and flung it as high as he could. It tumbled and flapped, the other crows swooping down after it, probably because they thought it was diving after another owl.

I was counting to see how many marbles I had left when one of the crows landed in a chokecherry tree right next to the blind. He was so close I could see his feathers shimmering sort of bluish when the sun hit them just right. Each time he cawed, he bobbed his head and gave his wings a little flit.

I loaded up a yellow cat's eye marble and zinged it glinting through the sun. Thump.

The crow lurched backward, flapping its wings. It caught itself and hung upside down, its wings fluttering and its beak open wide.

My hands shook so much when I shot at the crow again I missed it by a year and a half. Then I let fly a couple more times, cussing as each marble rattled through the branches overhead. About the fifth or sixth time, I heard another thump, and the crow squawked. Came a crashing and bending of branches down through the chokecherry tree.

"I got it! I got it!" Something like electricity tingled my spine. Here I was, a kid who'd never shot anything bigger than a starling—except a rat once at the Twenty-ninth Street dump. Out of the blind I charged, tearing through the underbrush and looking everywhere at once because I knew how fast a wounded bird could flutter out of sight. Then I saw the crow in some brambles trying to squeeze itself small against the ground. I crashed after it, and it started to flop away. Only it got tangled in the brambles and just lay there panting, its skinny tongue hanging out.

The crow couldn't have been more than five feet away, but my hands shook so much I missed my next shot. The second time, I held my breath and aimed like the crow was way up in a tree. I felt strange, kind of haunted, because the crow was watching me with shiny black eyes. Its throat sort of pulsed, as if its heart was beating there. I remember feeling kind of sick when it made little gagging sounds. It jerked as my next to last cat's eye marble slammed into its side.

The crow shivered with its neck straight out along the ground. Sunlight shimmered through the trees, and the crow's eyes glittered like wet stones, shiny and black. Then the funny upside-down eyelids that bird has slid up over its eyes. It curled up, then relaxed with its head under one wing.

"I got it! I got it!" My voice blurted so loud and squawky that it scared me, and I clamped my hands over my mouth. Only there weren't any more crows. Wally and Uncle Floyd had stopped blasting away too. Out in the corn stubble, something kept humping up, then flattening out along the ground.

It was a wounded crow. The wind sighed and rustled the crow's feathers until you could see grayish down underneath. Uncle Floyd walked all big and long-legged into the field, limping just a bit on account of his wounded leg. He picked up the crow, and it screeched and stabbed him with his beak.

"Ouch." Uncle Floyd laughed and grabbed it by the neck, then snapped it the way I'd seen Mom pop the dust out of a rag.

"Jeez," Wally said.

I felt kind of sick again.

There were a few other crows still alive in the field, some flopping around in circles, others lying still and waiting for Uncle Floyd to come by and snap their necks.

When we started home, I decided to take the crow I'd shot and show it to Mom and Dad. At first, I kept skipping around as we walked home along the North Shore railroad tracks that ran through woods and fields and then right past my house. "Barooooom . . . Barooooom!" I yelled, imitating shotgun sounds.

"Dow . . . Dow . . . Dow," Wally yelled back. "Did ya see the way them crows just sort of flew apart?"

"Barooooom . . . Barooooom!" I was carrying the crow in my hands, smoothing out its feathers and trying to make it look like it was alive. But it felt flabby and busted up, and its head kept flopping back and forth.

After a while, I stuck its legs under my belt and let it hang from my waist.

"Wow," said Wally. "Just like an Indian scalp."

"Yeh." But I felt a little queasy with it banging against my leg as we walked along the railroad tracks. And every once in a while, it came loose and flopped down on the white rocks of the railroad bed. Finally, I smoothed its feathers once more, then threw it in the weeds.

"Hey. Wudja do that for?" Wally asked.

"'Cause," I said. "Just because."

"Hey, I'm gonna get it then."

"No! Leave it be," I yelled. "It's mine. It's mine!" My voice was trembling, and it felt like something had wadded up in my throat.

"Well, jeez. Don't have a heart attack, fer crumb sake."

Wally and I didn't say anything to each other the rest of the way home. All you could hear was the big boot sound of Uncle Floyd's footsteps along with the scuffing of our tennis shoes across the white limestone rocks of the railroad bed.

Chapter 4

"C'mon, Ma. I gotta have one. I really do."

"Have what?"

"You know. A BB gun."

"Bee dee gum." Carson John looked up from the floor where he was smashing a piece of Melba toast with his toy fire truck.

"BB gun!" echoed Mom.

"Well, gee. It ain't like a shotgun or a .22."

"No. You do enough damage as it is."

"Aww, c'mon, Ma. Puhleeeez. Huh, Ma, huh?" It was a Saturday afternoon in the middle of summer, and I'd just come back from looking at the new Daisy pump-action BB gun in the window of Simon's Cycle and Hobby Shop. Mr. Simon even let me pick it up and stroke its blue-steel barrel and squint through its adjustable rear sights. Its real maple stock nestled smooth and cool against my cheek while I fingered the genuine imitation gold inlay along the pump mechanism and the trigger guard. With a gun like this, a kid could blast anything from frogs and grasshoppers to ground squirrels and mourning doves. A guy could shoot dents in stop signs and mailboxes and even knock chips out of power line insulators along the North Shore railroad tracks. All for only $12.95. Mr. Simon sure knew what he was doing when he let me fondle that Daisy pump.

"C'mon, Ma." My voice took on a kind of insect-sounding whine.

"No!"

"Awwwww."

"I said *no!*"

"Crud." I stuck my tongue out at Carson John, who giggled and whacked me on the ankle with his toy fire truck, which was made out of cast iron and weighed as much as a bowling ball. I thought of taking the fire truck away from Carson John and making him cry. But Mom wiped her hands on her apron and reached for a broom. I shagged out the back door.

"Crud." I started to slam the door but changed my mind, then jumped over the porch railing instead of going down the back steps.

"Sheeeeooooot." I scuffed my feet, kicking up clouds of dandelion fluff as I stomped across the yard. Flopping down on my belly, I scooted under the back fence and came up in the weed lot next door.

My slingshot was in my back pocket, so I took it out and bounced a rock off Mrs. McFarlan's storage shed that stood like a stubby tower of Pisa in one corner of the vacant lot. Well, if that was the way Mom was going to be about it, who needed a stupid BB gun? If a guy had to, he could hunt with slingshots, spears, a bow and arrow, and even rocks and clubs. Me, I'd be like the cavemen in one of my library books and roast bloody mammoth meat on a stick.

Another rock from my slingshot bounced off the shed. In my imagination, a woolly mammoth went *Breeeek!* and shook the ground as it keeled over dead.

"Yessiree." I flopped down in a patch of itchy ragweed and decided that when I was older, I'd run off and live with wild animals, like maybe gorillas and wolves. But first, I had to live in the weed lot for a while, hunting grasshoppers and mice to get in practice for the really big animals I'd hunt later on.

The more I thought about it, the more I made up my mind. I was going to be like the wild boy found running around with wolves over in China or India or someplace like that. This magazine article said they found him running on all fours, galloping so fast that the guys who caught him had to use horses to chase him down.

Now that would be fun—galloping on all fours. And if you got good at it, you could catch rabbits and chickens, maybe even sheep. Anyway, I spent about an hour that day with my head down and my butt end bobbing in the air, gallumphing back and forth with ragweed and goldenrod whapping against my ears and face. Grasshoppers and katydids buzzed off through clouds of pollen I kept stirring up.

Soon I started to sneeze. My hands hurt too, getting stabbed full of thistles and weed slivers until some of the skin was wearing off. I flopped on my stomach and licked my hands the way I'd seen lions lick their paws when Mom and Dad took me to the Racine Zoo. Then I got hungry, so I took off my T-shirt and swatted a big yellow-winged grasshopper off a goldenrod stem. I'd read about natives in Africa eating big locusts, so I figured I could eat one too if I was hungry enough. But just when I got around to taking a bite out of the one I'd caught, it spit tobacco juice all over my fingers. I nearly threw up and had to let the grasshopper go buzzing off through the weeds.

Still flopped on my belly, I heard someone giggling and saw Alice Croft and Shirley Baldini ambling down Galilee Street past my house. I crawled through the weeds and hid behind some dead branches piled next to the street.

Fat old Shirley and skinny Alice Croft—they dawdled right by me without knowing I was there. They were munching on licorice rope and giggling while bumping each other with their hips. Old Shirley, she was so hippo-fat she knocked poor Alice about a hundred feet each time they bumped hips. Their lips and tongues were black and sticky looking from the licorice rope.

It's fun to watch people who don't know they're being watched. Of course, Mom would have bawled me out for sneaking around and spying on people. But it was only Shirley and Alice, so I didn't care. When they passed by my hideout, I hunched down and growled, wolf-boy-style, deep in my throat.

Alice and Shirley crossed the street, disappeared over the railroad embankment, and a little later, I saw the tops of their heads bobbing up and down as they crossed the tracks. Shirley wore a red babushka, and Alice had her hair tied together in stringy braids. They giggled and threw white rocks from off the railroad bed at the green station house where people waited to catch the North Shore train.

I stood up and yelled, "Ya got a wing like a chicken," then scrunched down in the weeds again. Nobody looks sillier than a girl trying to throw rocks.

Shirley and Alice must not have heard me because they never turned around. They just went inside the station house.

Stupid girls. You didn't need to see them to figure out what they were doing. Probably smoking cigarettes and writing dirty words like "womb" or "uterus" all over the wall of the station house. I'd watched them once last fall while hiding in old Mr. Gushowski's grape vineyard on the other side of the tracks. Shirley had a cigar that time and kept coughing and waving smoke away with her hand.

I remember telling Arvey about Alice and Shirley fooling around in the station house, and he said I should have crawled under the platform and peeked through the cracks to see their underpants.

"Shoot," I said. "Why the heck would a guy want to crawl around under a dirty old train station just to get a peek at some stupid girl's underpants?"

Arvey chewed on his lower lip before squirting licorice spit between his front teeth. "Crud. Everybody knows ya gotta see what color the underpants a girl's got on every chance ya get."

"But why?"

"Well, shoot." A disgusted look scrunched up across Arvey's freckled face. "Because . . . pink pants stink and white pants bite. That's why."

Arvey was a year older than I, even though we were in the same grade. Also, he had two sisters, so you had to figure he knew all there was worth knowing about girls. But I told him I still didn't understand the importance of knowing whether a girl's underpants stunk or bit.

Arvey thought some more, then said I didn't know diddly about girls, and he sure wasn't going to take the time to explain.

Of course, that all happened before Arvey found a magazine with pictures of naked women playing volleyball at some place called a nudist camp. There were other pictures, too—pictures of some fat ladies wrestling without hardly any clothes on. That magazine was sort of an important document for a couple of kids like Arvey and me. We gawked and pointed and haw-hawed about how flexible those fat ladies were. And what it would be like to get sat on or rolled on if a guy was in the middle of a wrestling match like that.

Anyway, we got scared when Arvey's mom almost caught us studying the magazine, so we shoved it down the hollow handlebars of his Schwinn Roadmaster bike. A couple of days later, after we got over being scared, we worked like crazy trying to pry the magazine back out with a piece of coat hanger wire. But the magazine got pushed further in and never did come out.

So there I was sitting in the weeds, feeling kind of warmish while thinking about Shirley's underwear, as well as some other stuff—like how to get that magazine out of its hiding place, and also, how it might be fun but kind of scary to wrestle with those ladies who were kind of pretty, even though they were fat. All at once, I noticed a big spider web with a giant yellow-and-black spider inside. The spider looked big enough to eat anything, so I got up and started scouting around for a bumblebee, which is just about the easiest insect to catch when you happen to be near a bunch of hollyhocks. All you do is wait for your bee to crawl down inside the hollyhock flower. Then you close the petals around it, and you've got the job done. I was just getting ready to wrap up a bumblebee when something else moved at the corner of my eye.

It was a tomcat, a big dirty yellow one with orange stripes. The old cat lay bellied out with a grasshopper in his mouth. You could hear a little thumping sound as the grasshopper kept kicking him in the eye. Finally, he shut it and stared at me out of the other one.

My slingshot was in my back pocket, so I reached around real slow and eased it out. Then I hunkered down, feeling around for a pebble, or a cinder, or maybe a little hunk of dirt. I didn't want to get anything big enough or hard enough to hurt the cat—just make it yowl or run up a tree. Something like that.

Pretty soon, I found a cinder chunk, about marble size. Cinder is poor slingshot ammunition because it's not smooth, and when you let fly, it buzzes off in any direction, like shrapnel from a hand grenade. But it's okay to use it up close on dogs and cats because it stings and makes them run as if they had a string of firecrackers tied to their tails.

I put the cinder in my slingshot pouch and started edging around to get a good shot at the old cat's rump. But every time I moved, he moved too, so we stayed nose to nose. What an awful-looking cat. Torn-up ears. Chunks of fur ripped out of his skin. He growled and panted, as if he thought I was going to take his grasshopper away.

"Ssssssst," I hissed. I had my slingshot rubbers pulled back so far they were humming next to my ear. But I couldn't get a good shot at that yellow cat's rump. "Ssssst." I kicked at him a little so as to make him turn and run. He just stayed there, hunched up and staring at me through the weeds.

All at once, I got a good look at his eyes, which were the yellowest, most miserable-looking eyes you ever saw—all runny at the corners, as if he had a bad cold.

Something else about those eyes too. You could look right inside them and imagine all the miseries haunting that old cat. It was probably my imagination, but I felt him asking me not to shoot him because he'd had about all he could stand of people swatting him with sticks and brooms, or flinging rocks and dirt clods to chase him out of backyards and away from garbage cans.

All at once, I felt like a real Neanderthal: hunched shoulders, hairy knuckles, stupid grunts stumbling around in my throat. I mean, there I was, getting ready to shoot some poor old cat that hadn't done anything to me and probably never had a decent home and had to climb down inside raunchy garbage cans to gnaw on old chicken bones and rotten fish heads most of his life. Then I remembered the sound of a cat's eye marble slamming into the crow when it was just sitting there on the ground—and how Uncle Floyd walked around in his big boots snapping the necks of those other crows lying out in the field.

I'm not saying I changed my crummy ways right then and there and that I swore never to shoot living things ever again, but it's easy to shoot something when it's just a dot. When you're close enough to hear something whimper, it's different somehow.

I stuck my slingshot back in my pocket, then eased down on my hands and knees. "Here, kitty-kitty," I said, edging in his direction. Each time I moved, he let me get a couple of feet away before hunching backward through ragweed and goldenrod. He kept chewing on the grasshopper, trying to get it eaten before running away.

"Aw, c'mon. Nice old cat." I kept crawling along and talking soft until the old cat let me reach out and touch his head. After flinching a little, he laid his ragged ears back while I scratched between them and ruffled the fur along the back of his neck.

"See there. It ain't so bad."

Soon the old cat was leaning against me and humping up every time he felt my hand on his back. Then he began that funny little dance that cats do—waltzing around purring and rearing up to give your hand a nudge if you're not petting them often enough.

In another minute, he was in my lap, working his paws up and down and chugging inside like a motor boat.

"Wow," I told him. "You must have had about nine hundred fights." I was always having conversations with animals—cats and dogs and even gophers after I'd dug them out of their holes and was carrying them home in an old pillowcase. Anyway, I took a close look at that cat and saw just about anything you could think of tangled up in his scraggly fur: burrs, weed seeds, and a zillion wiggly bugs. When I pressed my face against him, my eyes watered and I started to sneeze.

After about half an hour, I went home, filled a pie pan with milk and brought it back, spilling some of it crawling under the fence but still having some left. Now I was a wolf boy, lapping milk from the pan with the old cat. Afterward, we hunted grasshoppers in the weeds.

At day's end, I thought about taking the old cat home and asking Mom if I could keep him for a pet. As long as I didn't want a Daisy pump, she'd probably say yes. But then I thought about the fun of sneaking food for him while keeping him in the weed lot as a special pet, a wild one nobody knew about except me. If I took him home he'd get debugged and brushed. No more hungry wildness in his eyes. He'd eat store-bought food and stop hunting for grasshoppers and mice. He'd get fat and tame, and anyone could pick him up. Just another lazy cat. Like lions in the Racine Zoo pacing back and forth. Or like Aunt Jane's twenty-five pound Angora that looked more like a sofa pillow than a cat. When I went home for supper that night, the old cat stayed behind.

Chapter 5

The next day, I named the old cat "Bum." And since he lived in a weed lot, I started calling him the Weed Lot Bum. That same day, the two of us went mouse hunting by turning over a pile of old lumber next to Mrs. McFarlan's shed. Instead of a mouse, we flushed out a little shrew no bigger than my thumb. Shrews can fight. If they were lion-sized, they could eat a whole zoo. That little shrew sprang up and latched on to the Weed Lot Bum's nose. The old cat squalled and snapped his head back and forth until the shrew tore loose, along with a chunk of nose. I wanted to take the shrew home for a pet. But before I could throw my T-shirt over it, the Weed Lot Bum pounced on it and ate it up.

Now in my Technicolor imagination, I was a wolf boy for sure, or sometimes a caveman. And the Weed Lot Bum was a saber-toothed tiger I had for a pet. I even made a couple of spears out of saplings. And a stone club too, made by tying a rock to one end of a stick. It was a pretty good weapon, except the head kept flying off every time I used it to hit anything with.

Aloneness: it allows you to crank up your imagination in funny ways. Like garbage cans in the alley. They were cave bears and mastodons to be sneaked up on and hit with spears and clubs. And the clanging noises they made were death cries echoing back and forth. Or sometimes I'd hunch down in the grass with the Weed Lot Bum and shoot cars with my peashooter as they whizzed by. Spaceships, that's what they were. And how they got mixed up in my imagination with cave bears and mastodons was no concern to me.

Like I said, there was this old shed in the weed lot next my house. Everybody called it Mrs. McFarlan's shed, and Arvey Hicks said it was chock full of gold, but if you tried to break inside, you'd set off about a ton of dynamite and blow yourself to kingdom come. Wally Hubble insisted it was full of dead bodies because old Mrs. McFarlan used to murder people, then hide the corpses in her shed.

But since I was a caveman, I was going to need a cave. And the best way to get one was to tunnel under the shed and maybe get inside. I didn't worry about the stuff that Wally and Arvey told me. They were always grinding out spooky stories like that. I borrowed Mom's garden trowel and commenced digging away. It was easy as pie because the dirt under the shed was soft. Wet and moldy too. Pretty soon, I wormed myself under the shed and found a space between the ground and the floorboards overhead. Just like a real cave, or maybe a tunnel leading to a treasure cave. Maybe even an old mine.

While I was grubbing around, the Weed Lot Bum made a rowering sound, came in, rubbed against me, started to purr, then disappeared. You could hear him rustling around overhead. Somehow he'd managed to crawl inside that old shed.

I shagged on home, got my Boy Scout flashlight, ran back, and scrooched under the shed again. The light wouldn't come on at first—you know how flashlights are—so I had to rattle it and bang it on the ground about a dozen times. But then it flickered on and lit up this spooky, spidery place with half-rotten floorboards that had been tunneled in to by carpenter ants. If you live in Illinois, you probably know about carpenter ants. They're big and black, and if you put one on a red anthill, it will bite the heads off three or four red ant soldiers before they tear it up and drag it away.

Anyway, I gawked around with the flashlight and found a place where the leg of an old chest of drawers stuck down through a couple of broken boards. After getting slivers in my hands, I managed to rip some boards loose and squeeze up inside the shed.

What a place. Just like a haunted house. Or maybe an Egyptian tomb. I saw hats with feather plumes on them, and high button shoes. There were leather-bound books with gold-lettered titles and old, old albums with pictures of people sitting as stiff as fence posts with their hands folded in their laps.

Dust covered everything, and you had to sneeze a million times whenever you picked anything up. Cobwebs dangled from the ceiling like ghost curtains sticking to your hands and face. Dried-up bird wings and piles upon piles of feathers and grasshopper legs covered the floor. Under an old three-legged stool, I saw a long naked tail—probably the remains of a giant rat. The Weed Lot Bum flopped down on the stool, his legs hanging over the edge while he gave himself a bath with his tongue. Maybe the shed had been the rat's den before Bum had come along.

I kept snooping around in that old shed and found even more terrific stuff: a bed pan, some old chairs, a couple of kerosene lamps, and an old Singer sewing machine that you cranked with your hand. Behind an old oak chest stood this thing called a dressmaker's dummy that scared me skinny at first because I thought it was a robber who was going to slit my throat with a knife. There was lots of other stuff, too—all the old, raggedy pieces of an old lady's life that she has got to leave behind when she goes off to an old folk's home.

I started thinking about all kinds of things while scrounging around in that old shed. Like growing old and dying, and stuff like that. I mean, here I was looking at things that really meant a lot to Mrs. McFarlan. Only other people would call it junk. And when she died, they'd probably throw it all away. Then I thought about what it would be like if Mom and Dad and Carson John and I got killed in a train wreck or something like that. People would come into our house to look after our things. And if they went in my room, they'd call most of my things junk: my butterfly net and my stack of *Captain Marvel* comic books. They'd probably take my aquarium and dump out the bullheads and bluegills. My ant colony too. All those poor ants and bullheads and bluegills just dumped on the ground, or maybe flushed down the toilet.

All of a sudden, I wanted to go visit Mrs. McFarlan in the old folk's home and tell her how much I really liked her stuff. And even if I was just a kid, I'd see that no one would just throw it all away. I never did go see her though. I'm always thinking about doing something special or important, but never getting around to doing it. You probably know what I mean.

I also found some old, yellow newspapers inside a trunk and used my flashlight to read about this German guy who wore a helmet like the one Wally had, only it had a funny-looking spike on top. They called him the Kaiser and said he started World War I. It's funny, because you'd think a whole lot of people would want a war before you could have one. But anyway, the paper said the war was the Kaiser's fault, so I guess it had to be true.

Then I found some copies of an even older newspaper printed a long time ago in Zion City, which is the town I live in. The paper was called *The Leaves of Healing*, and it was dated way back in 1902. It had a whole bunch of articles that proved the earth was flat, and that there were no such things as cavemen and dinosaurs, and that the devil had put dinosaur bones in the ground to make people not believe in God and think evil thoughts. Those articles disturbed me a bit. I mean, why couldn't a guy believe in both dinosaurs and God? Of course, you had to believe in God, or else you'd go to hellfire when you died. But a kid like me sure wanted to believe in dinosaurs too. Otherwise, what fun was there to pretending garbage cans were dinosaurs if those dinosaurs never existed in the first place?

Real head-scratchers, that's what those articles were. And there were other articles about the founder of Zion City, a guy named John Alexander Dowie. There were lots of drawings of him dressed up in long flowing robes. And he had a long white beard too, so he looked a lot like a magician, or even the way God might look if he was to come down to earth. According to those articles, Dowie could do the most amazing things, like walk into a whole room full of sick and crippled people, wave his arms, and make them all well. Sure enough, there was a drawing of Dowie standing behind a church pulpit with his arms spread, and beams of light were streaming down, probably from heaven, I guess. And behind him was this big pile of crutches and canes, medicine bottles, wheelchairs, and such. Under the drawing, in big letters were the words "Behold the power of faith."

Without letting on to Mom about being in Mrs. McFarlan's shed, I asked her about Mr. Dowie and about all the miracles he did.

"Well," Mom said, "Dowie was a faith healer who founded the City of Zion about fifty years ago. Supposedly, he could cure people just by a process called 'the laying on of hands.'"

"Wow," I said. "Is that really true?"

"Well. Maybe yes and maybe no. When I was a little girl, I knew a man who said he had been cured of a bad back by Dowie's prayers. But then, there was Dowie's own daughter, Esther. She accidentally set her hair and her clothes on fire using an old-fashioned hair curler that required alcohol and an open flame."

"Wow," I said, thinking about the time Wally and I'd dropped a lighted match into what we thought was an empty can of kerosene.

Mom nodded, as if she'd read my mind. "Esther was so badly burned that Mrs. Dowie wanted to call a doctor. But Dowie refused. Doctors were evil, according to him, and he was sure prayer and the laying on of hands would cure Esther."

"Gosh, Ma. Did it work?"

Mom got a sad look on her face. "No, it didn't. Dowie prayed and prayed. And all of the people in Zion prayed as well. Esther suffered badly, and finally, she died."

"Wow. What happened then?"

"Well. The people of Zion were divided. Some said that Esther died because she used burning alcohol, which was an evil liquid, to help her commit the sin of pride."

"The sin of pride?" I was wondering how alcohol could be evil if you didn't drink it.

"Yes, meaning that Esther was spending too much time thinking of earthly things like wearing pretty dresses and curling her hair using an alcohol flame to heat her curling iron. Instead, she should have been praying and devoting herself to God and the afterlife."

"The afterlife? You mean like heaven, with angels and harps and streets paved with gold?"

Mom smiled. "Something on the order of that."

I didn't say so, but I figured that thinking about angels and harps and golden streets wasn't nearly as exciting as earthly stuff like fishing at the Zion Pond or riding your bike to the Zion Theater for a Saturday matinee. Of course, avoiding earthly, prideful stuff like combing your hair all the time and dressing up in the itchy wool suit that my Grandma Sabine had bought me for my birthday—well, that was okay.

"Anyway," Mom went on. "Other people in Zion blamed Dowie. They agreed that prayer and the laying on of hands was good. But calling upon the aid of doctors would also have been all right with the Lord. They accused Dowie himself of the sin of pride. He was so taken up with his power as a faith healer that he refused the earthly assistance God made available to him as well."

"Yeah," I agreed. "Sort of like Grandma Hoover when she says, 'God helps those who help themselves.'"

"Sure," Mom said. "Or think about the songs you've been singing at school, 'Coming in on a wing and a prayer.'"

"Wow." I was getting excited about the word game Mom and I were playing. "And how about, 'Praise the Lord and pass the ammunition,'" I shouted, marching out of the kitchen, down the porch steps and off to the weed lot again.

Looking back, I could see Mom smiling and shaking her head.

"Praise the Lord and pass the ammunition." I kept on singing while whanging away with my slingshot at Mrs. McFarlan's shed. Now instead of being a woolly mammoth, it had turned into a German tiger tank.

It was so much fun playing in Mrs. McFarlan's shed with the Weed Lot Bum that I went there almost every day. I hid the tunnel opening by piling scraps of lumber against the side of the shed. Nobody could find my hideout, and I could sit in that old shed and read all the old newspapers and think about all kinds of things, like did the Germans have songs about God helping them win the war?

And if so, whose side was God on anyway?

Something else that started me thinking was a picture of Mrs. McFarlan when she was a pretty young woman wearing a long frilly dress with puffy sleeves and having her hair piled on top of her head, sort of like ice cream on top of a cone. She had a graceful long neck, like a bird has, and a kind of sad, wistful smile. What was she thinking about? Earthly thoughts? Or thoughts about heavenly things? And what kind of earthly thoughts would a pretty lady have? Certainly not thoughts about fishing for bullheads, or going to a John Wayne war movie on Saturday afternoon.

The more I looked at that picture, the more wistful I got. Now she was an old, old woman, probably sitting in a rocking chair someplace. But her picture, even though it had yellowed up some, was still beautiful and all. What was it going to be like to get old? And suppose you never looked in a mirror, ever. So then would you maybe not get old? So then you could go around doing youngish things like climbing trees, and then maybe the world around you would always stay the same. And you wouldn't have to be afraid of dying and all. And then lying in a coffin, all waxy and cold, and maybe wearing an itchy wool suit. Kind of stupid thoughts, they were. But I couldn't help myself.

While I was doing what Mom called "wrestling with the universe," the Weed Lot Bum sat on my lap and purred. Or maybe rubbed against me and meowed in that rusty old voice of his. And no one knew of my secret place, not even Mom. But she did wonder why all the spare flashlight batteries in the house began to disappear.

Chapter 6

Rain—a real Midwestern, gully-washer storm with thunder and lightning, along with hailstones the size of mothballs hammering out of the sky. It was about three days before Mom would let me out of doors. Right away, I sloshed over to the vacant lot, wet weeds soaking me all down the front when I crawled under the fence. Mud and dirt caked my wet clothes when I wormed under the shed. Mom would have a cow about my getting so dirty, but it was too late anyhow. Once you're already dirty, you might as well go whole hog.

"Here, Bum. Here, kitty." My flashlight beam made bat-winged shadows slide and jerk as I scooted down the tunnel on my back. A moaning sound made me stop.

"Bum?" I swung the light back and forth. "Here, kitty-kitty. C'mon."

Something hunched itself up in the dark. It was the old cat.

"Bum?" His eyes shone big and yellow—on fire inside his head. He yowled, hunching away as if the light cut into his skin. All doubled up, he hardly looked like the Weed Lot Bum.

"Oh jeez," I groaned, crawling after him through that awful, moldy-smelling dirt. He hissed and yowled and backed away, panting, his tongue hanging out like he hadn't had water for days and days.

I reached out and grabbed the scruff of his neck, figuring he was going to scratch me for sure. But I didn't care.

Instead, he dug his feet in the dirt while trying to pull further under the shed. Then he went limp, screeching like he was broken up with pieces of sharp glass inside. I was crying and soothing him, saying, "Nice kitty. It's okay," while dragging him through the dirt and hauling him from under the shed. His bones rubbed hard and skinny against my face as I stumbled bawling down the alley and through the back gate.

Our screen door banged open, and Mom flew down the back steps. She'd spilled coffee all over her red-and-white apron, and her brown hair flew in front of her eyes. She had the same tight-jawed look about her I'd seen when

I made a parachute out of an old bed sheet and gashed my knee open when I jumped off the roof of the green station house.

Mom ran down the sidewalk, flinging her arms around me and almost crying herself when she saw how Bum and I were smeared with a kind of horrible brown stuff leaking out of the old cat's behind. "Well, look what the cat's dragged in." She made herself smile as she petted the old cat. "Did he get hit by a car?"

"Ahh ahh ahhh . . ." I was bawling so hard I couldn't talk, so Mom whipped off her apron and wrapped it around the Weed Lot Bum.

"Well, never mind." Mom sort of put her arms around the both of us at the same time and steered us into the house.

I've got just about the best mom in the world. Not a word about where the cat might have come from, or about all the germs he'd bring into the house. Not even a word about how much we both stunk. She got a big cardboard box out of the pantry and set the old cat gently inside. With the hem of her yellow dress, she dug tears and dirt and other goop out of my eyes. "Go on upstairs now and take a bath. I'll heat up some warm milk."

A saw-toothed ache sort of rasped at my insides. And the putrid brown smears on me smelled so bad I almost threw up, even after I'd scrubbed as hard as I could and put on clean clothes. I remember wondering if that was what people smelled like when they were going to die.

Mom was on the phone as I got dressed, and then she called upstairs. "Dad's coming to take us all to the vet. Your cat's going to be all right." She tried to make her voice sound cheerful. "Just you wait and see."

When I got back to the kitchen, the Weed Lot Bum was out of his box and hunched over a bowl of warm milk. He didn't drink. His fiery eyes just stared at the milk.

Mom dipped her finger in the milk and held it to his nose. "Nice kitty. Come on." But he only sniffed at it, then stared way off somewhere, like he was looking through the wall and into the weed lot where we'd hunted grasshoppers and mice.

"He's gonna die, Ma. He's gonna die." I started sobbing again. Pets of mine had died before. But that was when I was little and hadn't really understood what it meant when you were dead. I petted Bum, and his eyes came back from the far off place they'd been. They were burning and kind of hollow, sort of staring down through a tunnel of pain.

"Now now," Mom insisted. "He's going to get well. It's really true, you know, that cats have nine lives." Mom was bustling around in the kitchen, washing dishes that were already clean, then wiping the counter off, even though she'd already done it half a dozen times. Her voice rang high and trembling, the way a mom's voice gets when she's worried but wants you to think everything's okay.

My old cat was going to die. I knew it for sure. Carson John knew it too, even though he was just a little kid. You could hear him whimpering and snuffing under the table, and every once in a while, he'd croon this little song that he kept time to by banging his head against the wall. He wouldn't even look at the old cat.

Pretty soon, Bum jumped up on the counter and hunched down inside the kitchen sink. He was panting, so we gave him water. But he just stared at it the way he'd stared at the milk.

"Come on, kitty. Please try," Mom coaxed. But it didn't do any good. I even grabbed his hard, scabby head and pushed it down. But he just took a few licks before shutting his eyes. It was awful—him just staring at the water, then shutting his eyes and making little ripples in it when he breathed.

Then Dad hurried into the house, and we put Bum in the box Mom had fixed for him. Dad was in such a hurry he still had his meat cutter's apron on, and it kept coming untied and getting in his way. He had on his old fedora hat too, the one he wore around the meat market to keep his bald head warm when he had to go in and out of the meat cooler all the time.

"Good Lord. You're a dandy sight." Mom grinned. "When that hat of yours wears out, I'm going to buy you a toupee."

"Now now, Fern." Dad was grinning too, even though he looked kind of sad. "A guy's got to keep his head warm so as not to catch cold." I had the Weed Lot Bum in his cardboard box, and Dad squeezed my shoulder as he opened the car door so I could get in the front seat.

"Warm my foot. You don't want all those pretty lady customers to know you're getting bald." Mom gave me a wink.

"Giddy bawd," Carson John said.

Dad kissed Mom on the back of her neck—the place he called her kissing spot. Then he helped her and Carson John get in the back. Even though there was lots of room, Carson John climbed on Mom's lap, bounced up and down and made car engine sounds. Goofy kid. If we were going to a funeral, he'd make car engine sounds.

Soon we were racing down Sheridan Road toward Waukegan with billboards and telephone poles swishing by, and Lake Michigan spread out all blue and peaceful on the far side of the dunes. It was a funny thing. About the weather, I mean. Here it was, after three days of rain, such a beautiful day. Only this really monstrous event was swallowing Bum and me. Like maybe God just didn't care. You know—with the sun shining and the lake so blue, mixing in with the sky, and the dunes so white and clean.

We got to the vet's office and sat next to a skinny lady with a little white dust mop of a dog whining and trembling on her lap. Then we went in this room that had a smooth, metal table the Weed Lot Bum slid around on as he tried to get away. He yowled and started oozing more of that putrid brown stuff when the doctor grabbed the scruff of his neck and shoved a thermometer up his rear end.

Then it was as if the world slowed down until it turned into a big rusty wheel just grinding away while I held Bum and the doctor took his temperature and squeezed him gently underneath. Sick, gurgling sounds poured out of him, along with more oozy brown stuff.

"Poison," the doctor said. He shook his head. "Probably rat poison of some kind. And it looks pretty bad." He had big rough-looking hands. But he was gentle, and he kept petting the old cat.

"Is there anything you can do?" Dad squeezed my shoulders as he spoke.

"I'm sorry." The doctor went to a metal sink and washed his hands. "The poor old guy is so dehydrated there's no way I can keep him alive." Then he looked at me. "The best thing we can do is to put your kitty to sleep."

Now I was crying so hard my stomach hurt. "I'm sorry. I'm sorry," I said to Bum. I hugged him and pressed my face against his scraggly fur that smelled like dirt and weeds. Bum purred a little, even while gasping for breath.

Then Bum got taken away, his scared, yellow eyes staring at me over the edge of his cardboard box. When the back door to the examining room swung open, you could see a lot of cages with cats and dogs inside. The dogs started barking, and their throats sounded full of gravel and worn-out, like they'd been barking for days. The door closed, and the barking sounded far off.

Dad and I turned away and went outside. Mom had stayed in the car with Carson John, but she came in the office and hugged me and ruffled my hair while Dad signed some papers and paid the bill.

We went outside. I got in the backseat, and Mom got in the backseat too. She put Carson John in the front seat with Dad. And when Dad started driving, Carson John went, "Rummmmmmm rummmmmmm," and bounced up and down while hanging on to the top of the seat. Every time he bounced up, I could see his round, pudgy face appear and disappear over the top of the seat. We'd left for the vet in such a hurry that Mom forgot to wipe Carson John's face, so he had Skippy's Peanut Butter smudges at the corners of his mouth. He kept grinning at me with that peanut-buttery face of his, like he was trying to cheer me up because he knew how bad I felt.

After we got home, Dad got a wheelbarrow and a shovel out of the basement, trundled out the back gate, into the ally, then into the vacant lot. I got a shovel too and helped him dig up some dirt from one corner of the lot, then haul it to the shed and fill the hole that went underneath.

After Dad and I filled the hole in, I started beating the dirt down with my shovel as hard as I could. The wet, raspy sound of my own breathing was loud and fierce in my ears. And I swung the shovel so hard the force of it slamming on the ground jarred up through my wrists and arms and all through my whole body, almost. The tears just wouldn't stop coming, and everything I saw was silvery and trembling each time the shovel swung down against the dirt.

I didn't feel much like playing in the weed lot for quite a while after that.

Chapter 7

"Wow!"

It was almost a year after the Weed Lot Bum had died. I was down in the woods with my head tilted so far back that the big white oak I was staring at kept spinning around and around.

"Yeah. It sure is high." Arvey Hicks stood beside me, his mouth open so wide you could see the chip in his tooth from when he'd ridden his bike off the bridge to a place we called Turtle Island in the middle of Zion Pond. Old Arvey was a pudgy, freckle-faced kid with messy red hair smeared all over the top of his head. His blue jeans had a big rip out of one knee.

I looked up again, squinting from the sun in my eyes. In my imagination, that tree looked like the big redwoods you see in books. The kind of tree you could drive a car through and all.

"Ya don't gotta do it," Arvey said. "I ain't daring ya to." Good old Arvey. He had all kinds of ways to make you do stuff you didn't want to do. Like sticking your tongue against an electric fence, or riding your bike down the hill and into the frog ditch beside the North Shore Railroad tracks.

"Ya sure there's a crow up there?" I asked.

"Yeah. I seen the mother crow land up there last Saturday. And there was all kinds of funny noises when she sat on the nest." Arvey was bent over, scratching at a scab through the rip in his jeans.

I hugged the big white oak. A whopper for sure, it was as big around as the brine barrels my dad used for aging corned beef in the big walk-in cooler at his meat market.

I stepped back, letting my eyes climb up the big tree. It was over a year since the crow shoot, and I'd given up pestering Mom and Dad for a Daisy pump. Now I wanted a pet crow. And Arvey did, too—a talking crow just like the one living in a cage not far from Elmwood School. If you stood in front of the cage long enough, you'd hear it say, "Hello" and "Poor Joe." It laughed, too—a screechy, little-old-lady kind of laugh, and it caught pieces of tinfoil tossed through the chicken wire sides of its cage. Wally Hubble said Arvey and I were nuts to want pet crows because you had to keep them in cages all the time; otherwise, they'd fly off. But Arvey and I didn't care. We wanted pet crows.

"See. Right there." Arvey backhanded a weed patch of red hair out of his eyes, then pointed up. Sure enough, I saw this big pile of sticks jammed in a fork way near the top of the tree. Something stirred in the stick-pile, like maybe a wing had opened, then closed.

"That's the mother, I bet." Arvey squirted licorice spit, then kicked dirt over it with the toe of his P.F. Flyer tennis shoes. "Like I said, I think I heard the babies inside last time I was here."

"Ya sure?"

"Cross my heart an' hope ta die." Arvey traced a big X across his stomach with his thumb.

I took my slingshot out of my back pocket and dropped it on the ground. Then I took my magnifying glass and my bar magnet and my Captain Midnight decoder ring out of one front pocket and dumped them on the ground. From my other pocket I took twelve cents, a pack of Tootsie Rolls, a mouse skull, some marbles, and half a Babe Ruth candy bar.

"I'll give ya a boost," Arvey volunteered.

Up I went, hunching and pulling while Arvey shoved against my behind. Then I started climbing on my own, hugging the tree and jacking myself higher and higher while bark dug into my bare arms, some of it scuffing off the tree and sifting down inside my pants. Partway up, I stopped and pressed my face against the trunk while hugging it for dear life. My heart pounded. My belly pumped in and out.

"Ya okay?" Arvey's voice sounded like he was a hundred miles away.

I couldn't very well nod my head, and I was breathing too hard to yell back—so I just started climbing again.

By this time, sweat was stinging my eyes, my skin was hot and scratchy, and little chunks of bark kept sticking to the sweaty places on my head and neck.

Finally, I got to a big branch and pulled myself up. Way below me, like part of a toy train set, were the railroad tracks crossing Wadsworth Road. They traced a pair of shiny streaks through green corn and alfalfa, then curved past my house with its red roof and the big cottonwood tree lofting higher than the chimney top. And just about straight below me rustled the tops of some big maples growing down in the ravine where Arvey, Wally, and I'd met up with a skunk earlier that spring. Mom had burnt my clothes, then scrubbed me with a mixture of lemon and tomato juice.

"Whoooooooooeeeeeee!" Old Arvey was waving about nine hundred miles below.

"Ohhh jeez," I groaned. Even though there wasn't much wind blowing, it seemed like that old tree was waving back and forth and creaking as if it was going to break right in half. I waved back at Arvey, then squeezed my eyes shut to chase the dizzy feeling away. When I opened my eyes again and looked up, it seemed like I still had almost halfway to go.

Now I could see the mother crow cocking her head to get a good look down to where I was at. A couple of times, she spread her wings as if she was going to fly off. But she settled down in the nest again.

Now there were more branches to grab while I climbed. And the trunk wasn't so thick anymore, so I could hug it better with my arms and legs. I kept hauling and grunting, stopping every so often to look around and tell myself this was the tallest tree in the whole woods.

Then this monster shadow flapped across the sunlight that was making the sweat glitter like silver in my eyes. *Caw caw caw.* The mother crow swooped so close I heard her wings swish. Her screams echoed inside my head.

Arvey yelled, "Look out!" His slingshot rubbers *thwaped*, and a marble rattled through the branches over my head. With my face pressed against the tree, I waited until the cawing and the black shadow didn't seem so close.

"Whoooooeeeee," Arvey whooped.

Caw caw caw! If there'd been eyes in the back of my head, I bet I'd have seen that monster crow come swooping back down, just like a vulture, or maybe a giant vampire bat. Her floppy shadow flickered, and the wind from her wings cooled the back of my sweaty neck.

All at once, I started horsing around, pretending I was King Kong by grabbing what turned out to be a rotten branch with one hand while leaning back a little so as to beat on my chest with the other. I let out a gorilla yell, a real boomer that echoed all over the woods.

Of course, the rotten branch I was hanging on to broke, and I almost fell. Good thing my legs were wound around the tree trunk because I slid down until another branch wedged itself under my rear end.

"Look out," Arvey yelled.

"Ooooooh." If you've ever come close to falling out of a tree, you know how my stomach felt: light and queasy but heavy at the same time. I let go of the broken branch and heard it rattling and crashing down while I hugged the trunk of that big old white oak.

"Take it easy fer jeez sake." By this time, Arvey was so distant he sounded like someone hollering from inside a well.

About a hundred years later, you could hear that broken branch shatter into a jillion pieces when it hit the ground. From far off somewhere, another crow cawed across the tops of the trees.

Well, it was wet-your-pants time for sure. Why is it that when a guy is showing off, he winds up looking like a spastic moron instead? Anyway, I sucked in a deep breath and started climbing again, not looking up or down or stopping to rest until my head just about bumped the bottom of the nest.

There was a stinky, bird doo-doo smell about the nest as I grabbed one of the branches it was resting on and pulled myself up over the top.

There they were—a bunch of baby crows. Bald-headed, bug-eyed, naked baby crows. They looked more like lizards instead, and they charged right at me too, waddling and bobbing and shoving, their bald heads waggling back and forth on the scrawniest set of necks you'd ever want to see.

Ong ong ong. The one nearest to me opened a giant, baby-bird mouth, and before I knew what was going on, he had me right by the nose. What a putrid smell: dead bugs and moldy leaves. He began thumping his skinny wings against my face.

I let out a yelp and ducked under the nest, the mother crow taking another swipe at me while I wiped my nose on my sleeve. While that was going on, a funny gurgling sound came from overhead as one of the baby crows hoisted its rear end over the edge of the nest. A giant glob of bird dung plopped down and made a grayish white streak on my pants.

"Sheeeeeoooot!" I lunged back over the edge of the nest and grabbed the first warm thing I felt. It was wiggly and naked, with a strange, squishy feeling to it—like the overripe pear I'd hit June Morris with, right in the back of the head. When I lifted it out of the nest and put it on my shoulder, it dug its claws into my T-shirt and screeched in my ear. Then it made a wet, swallowing sound and took part of my ear in its mouth.

You can't believe how fast I bailed out of that old white oak. A baby crow was digesting my ear while its mother dive-bombed my head, and tree bark wore most of the skin off my arms as I went sliding down.

I was up the creek without a paddle, as Dad would have said if he were there. Down I slid, while chunks of skin peeled off my arms and stuck to the tree. All that sliding pulled my T-shirt up over my chest, so the skin started wearing off my belly too.

I really don't remember—but Arvey said later that I yelled and cussed all the way down. I do remember that my blue jeans were frying-pan hot between my legs.

Then the ground jumped up and hit me—one, two, three—on my heels, on my rear end, then right on the flat of my back.

"Woweeeeee!" Old Arvey's freckle-faced grin swam and woozied around overhead while I lay blinking and wheezing like a box turtle tipped over on its back. "Ya okay?" Arvey asked.

"Yeah." I sat up and felt around for all the hot, peeled-off places I could find. Everything started to clear up as my brains jiggled back down to where they belonged.

A loud screeching noise made me look down to where the baby crow was still hooked to my T-shirt. Upside down the way it was, it reminded me of a vampire bat. You know, like in the movies where they suck all the blood out of a lady who has on a long fluttery nightgown and sleepwalks through an old mansion at night.

"I only got one," I told Arvey. "You can have it, though."

Arvey frowned as I unhooked the baby crow and put it on the ground. It sort of looked like a little old man in long underwear as it lurched around, flubbing its scrawny wings and wobbling its head from one side to the next. "Naw. It's okay." Arvey made a face. "I didn't really want one anyhow."

By this time, it seemed like the sky was black and spinning with crows, all swooping and screaming while I peeled off what was left of my T-shirt and wrapped it around the baby crow. Arvey helped me cram all my stuff in my pockets, and then we ran lickety-split through the woods. Both of us kept looking up at the crows and not paying attention to where we were running so that spider webs and branches brushed and snapped at our faces and chests. The raggedy flapping of Arvey's torn pant leg was right next to me too. When the mother crow screamed, it sounded like she was yelling, "Sam! Sam!" My new pet had a name.

Chapter 8

"**W**hat in heaven's name have you got now?" Mom asked when Arvey and I thundered, whooping and sweating, up the back steps and into the house. She was poking Gerber's vanilla custard into Carson John's mouth while he jigged up and down in his high chair.

"Ut oo dot mow?" said Carson John.

"His name is Sam." I pulled the folds of my T-shirt back.

"Not in the kitchen." Mom was fairly courageous, as far as ladies go. But she picked Carson John up and backed off. I guess she still remembered the time I caught a possum and brought it home. It nipped her on the ankle, then climbed the drapes and wrapped its tail around the curtain rod. Another time, Arvey and I'd caught a woodchuck, stuffed it in an old suitcase, and left it in the hall closet. We'd meant to take it back down in the woods and turn it loose before Mom came home. But we forgot.

So now Mom is protecting Carson with one arm and pointing to the door with the other. "Out! Right now! Out!"

"Wait," I said. "It ain't a big animal or a frog or anything slimy like that. It's a baby crow."

Mom edged forward, then backed off again. "That? That's a baby crow?"

"Sure. I think so, anyway." I reached out with my finger and gave Sam a poke.

"Got it out of a crow's nest," Arvey explained.

Mom wiped Carson John's face with a wet rag and stuck a piece of Wonder Bread toast into his hand. Then she bent over, sort of frowning and suspicious, and examined Sam. "Maybe it's something the crows picked up and carried home to eat."

"Chickum . . . Chickum," gurgled Carson John.

Now Sam was thrashing around in my T-shirt, cranking up a whole dictionary of gurgling sounds. Then he backed up, hoisted his hind end in the air, and wiggled it back and forth.

"Oh my god!" Mom had a strong stomach for most things. But what Sam did to her red-and-white-checked tablecloth would have made an ambulance driver pass out.

Wa wa wa! Sam yelled.

"Poo poo!" whooped Carson John.

Well, Sam yelled all the way to the basement. He yelled while I got an old hatbox, crammed it full of toilet paper, and put him inside. He kept right on yelling while Arvey and I stood around trying to figure out what to do next.

"He's hungry, I bet." Arvey scratched the top of Sam's bald head. "What do baby crows eat?"

"Worms and bugs and stuff. Lots of them, I bet. In this book I got, it says baby birds eat two or three times their weight every day."

Meanwhile, Sam began flubbing and wallowing around in his toilet paper nest. He was screaming too, like a baby wanting its bottle or needing its diapers changed.

"Wa-wa! Wa-wa-wa!" Sam's voice followed after us and clawed against our eardrums when we went bug hunting under the scrap lumber next to Mrs. McFarlan's shed.

"Wow!" Arvey kept shaking his head and looking overhead. "I bet he might call his ma all the way down the railroad tracks."

Soon we went back to the basement with a whole army of worms and earwigs and even a centipede wiggling around in a tin can. "Now what?" Arvey shook the can of bugs while frowning at Sam.

"Just drop them in his mouth, I guess." Being careful not to be bitten by the centipede, I grabbed a worm and held it over Sam's mouth.

Came a funny *glubbing* sound. The worm got sucked away like a spaghetti strand.

"Gosh." Forgetting where he was, Arvey squirted licorice spit on the basement floor.

Meanwhile, Sam was screaming and eating worms without stopping to catch his breath. They all disappeared like food scraps flushed down the drain of a sink.

"Holy cow!" Arvey shifted his licorice wad from cheek to cheek. "Ya gonna give him the centipede?"

"Shoot yes. Why not?"

"Well. I dunno. Centipedes are poisonous. Might bite him on the insides or something like that."

"Naw. Sam'll eat it in nothin' flat." I waggled my finger in front of Sam who stretched out his neck and tried to swallow it as if it was a worm. Looked as if I had about the best pet a kid like me could hope to have.

So we went digging around in Dad's toolbox and found a pair of needle-nosed pliers to hold the centipede with.

"Bombs over Tokyo," yelled Arvey as we dropped it in Sam's mouth. Well, anybody who's fooled around with centipedes can tell you how fast they run. This was a big one, too—squiggly and rubbery, with at least nine hundred legs diddling around as it tried to climb out of Sam's mouth.

But Sam started to swallow. *Glub glub.* With each *glub*, the centipede lost ground. After the fifth or sixth gulp, it rolled into a ball and tried to clog up Sam's throat. But my new pet hunched down, then shot his neck straight out in one gigantic *gulp.* The only thing left of the centipede was a little bulge sliding down Sam's neck.

"Jeez," Arvey said. "Let's go get him a bunch of wasps."

Meanwhile, Sam had a thoughtful look, as if he was counting all the bugs sloshing around inside. Then he opened his mouth and let out a noise I was going to hear a lot of for the next few weeks: "Wa-wa-wa-wa-wa!"

Arvey and I must have spent at least another hour or so hunting bugs. We turned over old boards and slapped our hands down on crickets before they hopped away. We got a stick and an old jelly jar and rounded up more centipedes. We took off our T-shirts and swatted grasshoppers before they could buzz off. We trapped bees in hollyhock flowers, squashed them through the petals so they couldn't fly, then dumped them in the jelly jar with the centipedes and other bugs. The bees buzzed around and around on their backs and tried to sting the grasshoppers, the partly mashed crickets, and the centipedes. Sam ate them all, down to the last feeler and leg.

Mom and Carson John came out and gave us a hand. Mom had on a floppy straw sun hat with yellow crepe paper flowers around its crown. She wore rubber gloves for protection against the feeling of worms against her bare skin. Carson John helped catch bugs too. Most of the time, he mashed them so bad with his fire truck that there wasn't much left to dump into the jelly jar.

Finally, Sam started to fill up. You could tell by the gurgling, digesting sounds. And the last worm Arvey dropped in his mouth didn't go down very fast. It just hung out the corner of his mouth and thrashed back and forth.

Arvey and Mom and I looked at each other and grinned. Then Arvey and I went outside and washed our hands with the garden hose. After that, we went back down in the basement and took turns scratching Sam's bald head. His eyes goggled, and wet, gurgling sounds spilled out of his throat.

Mom laughed. "He does look kind of cute."

"Yeah." Arvey and I agreed.

All at once, Sam started to fret, mumbling and gurgling in what seemed like an absentminded conversation with himself—as if maybe he was doing arithmetic and running through the multiplication tables under his breath. Then his tail wiggled up in the air again.

"Oh oh." Mom yanked Carson John away from the box.

"Pooooo pooooo." Carson John laughed and clapped his hands.

Chapter 9

It isn't easy being a mother crow, especially if the mother has to go to school, do homework, and take the garbage out. At night, when the other kids were listening to *The Lone Ranger* or playing kick the can, I'd be lurking on the back porch picking bugs off the screen, or maybe in the garden with a flashlight grubbing for night crawlers on my hands and knees.

Mom helped out, especially when I was at school. Protected by rubber gloves and an old apron, she used a pair of pliers to pick up worms and bugs. Carson John wanted to feed Sam too. But Mom was afraid he'd eat the bugs instead.

All those bugs sure made Sam grow. His feathers sprouted like an unmowed lawn, and in about a week, he was out of his box clumping around on Dad's workbench and then on the basement floor.

Poor Sam. Sometimes he'd get lost in the coal bin, or tangled up in the lawn mower blades. Once, he fell behind the workbench and got trapped in some boxes of old wire and parts of busted radios we had stored away.

"He needs a place to perch," Mom said one day when she heard him screaming and flapping around. "Go bring him upstairs."

"Wow!" Figuring she'd forgotten about the possum on the curtain rod, I ran down to the basement and hauled Sam from the inside of a rolled-up piece of linoleum. When I took him upstairs, Mom had finished spreading the society pages of the *Chicago Tribune* on the tabletop.

"There. Now bring me that chair." Then she gave me the funny wink she'd give a person when she was ready to do something strange, like roller-skate in the house or let my pet snapping turtle swim in the bathtub for a while.

I dragged a chair across the floor, then stood around grinning while Mom put it on the table. "That's so your brother won't get in the mess Sam's going to make," Mom explained.

"Ain't it awful high?" I untangled Sam's claws from my T-shirt and handed him to Mom.

"Don't be silly," she said. "You found him in a tree, not in a gopher hole"

So there was Sam, part of the family now. At first, he wobbled on his perch, gawking his neck and flubbing his stumpy wings up and down. Then he steadied up and looked around, screeching for food every time anyone came by. *Skeeeek!* He yelled, stretching his neck out like the noisemakers you blow at birthday parties and on New Year's Eve.

In the sunlit kitchen, you could see how much Sam's feathers had grown. But they were still clumpy and frazzled, as if he was a kid whose mom had given him one of those awful homemade haircuts a guy gets once in a while.

Sam flopped and squawked on the back of the chair all afternoon. He was still there when Dad came home from work, lugging two big bags of groceries, one in each arm.

Scraaaw. Sam tried to eat a radish leaf hanging over the top of one of the bags.

"Lord love a duck." Dad just stood there gawking at Sam who was imitating one of those pterodactyls you read about in dinosaur books. Then Dad groaned as Sam went to the bathroom on what was about the fifteenth layer of newspaper Mom had put down. He was going to put the groceries on the table, but changed his mind and set them on the drain board next to the sink.

"Hello, Dear." Mom winked at me, then skated over to Dad and kissed him on the cheek. Taking his hat off, she rumpled the hair around his bald spot.

"Chickum . . . Chickum." Carson John toddled over to Dad, grabbed his thumb and led him over to Sam's perch. "Chickum," he said again, laughing and hopping up and down.

Poor Dad. He shook his head, sat at the table as far away as he could from Sam's perch, and grinned stupidly while Mom brought him a cup of coffee and some vanilla cookies on a plate. Pretending to be upset, he couldn't stop grinning, no matter how hard he tried. Every time he ate a cookie or sipped coffee, Sam opened his mouth and let out an insane, witchy-sounding screech.

With every screech, Carson John yelled, "Chickum! Chickum," and jumped in circles next to Dad.

Then Sam went to the bathroom again, and that really fired Carson John's engine up. "Pooooo pooooo!" He spun around, lost his balance and fell on his behind.

Poor Dad. He kept sitting there, hammered into place, rubbing his forehead with his fingertips every now and then. Finally, he gave up and started to laugh. Then he imitated Sam by flinging his mouth open as Mom rumbled by on her roller skates. "Wa . . . wa . . . wa!" He pointed to his mouth and then at the empty cookie plate.

Mom delivered more cookies, and Carson John climbed into Dad's lap. Each time Dad yelled, "Wa . . . wa . . . wa," Carson John dropped a piece of cookie in his mouth.

"Say now"—Mom skated over to where Dad was sitting, made a fancy spin, and sat on his lap too—"why don't we eat outside? The kitchen is such a mess anyway"

"All right," Dad agreed. When Mom got off his lap, he gave her a toy car push and sent her rolling toward the refrigerator.

"Oooooooooeeeeee!" Carson John took off after her, stumbled, fell, then left peanut-butter-and-jelly skid marks as he slid on his hands and face. He lay there blinking, sort of waiting to see how Mom would react. Maybe it would be "Oooooo!" and "Ahhhhh!" and "Let Mommy kiss it where it hurts." If so, he had about a tank- or truckload of tears along with enough yowls and blubbers to turn on the mother instinct of every female creature—cat, dog, or human—in the neighborhood.

But Dad got there first, patted his rump, and set him right side up. "Hey, kiddo," he laughed. "Let's have us a picnic. All right?"

"Pic pic." Carson John took off running again, tripped one more time, and hit his head against the refrigerator door.

While Mom oohed and aahed and smeared Carson John's blubbers and sniffs around with a wet cloth wiped back and forth across his face, Dad and I took Sam's chair off the kitchen table, then carried it outside while he screeched and flapped his wings. Then we picked up the kitchen table and carried it outside too. Carson John had recovered by that time and tried to help by grabbing one of the table legs and toddling along underfoot.

"Atta boy," Dad said.

After Dad, Carson John, and I set the table on the lawn, Mom got out an old tablecloth and some unmatched dishes we hardly ever used.

"Bomb! Drop it, and it'll explode!" A white dish with yellow flowers on it spun toward me from several feet away. I caught it and set it on the table just in time to catch the next one Dad threw. We, Dad and me, set the whole table that way. We dropped just one dish. But it didn't break. "Good thing she was a dud," Dad explained.

Dinner was crisp pork chops, along with mashed potatoes in giant gobs, the kind you can dredge into a saucer shape and make a gravy lake inside. We stuffed ourselves with green beans and a giant salad too.

Sam kept bobbing up and down on the back of his chair, which was placed next to me, since I was his mom. He screeched and went to the bathroom while gobbling bites of pork chop, mashed potato, and green beans I pitched into his mouth.

Dad kept his hat on, and even though Mom teased him about it, he said, "I don't give a rip. Always wanted to wear my hat during a fancy dinner. Now's my chance."

After dinner, Dad tried another funny stunt. Instead of taking the dishes inside, he lugged an old galvanized washtub from the basement, dumped everything in it, along with a ton of American Family Flakes, then turned on the garden hose. "Fire in the ammo locker," he whooped. "Let her rip!" We blasted away at those dishes as if they were on fire, and it wasn't too long before the tub overflowed and spewed water and fizzy soap suds all over the lawn.

Mom swatted Dad on the back of the neck with a wet dishrag and scolded, "Theodore! Stop fooling around."

"Fooooolingownd . . . fooolingownd." Of course, Carson John was in the middle of everything, soaking wet and all plastered with soap. Dad laughed and snapped Mom on the behind with his dish towel and said, "Never mind. Just wait 'till next time. We'll just dump them in the washing machine." By this time, the sun was setting all lopsided on the horizon, and the sky had turned orange and pink. Robins clucked from the tree shadows, and then the nighthawks started in, their voices soft and trembling, a little lonesome too. Just listening to nighthawks can make a person feel sad and happy at the same time. Nighthawks—they'll do that to you every once in a while.

Mom went into the house, brought a blanket outside and wrapped it around Carson John who fell asleep on her lap. Sam nestled down in the hatbox nest we'd made for him and fell asleep too.

Then it darkened, velvety and cool, with greenish yellow fireflies winking on and off above the lawn. June bugs and hawk moths rasped and hummed through the air, and just listening to them made me think about how bugs only lived a little while, then died. I felt really sad about the bugs dying so soon—just little specks of life that they were. And then I got to thinking what it would be like if Mom and Dad got killed in a car wreck or something like that. Then Carson John and I'd have to go to an orphanage and eat porridge and wear old clothes the way they did in this library book I once read. And if you were still hungry and asked for more porridge, a big fat woman and a skinny guy with a tall hat would beat you and lock you up in a dark closet someplace.

Then Dad lit a cigarette, and that made me feel better right away. The tip of Dad's cigarette glowed bright red, faded, glowed bright red again each time he took a puff. When Dad talked, he used his hands a lot. Like a red firefly, the cigarette danced in the night.

We started talking about fireflies, Dad and me. And he told me how he used to make firefly lanterns when he was a kid. I wanted to do that too, so we got my butterfly net, started catching fireflies, and putting them in an empty Skippy peanut butter jar. Soon we had us about two dozen fireflies that lit up the jar with a sort of electric-green glow.

"Hey, look." Dad grabbed my shoulder and pointed to where some bats were swooping back and forth, with their wings making a silky fluttering in the dark. "Let me show you a neat trick," Dad said. I followed him as he picked up the firefly lantern, took it around to the driveway, and set it on the ground.

"Now watch." Dad picked up a bit of pea gravel and tossed it in the air. Right away. I heard a faint fluttering sound and saw a bat swoop overhead. "That old bat thought that pebble was an insect," Dad explained.

It sure was a party fooling those bats. They dived and swooped at those phony bugs the way that flock of crows went after Uncle Floyd's fake owl. Only no bats were being hurt or anything like that. Soon Mom came around to the driveway and laughed when we showed her our trick. "You know," she said, "when I was a little girl, I thought bats would dive at a person and get tangled in their hair."

"Just an old wives' tale." Dad's cigarette tip glowed, and I saw his arm swing up and down as he threw more pea gravel into the cool dark overhead.

"Oh, I know." Mom had me in a playful headlock and was mussing up my hair. "But when I was a little girl, bats frightened me half to death. Maybe that's why it's so important for little girls to become women and have grubby little boys to raise."

"Why is that?" We heard Dad chuckling in the dark.

Mom gave one of my ears a little tug. "Well, the little boys bring home all kinds of wonderful animals. That way they teach their mothers not to be quite so afraid of frogs and snakes, baby crows, and even bats.

"And possums?" interrupted Dad.

"And possums," Mom agreed.

I felt good about the way Mom and Dad were talking, so I hugged Mom and gave her the firefly lantern to hold.

"Magic." She lifted it up to her face.

Sure enough, she looked like a fairy queen, with greenish hair and skin.

Pretty soon, we went back around the house to where Carson John was sleeping with one finger stuck up his nose and a thumb crammed in his mouth. Sam was nestled beside him, tucked down in his toilet paper nest.

"Twins," Dad said.

Carson John woke up crying when we sat down on the porch steps, so Mom picked him up and rocked him back and forth.

"Fash light. Fash light." He reached for the firefly lantern, so I gave it to him, and he giggled and hugged it against his cheek.

Now he was green, like glowing in the dark; and all at once, I decided if Mom and Dad were killed in a car accident, I'd be able to take care of Carson John. What the heck. We could go live at Grandma Hoover's house. And if she died too, we'd live in the woods. With my slingshot, I'd hunt squirrels and other animals to eat. Maybe by that time, I'd have me a Daisy pump.

Getting sleepy, I went inside, got an old patchwork quilt, came out, and rolled up in it on the front porch. Dad's cigarette bobbed and swooped through the night while he explained to Mom and me about bats. How they use something like radar, or maybe sonar to find insects and also to keep from bumping into things like tree branches and other stuff while fluttering through the night. Dad's voice made me feel safe and comfortable as it fingered its way toward us through the dark. So even though I was interested in what he had to say about bats, I started falling asleep. The last thing I remember seeing was a green firefly winking on and off in the night.

Chapter 10

It was the next Saturday afternoon that I took Sam to visit the talking crow that lived in a cage near Elmwood School. I carried Sam in a box, balancing it on my bike handlebars as I rode along. Sam's partly bald head, with his goo-goo eyes and his big cave of a mouth, stuck over the edge of the box. His screechy voice sounded rusty and worn-out. Blue jays scolded overhead and dive-bombed us a couple of times as we rode past Arvey's house and turned down the alley behind Elmwood School.

The talking crow lived in a big cage built between a tool shed and an old garage. When Sam and I got there, it was down on the cage floor pecking at an ear of corn. Sort of gurgling and squawking, it flew up to its perch. "Hello." It tilted its head back and sounded like it was talking and gargling at the same time.

"Hello yourself." I grinned at the old crow as I lifted Sam out of his box and let him perch on my arm. Wobbly-legged, bug-eyed Sam. He sure didn't look like much of a crow. With those clumpy feathers of his sticking out everywhere, he looked like he had a rumpled sweater on.

The talking crow flew over to the side of the cage where Sam and I stood and hung on to the wire mesh. Even though he was about ten years old, he looked shiny and new, like a piece of satin in the sun. I had a hard time telling myself that old Sam would ever look that good.

"Hello," I said again, holding Sam out so he and the talking crow could give each other a good look. *Eeeeerrooooozzzzook,"* Sam said, sort of imitating a static-filled radio. He flung his mouth open and stuck his neck through the chicken wire.

You never saw such a look come over a bird's face in all your life. That old crow must have thought Sam was accusing him of being his old man or something, because he let go of the chicken wire and did a back flip down to the ground. Then he fluffed his feathers up and skittered back and forth, screaming loud enough to just about make the wires of his cage hum.

Sam was screaming too. *Waaaaaaaa waaaaa waaaaa!*

By this time, the guy who owned the talking crow came charging like sixty out the back door. "Hey, kid. Git yer butt outta here!" He was red-faced, with a big belly, and he had a greasy undershirt on. I wanted to show the guy how I had a pet crow too. Only he looked so mad I pulled Sam away from the cage and tried to shove him back in his box. Except he got one of his claws hooked on my T-shirt front.

"Go on! Scram outta here!" The guy slammed his screen door shut and reached for a broom leaning against the railing around his back porch.

I managed to get almost all of Sam in his box, except for the part of him hooked to my T-shirt. Then I piled on my rusty old Schwinn bike and shagged off down the alley, weaving all over the place with Sam still snagged on my shirtfront. And when I reached down to pull him loose, he swallowed my little finger halfway down his throat.

"Le'go!"

But old Sam kept swallowing and flapping and started climbing right up the front of my T-shirt with my finger still jammed down his throat. Then we hit a pothole, and that jerked my finger loose. I couldn't keep my bike going straight, so we sideswiped a picket fence and crashed headfirst into a garbage can.

It was like slow motion after that: me sailing through the air, right over the handlebars with my hands out in front of me so as to break my fall and to protect Sam. When we landed on the garbage can, the lid flipped up like a tiddly wink and clanked me on the head. Then I felt myself sliding across the ground on top of a mess of old coffee grounds and eggshells mixed up with something that smelled like week-old potato peelings and rotten fish.

I was hurt just enough to make me mad. "Ding blast it!" I got up, gave the garbage can a kick, then picked Sam up from where he was wallowing and flopping around in what looked like a gob of potato peelings and fish scales pasted together with bacon grease.

By the way Sam screeched and fluttered, you could tell he wasn't hurt much, so I just stuck him on my shoulder and waded through the garbage and picked up my bike.

"You there! Hey!"

I turned around and saw a lady running across her backyard. She had on a floppy, blue robe, and about nine hundred pin curlers jutted like radio knobs out of her head. "You there! You get right down off that bicycle and clean up this mess!"

Mom and Dad had tried to raise me right. When a grown-up told me to do something, I was supposed to do it without giving anyone any sass. But I'd had just about all the yelling at I wanted to take, so I just piled on the old Schwinn and took off.

"You there! Hey!"

"Aw, go soak yer head."

The blue jays were scolding again too. And a flock of starlings and blackbirds screeched from one telephone pole to the next.

I was riding lickety-split, even though my handlebars were twisted just about halfway around. And Sam was squawking and flopping and hanging on to me like a vampire bat. I was scared he might fall off and maybe get run over or tangled in my bicycle spokes. But then something warm started soaking through my T-shirt, and after that, I didn't give a fig about what might happen to that dumb old bird. With my head down and my teeth grinding together, I just kept peddling hard and fast.

And even though I was madder than a sack full of cats, I got to pretending I was a Pony Express rider with a whole tribe of Apaches on my trail. "Dum dum dum dum . . . Dum dum dum dum." They were whooping and beating their drums, and when I slid around the corner at Marshall's grocery store, I almost ran over Mr. Marshall when he stepped outside his front door. He had a water bucket in one hand and a squeegee in the other, and when he jumped out of the way, he slopped water all over his brand-new alligator shoes.

Even though Mr. Marshall and I were good friends, I could tell by the way he was shaking his squeegee I'd best not stop. He ripped off a scorching cuss word too. Nothing as tame as "Ding blast it." That's for sure.

By now, five or six arrows were stuck in my back; and the warm, oozy stuff deposited by Sam had turned to blood. The Apaches were whooping right behind me, so I turned partway around and opened up with my big old peacemaker .44. "Dow dow dow!"

Then I saw the big cottonwood tree in my yard, and behind it was the red roof of my house. Sam kept screaming in my ear, so I pretended he was an Apache ready to bash my head in with a tomahawk. Imagining stuff is really fun. How else can a kid put up with his bike handlebars being twisted halfway around, and everybody is yelling at him while a baby crow is messing down the back of his neck?

Mom had her floppy hat on and was weeding her iris bed when Sam and I rattled down the alley like a junk truck and sideswiped a garbage can as we turned into the back gate. She stood up, and then a kind of tired look drifted across her face as I bailed off the old Schwinn and let it fold up and crash-land beside the back porch.

"Well. Kill the prodigal son. The fatted calf has returned. You want a glass of milk?"

"Naw." I squirmed around, trying to unstick my T-shirt from the middle of my back. "I ain't hungry right now. Really, I ain't"

Chapter 11

About a week later, Mom and Dad invited some friends and relatives over to the house. One of them was a lady named Mrs. Porter who, except for Wonder Woman, was the most gorgeous female I'd ever seen in my life. She was even more beautiful than the female dummies that stood with their wrists and elbows all twisted around in delicate but kind of impossible angles in the window of the Leader Department Store. She had curlicued yellow hair, red lips, and big blue eyes that belonged to one of those fancy dolls that says "Maa maa" and wets its pants when you turn it upside down. Her cheeks and eyebrows looked like they'd been painted on with a brush. Kind of fake, maybe. But gorgeous just the same.

One night, when I had my ear against the register between the bathroom and Mom and Dad's bedroom, I heard Mom giggling and telling Dad to stop talking like that when he said that sleeping with Myra Porter would be like sleeping in a drawer full of wigs, lipstick tubes, perfume bottles, and china plates.

Anyway, Mrs. Porter was sitting there in our living room, sort of gracefully decorating the party while the rest of the grown-ups slouched around laughing and having a good time. Her dress was white with pink flowers on it, and her shoes were bright, shiny red. She wore her hair piled on top of her head so that every time she stood up, she looked like she was about ten feet tall. Every time she moved, all the bracelets she had on tinkled like those wind chimes people hang up on their patios in the summertime.

Mrs. Porter's husband was a carpenter who just dressed like regular folks. I figured he must have loved Mrs. Porter a whole bunch because he was always holding her hand or putting his arm around her waist. Or maybe he had to do that to keep her from tipping over on account of the wobbly high-heeled shoes she always wore.

Mr. Porter was a poker buddy of Dad's. They played penny ante poker with my uncle Norm and uncle Ken, and sometimes they'd give me thirty or forty cents and let me sit in. I was really in the game that night because I'd gone hiking along Lewis Avenue and picked up sixty-five cents worth of Canada Dry ginger ale bottles and turned them in at Marshall's store.

So there we were, playing and cracking jokes in the living room while the ladies drank coffee, gossiped, and did whatever else it is that ladies do. Only Mrs. Porter wasn't joining in. She just sat there with her ankles crossed and a kind of love-goddess smile painted on her face.

That smile of hers was strange, as if she had a little dial in the middle of her back, and when she decided it was time to smile, she'd reach back like she was going to scratch and give it a quarter turn or so. You could rip off a terrific joke, and everybody except Mrs. Porter would be laughing and hooting like a tree full of owls. Then it would dawn on her that something funny had just whizzed by, so she'd give her dial a twist. If the joke was just an ordinary joke, she'd turn her dial to Medium. But if everybody was wheezing, holding their sides and turning red, she'd crank herself up to Medium High.

So there we were—Dad, Mr. Porter, Uncle Ken, Uncle Norm, and me—all laughing and betting while Mrs. Porter had her dial set on Medium Low. I had three aces in a seven-card stud game, so I bet the limit—five cents.

"Well." Uncle Norm frowned at his cards, put them down, lit a cigarette, and stuck it in his ear. "I'll see that and raise you another nickel along with my bottle cap factory in Chicago and my house of ill repute in Kankakee."

Everybody was in. Dad saw the raise and upped it three cents along with his ice cream stand in Nome, Alaska, and his refrigerator dealership at the South Pole.

Meanwhile, Mom and my aunt Jane and aunt Margo were trying to warm Mrs. Porter up with all the latest gossip: how Aunt Jane lost ten pounds in one week, how the mayor's wife used henna rinse on her hair, how Great Aunt Lilly got drunk on her eighty-sixth birthday and flushed her false teeth down the toilet when she threw up. Nothing was working, though. Mrs. Porter just sat there, her back straight and her hands folded on her lap. While Dad was hauling in the pot with a flush, I looked over and saw she had her dial turned down to Low.

All at once, it was as if the whole house was being bombed with gigantic chunks of noise. *Skreeeeeek skreeeeek skreeeeeek!*

Mrs. Porter blinked and unfolded her hands. "What in heaven's name?"

Again: *Yaaaaaaaa yaaaaaa!* Like maybe an insane asylum full of maniacs were trapped in the furnace and yelling up through the pipes.

Dad grinned and tossed me a wink. He had his hat on, and he slid it back on his head. "Sounds like that crazy brother of yours is acting up again."

"Brother?" Mrs. Porter frowned and screwed herself around in her chair so as to get a better look at Dad.

"Family secret," Dad said. "Poor brother Sam. Fell out of an oak tree when he was a little kid."

Skawwwwwww awwwww awwwww! Skreeeeeooook!

"Oh oh." Dad threw down his cards. "He's coming up the basement stairs. Get the mattress out of the closet so we can all pin him to the wall when he busts through the door."

"Oh dear." Mrs. Porter whimpered, tucked her feet up, and grabbed the arms of her chair as if six inches of swamp water had oozed into the living room. She looked a lot older all at once because she'd set her jaw so tight that the muscles stood out on her neck.

"It's not the yelling that bothers me so much," Dad went on. "It's the way he slobbers all over everything and messes his pants."

Eeeeeeyowwwwwooooop!

"It's all right, Myra." Mom came out of the kitchen with dishes of strawberries and shortcake on a tray. "That's Sam, our pet crow."

Mrs. Porter flung Dad a jagged look that could have sawed him in half. Her mouth screwed up into a little O. "In your basement? A pet crow?"

About this time, old Sam let out another screech, so I took off for the basement before Mrs. Porter could turn her dial all the way down to Disgust.

I flicked on the light and found Sam flopping around at the bottom of the basement stairs. What a crow. I teased him for a while by letting him swallow my little finger as far as he could, then pulling it out of his throat. Afterward, I found his bug can and fed him a handful of worms and crickets and partly squashed bumblebees. He screeched for more when they were gone.

I was letting him swallow my finger again when a shadow swept across the top of the stairs. "Bring Sam upstairs!" Mom hollered down. "Mrs. Porter wants to see what he looks like."

I put Sam in his box, then straightened the toilet paper up, fluffing it and turning it so Mrs. Porter might not notice the ripe greenish gray mess underneath. Then we went upstairs, me feeling real proud and Sam goo-gooing and gawking over the sides of his box. Dad was right. He did look kind of slow.

You'll never guess what happened as soon as we got upstairs. Mrs. Porter took one look at Sam, picked up a short in her wiring, and wound up with her dial cranked all the way over to Pure Joy. All her bracelets tinkled as she stood up and reached out for Sam. "Ooooh! What a darling little bird."

She squealed and crooned and made all kinds of baby talk as she scooped Sam up and cuddled him just as if he'd been hatched out of an egg that she herself had laid. "Aw. Id um a wittle cheepy bird?"

Dad and Uncle Norm got all red-faced from doing their best to keep plugged up so as not to laugh. Uncle Ken started wheezing, then got up and headed for the bathroom, saying something about getting a cookie crumb caught in his Sunday throat. It was the first time anyone had ever seen Mrs. Porter's nervous system get out of control.

Gleep. Sam ruffled his feathers, looked at Mrs. Porter, and blinked his googly eyes.

"Awwww." Mrs. Porter clucked and chirped and coochy-cooed and scratched the top of Sam's partly bald head until he rolled his eyes in pure baby-bird joy.

To make a long story short, Mom sent me into the kitchen to get Mrs. Porter a fresh cup of coffee, and when I got back into the living room, I saw something that set my stomach to crawling and made me want to run away from home. Mrs. Porter had Sam perched on her arm and was feeding him sugared strawberries from off the top of her shortcake. Well, if you were to ask anyone who knows anything about birds to draw a picture of a baby crow's insides after it's swallowed fruit of any kind, you'll get a picture of a greased pipe running straight through without a single bend. Worms and bugs go through quick enough, but fruit slides through in about half a minute. Maybe less. And there was good old Sam, "Ong-onging" and swallowing strawberries with his rear end hoisted like a bomb bay door over the center of Mrs. Porter's lap. The coffee cup and the saucer in my hand started to clatter as I drew a picture inside my head of the mess Sam had splattered all over Dad's workbench. Then I imagined that mess decorating the lap of Mrs. Porter's pink-flowered dress. There wasn't a setting on her dial that could match what was going to happen to her in about two heartbeats and a shriek.

I wasn't much of a baseball player when I was ten years old. Ground balls always took lopsided hops. Fly balls disappeared into the sun, or got wind-gusted over my head. But that night, probably because I was so scared, I got really well coordinated all at once and made a move that enshrined me forever in the Sabine Family Hall of Fame. With Mrs. Porter's coffee cup and saucer balanced in one hand, I scooted forward, bent low, the other hand reaching out.

Out of the corner of my eye, I saw sparks fly off the end of the Lucky Strike cigarette tumbling from Uncle Norm's wide open mouth. "*Oh my god!*" Mom shrieked. At the same time something warm and odorsome plopped into the palm of my hand. Joe DiMaggio couldn't have made a better catch.

Chapter 12

"School's out
School's out
Teacher's let
The monkeys out"

June sixth. Out the door of Miss Bird's classroom we charged, then down the stairs and out the doors of good old Elmwood School. "Yaahoo . . . oops." I tripped over the laces of my P. F. Flyers, fell down and tore a hole in the knee of my new corduroys. Arvey helped me up while June Morris danced around teasing, "Lead-foot, lead-foot. Didn't your mother teach you how to tie your shoes?"

"Prune face." Arvey yanked one of June's pig tails one more time—just to last her through the summer, then piled on his bike and did a wheely in the middle of the schoolyard.

"Lard butt." June ran after Arvey and cracked him in the side with a black metal lunch bucket decorated with Wonder Woman stickers on the lid.

"Aaaaa . . . oooo!" Arvey crashed, then sat on the ground, the rear wheel of his green bike still spinning and glinting in the sun. The scab left over from the time he rode his bike into Sharon Park Creek had been knocked off his elbow, so he was trying to stick it back on. His hands were dirty and scratched from the cinder gravel he'd slid across. A bloody knee peeked through the fresh hole in his blue jeans.

"Serves you right." June crossed her eyes and stuck out her tongue. A real, honest-to-goodness weapon, that tongue. Purple and about two feet long.

"Prune face." Arvey kicked the front fender of his bike, so it wouldn't rub against the wheel, then started riding home. I got on my bike, peddling fast to catch up. A warm lilac breeze sort of brushed against my cheek. The sun was warm on the back of my neck.

"What're we gonna do this summer?" Arvey asked while shifting a wad of Tops Bubble gum back and forth from one cheek to the next.

"Oh, jeeez." I laughed and shook my head. Arvey had asked me that same question about fifty times already, maybe because he was all excited about all the plans we'd hatched. First of all, Wally and Arvey and I were going to build a raft and go floating through Dunes Park, into Dead River, then out on to Lake Michigan. Then we planned to sail south, maybe as far as Waukegan, six miles down the coast. Also, we were going to fish at the Zion Pond with a new dough-ball recipe and catch bullheads and giant carp that were so heavy you could barely haul them on to the bank. Besides that, I was going to teach Sam how to fly and how to talk. Then he'd be a better pet than the talking crow belonging to the old grouch who lived next to the school. Anybody could keep a crow in a cage, but mine would fly around loose and come land on my shoulder and talk to me every time I called. But before Sam could fly around loose, he had to learn how to fly. And since I was his mom and dad rolled into one, it was my job to teach him how.

"Ya sure it's gonna work?" Later that afternoon Arvey was scratching his head and squinting suspiciously at the launching tower we'd built for Sam.

"Sure it's gonna work," I said. "Why not?"

"I dunno. Looks kinda rickety to me."

"Aw, it ain't rickety. Look." I climbed up on the folding card table we'd set up on the lawn. Then I started up the stepladder that wobbled on the tabletop. Everything trembled as if I was standing on a pile of Jello, but I grinned and hung on tight. "See," I gulped.

"Okay." Arvey shrugged and squirted licorice spit. "But how come we need a tower anyhow?"

"Cripes, Arv, I already told ya that. We gotta have a high enough place ta throw Sam off so as he can get his wings flapping up an' down."

"Yeah. But we don't need no tower for that. Why don't we just fling him off the porch roof or out yer bedroom window instead?"

"Jeeez," I groaned. Arvey was a good kid. But his imagination was weak. "Ya gotta have a tower," I explained, climbing back down. "Ya just can't go an' fling him out a window or offa roof."

"Why not?" Arvey had big ears, and freckles peppered his face. He ripped another bite off his licorice stick.

"Well, because ya can't. Ya just can't." Poor Arvey. He just couldn't see the sense in anything, even when you spelled it out.

Arvey kept shaking his head as we went up on the back porch. His oversized socks were rolled down and flopped over the tops of his tennis shoes as he walked. "Don't worry," I told him. "It's gonna work."

Mom, Carson John, and Sam were on the back porch. Sam was flapping his wings and screaming at Carson John who was saying, "Car . . . car," while pushing a June bug back and forth across the porch floor.

"Rummmmmm rummmmmmmm. Rummmmmmm rummmmmmmmm."
Carson John had pretty much rubbed the legs off the June bug, so he ran over
it back and forth with his fire truck. Then he gave the June bug to Mom to feed
to Sam, then got another one to play with for a while.

Mom was sitting on the porch steps reading a book titled *Caesar's Gaelic
Wars* that she'd found at a rummage sale. For Mom, the older a book was, the
better she liked it. If it had a musty smell, a moldy cover, and yellow pages with
skittery little bugs hiding in them, she'd buy it for sure.

"Be careful," she said when I took Sam off the back of his chair. Sunlight
glinted off her glasses as she sighed and shook her head.

Urk urk urk. As soon as I picked Sam up and set him on my arm, he edged
his way up to my shoulder and tugged on my ear with his beak. He'd sprouted
lots of new feathers, and his eyes turned from blue to shiny black. He saw
Arvey tearing another chaw off his licorice stick and begged for a bite.

"No sir," I said. "No food for you. Not until ya fly."

Muttering what sounded like swear words mixed in with radio static, Sam
pecked at my fingers when I took him off my shoulder and set him back on
my arm.

"Yer right," Arvey folded the rest of his licorice stick and stuck it in his
pants pocket along with the pelt off a field mouse he'd skinned the day before.
"One more bite of food in him and he'll have too much ballast to fly."

I was all prickled up with excitement by now because Sam had grown a
lot in just two weeks. When he sat on my arm with his wings spread out, he
looked like one of those falcons that Arab sheiks used for hunting and stuff
like that.

By this time, Wally Hubble had jogged over from next door and was waiting
at the launching site. Here it was, about ninety degrees in the shade, and Wally
had his German helmet and his army jacket on. His lips were purple from the
gallon of Kool-Aid he'd already guzzled that day. "Hey," he suggested, "why
don't we just take him over to my place an' throw him off our garage roof?"

By now, I was having what Grandma Hoover would call "an attack of the
grumps." Throwing Sam off a garage roof would be like launching the USS
Missouri with Dr. Pepper instead of champagne. "Because," I said. "That's why."

Wally grinned while ripping up a handful of grass and throwing it up to
see which way the wind was blowing from. "Oh boy. There's a really good
breeze. He's gonna take off like a P-38."

"Yea," Arvey agreed. He and Wally started making airplane sounds.

"Rooooooooomm . . ."

"Errr oooooowwww . . ."

"Hey. Wait a minute," Wally yelled, taking off for the back gate. "Le'me go
get my bike, so I can chase after him if he flies too far."

"Okay. But hurry up." My heart was pounding like a tom-tom inside my ears. What if Sam did fly off and never came back? What if a hawk got him, or some guy shot him, just to be mean? Maybe I ought to clip his wings and keep him in a cage. Only somehow it didn't seem right. Like sending a kid to dancing school, the way Francis McArthur's mother had done. Or making him practice the piano three times a week. I took another look at Sam who was trying to eat the Sears Roebuck label off my T-shirt while gurgling happy, Chinese-sounding noises to himself. No. No cage for Sam. I'd take my chances, even if he flew off and never came back.

Arvey and I waited until we saw Wally riding around in circles in the middle of Thirty-third Street.

"Okay. Let 'er rip."

Vaaaarooooom vaaaarooooom.

Aaaarowwwww. Both the step ladder and the table wobbled as I started to climb, even though Arvey held on to everything as tight as he could. Sam must have known he was going to have a brand-new experience because he dug his claws in my neck and tried to climb up on my head, squawking like an about-to-be-slaughtered chicken all the while. He sure seemed heavy and clumsy for a bird that would soon be swooping through the air.

"Hey. Cut it out." I grabbed him and stuck him under my arm like a football. Then I started cussing because Sam bit me on the thumb and wouldn't let go.

"Look out," Arvey yelled. "Yer gonna fall an' bust yer butt."

"I grabbed the ladder with both hands, so Sam got loose and climbed up my T-shirt front, flapping his wings against my neck and face. His yelling and flapping reminded me of Wally's sister Joan when she fell off the bridge at the Zion Pond and learned to swim all by herself.

I got my balance, braced myself against the top of the ladder and unhooked Sam from my shirt. "Okay. Here he comes."

"Not like that." Arvey shook his head. "The other direction. Ya gotta throw him up against the wind."

Poor Sam. He flapped loose and started to fall. I grabbed him by one leg. "Hey! Look out."

I looked down and saw Arvey's mussed-up hair and the licorice gob in his wide open mouth. The ladder tipped. I flung Sam in the air, jumping at the same time.

Vaaaaarooooom!

"Whacko!"

"Doing!"

The wind jolted out of me when I landed on all fours and rolled over on my back. Then down came Sam—not really flying but crooked and fluttering, like Wally's kite when Arvey and I pretended it was a Jap Zero and used our slingshots to blast it out of the sky. Sam landed on my stomach, bounced, and rolled off on the ground.

Waaaaa. Wa wa wa wa wa. Bug-eyed, he hopped up to my face. *Waaaaa.* His breath smelled like dead bugs.

"Told ya we should of flung him off the roof." Arvey laughed and squirted licorice juice.

"Crud." I jumped up and cracked my knee on the ladder when I picked it up and heaved it on the table again. Scared now, Sam pecked my fingers when I grabbed him and climbed up the ladder again. Next time, I flung him hard. Hard and mean. He flopped and tumbled like a kid going off the diving board for the first time. He landed rear end first, rolled over a couple of times, then sat there blinking and ruffling his feathers up.

"Crud." After all that work, what did I have? A fat moron of a crow that sat around screeching and spreading doo-doo all over the place. Stupid bird. He'd never learn to fly.

Wally was laughing and doing wheelies in the middle of the street.

"Aaaaaarowwwww . . . bonk!" Arvey flapped his arms, making fun of the way Sam had crashed on the lawn.

"Aww poo." I jumped off the ladder, landed on the lawn, then rolled over on my back again. I just lay there, looking up through the branches of the big cottonwood tree in our backyard. The sky was blue, and a couple of purple martins were darting back and forth.

Rrrooo aaarrrrowwww. And there was old Arvey doing one of his stupid imitations again.

A second or two later, Sam came stumbling and fluttering toward me across the grass. His clumsy flapping and fluttering knocked loose some dandelion fluff that blew away across the lawn. "Go away." He tried to climb up on my stomach, but I pushed him away and stood up.

Sam started wailing, like a baby wanting its mom. After sitting on my foot for a second, crying, and looking up at me, he let fly a plop of doo-doo and tried to claw his way up my pant leg.

So there I was, all at once feeling jerky and mean. Because how would I have liked it if Mom had been nasty to me every time I fell down while learning to walk? And I remembered how long it had taken me to learn to ride a bike without doing kamikaze crashes into fences, ditches, and trees. And how I'd shot a crow, too—then flung it in the weeds.

By this time, Sam had climbed about halfway up my pants. He was sort of crying, as if trying to call his mother out of the woods. Poor Sam. He was an orphan, and it was all my fault.

Then I remembered a book I'd read about a kid named Oliver Twist who lived in an orphanage, and how he was hungry all the time, and how they were mean to him and threw him down in the basement when he asked for more food. I almost started to cry on account of feeling like such a jerk.

Meantime, Sam had given up climbing and was just hanging upside down from where he'd hooked one claw in the ripped knee of my green corduroys.

"Aw heck." I picked him up and felt how soft and warm he was when I hugged him against my neck.

Sam gurgled and cooed as he fluffed up his feathers and cuddled under my chin.

"There there," I told him. "It's okay." If they wanted to, old Wally and Arvey could jump and flap around and make dim-witted noises for the rest of their lives. No one, especially me, was going to be mean to Sam again.

Sam must have figured out what I was thinking because he started making happy little clucking sounds. Arvey grinned at me as Sam pecked my ear.

Chapter 13

Even though Sam flunked his first flying lesson, Mom decided he was still big enough to spend most his time outdoors. That was okay with him because he could scream at Jim the mailman and scold all the cats and dogs. In the morning, I'd put him in the lower branches of the fir tree and lilac bush hedge that grew all mixed up together along the fence in our front yard. He explored his jungle, hopping branch to branch, then losing his balance and falling like a sack of cement on the ground. I guess Sam figured if you're a fat lazy pet crow, you don't need to fly. All you need to do is learn how to bounce.

Once on the ground, Sam hopped around after robins, trying to beg food from them as they yanked up worms. He also pestered sparrows, starlings, door-to-door salesmen, cats, and dogs. As far as Sam was concerned, anything that moved was a mother crow. He even chased after the Jehovah's Witness ladies who came once a week to hand out copies of *The Watchtower* and debate religion with Mom on the front porch. They quit coming after a while, though. I guess it's hard to talk about the Second Coming while some creature that looks like a pterodactyl is screaming at you while trying to climb your leg.

The person Sam liked to follow most was Carson John. By this time, my little brother was two and a half, and you hardly saw him without a load in his drawers. Mom did her best, but old Carson John could grind out loads faster than two or three moms could rinse diapers out. He usually had his face smeared with baby food as well as jam and peanut butter. Wally figured that Sam followed Carson John because he smelled so good to eat. Whatever the reason, Sam screamed and flapped after Carson John, pecking at his bare legs and sometimes at his droopy drawers.

It was just like a regular zoo, or maybe like the Sam Katzman jungle movies Arvey and I went to see on Saturday afternoons. Sam would screech and flub his wings up and down while Carson John yelled, "Num num" as he picked up interesting stuff to drop in Sam's mouth. Half of what he gave Sam was edible. The rest just slid on through without doing any harm and came out looking about the same as it did going in. I worried at first. Then I noticed that Carson John never gave Sam anything he wouldn't eat himself.

Now that Carson John was cramming all that extra food into Sam, it seemed like he was growing a hundred times faster than before.

"When's he gonna fly?" I moaned.

"He'll fly," Dad told me. "Wait and see."

So we waited and waited. And then, sure enough, everything seemed to happen all at once. Sam learned how to fly, Mom sprained her ankle skating down the front steps, Wally got bitten by a centipede, and Dad cut his big toe on a martini glass when he fell off his horse.

Probably the best way to begin the whole story is to tell about Dad and the horse. Dad really liked horses, all kinds—pintos, Arabians, quarter horses, thoroughbreds—even old plow horses with swayed backs. One afternoon, we were driving in the country, and Dad just stopped the car and spent about ten or fifteen minutes looking at horses munching grass in a field.

"Well, look, hon," Mom took Dad's hat off, patted his bald spot, and gave him a peck on the cheek. "If you like horses so much, why not buy one of your own?"

Dad smiled, kind of wistfully, then shrugged his shoulders and started the car again. "Well," he said, "the first time I went riding, I got bucked into a gravel pit. And the second time, the horse I was riding got rid of me by galloping under the low-hanging branches of a crab apple tree." According to Dad, you had to be smarter than the horse before you could get on its back and tell it what to do.

But one day, Dad actually wound up owning a horse, an old plug named Bucephalus, which belonged to Mr. Phidias, the vegetable peddler who owned a big truck garden and fruit orchard just north of town.

Old Bucephalus had been pulling Mr. Phidias's vegetable cart for as long as I could remember. He was a kind of tired gray color with brown speckles on his sides, and he'd stand patiently with his head down while Dad and I helped Mr. Phidias unload the vegetables and carry them to the back room of Dad's grocery store. Sometimes Mr. Phidias took a lunch break behind the store. Then he'd play songs on an old concertina, eat garlic sandwiches, and drink homemade cherry wine from an old vinegar bottle with a rag stuffed down its neck. When Mr. Phidias was in a good mood, he gave Bucephalus sugar cubes and let him lap cherry wine from his hat. But when Mr. Phidias got a case of the grumps, he swore at Bucephalus, hit him with a stick, and gave a mean jerk on his reins. Poor old horse. He was sway-backed from pulling the vegetable cart all those years. He had watery eyes and a runny nose too. Like having a cold that never went away.

Finally, Mr. Phidias bought a truck and then told Dad he was going to sell Bucephalus to a factory in Kenosha that made dog food and glue. Well,

Dad got about as mad as I've ever seen him get. "Ungrateful old fart," he said, stabbing a boning knife into the rump roast he was trimming on his chopping block. "That poor horse has busted its butt for you all its life. If you sell him that way, you can take your damn cabbages and onions and shove them where they'll do the most good."

What finally happened was that Dad bought Bucephalus for ten dollars, plus he got free delivery from Mr. Phidias who brought the old horse out to the house in his new truck. But it really wasn't a new truck. What it turned out to be was an old 1926 chain drive Winther that wouldn't go much faster than Bucephalus when he was feeling his oats.

Dad claimed it was poetic justice when Bucephalus outlived the truck. Mr. Phidias forgot to put water in its radiator so that it overheated one day and threw a couple of rods. There were no spare parts for a 1926 Winther, so Mr. Phidias just left it alongside the road. Whitey Sloan sideswiped it with his Colonial Bread truck, and Mr. Phidias had to pay damages, plus a fifty-dollar fine.

Anyway, now that Dad had a horse, he had to figure out where to put it. Uncle Norm suggested Dad ought to enlarge the cellar door by knocking a hole in the side of the house and turning the basement into a stable. Mom laughed but wouldn't go for that idea, so Dad finally talked to Mr. Richardson who lived catty corner from us across Thirty-third Street. Mr. Richardson had a barn with a couple of cows, plus a spare stall. Also, there was an alfalfa field out back. Bucephalus had himself a retirement home.

And at last, Dad owned a horse he wasn't afraid to ride. Bucephalus was so old and fagged out that he probably hadn't come close to bucking in fifteen years.

Most of the time, it was all he could do to plod along for a hundred yards or so before stopping and closing his eyes. Dad never whipped him when he did that. He just sat patiently, admiring the scenery and waiting for Bucephalus to rest up and get going again.

Another thing about Bucephalus was that he couldn't plod and go to the bathroom at the same time. According to Wally, who knew all about horses, a really good horse could go to the bathroom at full gallop or when jumping fences or bucking off cowboys at a rodeo. Even a nag could do its business if it slowed to a cantor or a trot.

But not Bucephalus. You could ride him for maybe a hundred yards or so; then all of a sudden, his stomach would start rumbling like a Ready Mix cement truck. He'd give off a sort of wet sigh, then stop, put his head down, close his eyes, and go to the bathroom.

So there you'd be, sitting on Bucephalus, listening to his stomach, and wondering how long before he'd start up again. Wally, who'd got an A in history, said it was a good thing Paul Revere wasn't riding a horse like Bucephalus.

Otherwise, we'd be an English colony to this very day. Actually, it wouldn't take more than a minute or so, and then the old horse would take off plodding again with those insides of his gurgling and complaining until he had to stop yet another time. You never did see a horse that was better than Bucephalus at saving it up and doling it out in little piles.

Mr. Richardson laughed and said that Bucephalus hardly ever went to the bathroom in his stall. Instead, he saved it up to use whenever someone wanted to go for a ride. "That old plug could use a good whipping," Mr. Richardson advised.

"The hell with that," Dad said. "Only a no good so and so would whip a thirty-year-old horse when it's going to the john."

Dad and Bucephalus got along very well. Sometimes Dad would saddle up Bucephalus and not even ride him. Instead, he'd just take him for a walk in the alfalfa field. Sometimes Wally and Arvey and I'd go with them and take turns sitting on Bucephalus and pretending we were Pony Express riders while he went to the bathroom and ate grass. Other times Dad would bring Bucephalus home and tie him to the front porch. Mom complained sometimes about the manure, but Dad just laughed and gave me ten cents to shovel it up.

The one thing Dad liked most to do was to fetch Bucephalus from his stall after he got home from work, stand him out in the yard, then sit on him while sipping a martini, or maybe a glass of scotch. Sometimes Dad sat there for half an hour enjoying our big yard with all the birds and flowers and the half-tame squirrel that sat in the big cottonwood tree beside our house and scolded Sam. To some people, Dad and Bucephalus must have been a strange sight. I mean there was this old nag grazing on our lawn, and just sitting on it was this guy wearing a fedora hat and sipping a drink. But to those of us who were used to the sight, Dad and Bucephalus were just a couple of old friends relaxing and having a good time.

Anyway, it was a Saturday afternoon. Dad had come home early from the grocery store and saddled old Bucephalus up. It was too hot for riding, so he brought Bucephalus into the yard and tied him to the front porch. Then he put on his bathing suit, fixed a martini, and climbed on the old horse's back.

Meanwhile, Wally and I were burning ants on the sidewalk with magnifying glasses we'd bought at the new Woolworth's five and dime. By the way, you've really missed something if you've never burned ants with a magnifying glass. They'll be scooting along at about ninety ant-miles an hour, but if you can focus sunlight through the glass just right, they'll sort of crinkle up into a little ball, then explode with a sizzling pop.

So Wally and I are pretending we have death rays aimed at an army of Venusians invading Earth. "Zap! zap!" It's a scorcher of a day and we're frying Venusians like mad and having a load of fun. Except that Wally always got to be the general because he had his German army helmet on.

All at once, Wally shouted, "Hey, look," jumped up, and knocked over a jar of spiders and centipedes we'd collected under the back porch.

"Oooooooooeeeeeee!" At the same time, Carson John let out a whoop.

I looked up from where I'd just finished frying a daddy long legs to see Carson John jumping up and down and waving a piece of Melba toast at Sam who was about six feet in the air and flapping across the lawn. My pet crow was actually teaching his own self how to fly.

"Oooooooo ooooooooooh! Chickum fry!" Carson John was running after Sam. Only he had such a whopper of a load blundering around in his drawers that he lost his balance and fell. About the same time, our cyclone fence vibrated with a wiry, ringing sound as Sam crashed into it full tilt.

I was so flabbergasted I just stared at Sam as he sat on the lawn, blinking and rearranging himself the way Wally did after making a bed-sheet parachute and bailing off his garage roof.

Seconds later, Sam lit out hopping across the yard again, sort of gunning his engines and squawking encouragement to himself. After six or eight big froggy hops, his wings caught the air and he was flying again.

"Yahhooo!" My pet crow was learning to fly. And all by himself besides. Dad was cheering too, lifting his martini glass and tipping his hat to Sam as he flew past the front porch, then crashed into a fir tree next to the front gate.

Sam wasn't in the tree more than half a minute before he bailed out and took off flying again. "All right! Aaaaaaoooooow!" Wally yelled. It was then that some kind of bird, maybe a robin or a brown thrasher, dived down and sideswiped Sam who turned ninety degrees and headed straight at Dad.

"Hey," Dad yelled. "Hey!"

After that, it was one of those slow motion kinds of things, sort of like a whole bunch of events were happening underwater—something like that. Sam let out a squawk, crashed into the side of Bucephalus's neck, and clutched at his mane.

"Whoa!" Dad tried to grab Bucephalus's reins. But it was too late. The old horse did something it probably hadn't done since before I was born: it bucked.

Poor Dad. You could see it was going to be worse than the gravel pit and at least as bad as the crab apple tree. First, he lurched forward and got tangled up with Sam who was still hanging on to Bucephalus's mane. With a squawk, Sam turned loose of the mane and clawed his way on top of Dad's hat. The hat slid off, so Sam jumped on Dad's head. Bucephalus whinnied, bucking and rearing like a rodeo horse. Dad, still holding on to his martini, did a most glorious backward summersault, landed on his heels, then sprawled on his back beside the front porch. The martini glass bounced beside him, then landed on the sidewalk and broke into skittering bits.

Meantime, Sam had slid off the slick surface of Dad's bald head and was screaming and flapping on Bucephalus's back. Bucephalus reared again, then galloped off around the side of the house.

"What in the name of God's pearly gates . . ." Mom skated out of the house, caught a skate on Carson John's fire truck, spun around, and sort of skated backward down the stairs.

"Jesus H. Christ!" Dad was yelling and cussing, and just as he got up, Mom bumped down the stairs and knocked him down again.

Dad got up, saw that Mom was okay, then took off after Bucephalus. Since he was in his bathing suit and barefooted, he cut his big toe on a chunk of broken martini glass. Mom also cut herself when she sat on one of the chunks. But mostly, it was the sprained ankle that bothered her for about a week. She wasn't sure when she got it, though. It could have been when she bumpity-bumped down the stairs. Or maybe it was when she skated after Dad and Bucephalus when they took off down Thirty-third Street.

As for me, I didn't know what to do. I mean, there were too many things going on all at once. Carson John was yelling, "Chickum, chickum," while running barefoot toward the broken glass. Sam had been brushed off Bucephalus and was screeching upside down in a lilac bush. Wally was white-faced and groaning about being bitten by a black widow spider or maybe a centipede.

Mom decided it for me. "Take care of your brother," she yelled while skating out the front gate.

I didn't miss too much of the chase. Old Bucephalus was so worn-out from bucking he only galloped for about a block and a half before stopping and going to the bathroom in the middle of the street. Dad and Mom caught up to him and led him back to his stall. Then they came on home, and Mom bandaged Dad's toe while Wally and I cleaned up the broken glass. Wally's thumb was swollen, but since it didn't hurt much, he decided he wasn't going to die after all.

After Dad got his toe bandaged, he made another martini and limped back outside and sat on the porch steps. I was afraid he was going to yell at me for what happened, but he didn't. He just sat there for a while, chuckling and shaking his head. After a while, he gimped back into the house, got a wet cloth for his forehead, and flopped down on the couch with a folded pillow propped under his cut toe. "Hey, Fern," he yelled into the kitchen. "Wake me up in about thirty years." But he never did get a nap because the great bird war of the century started right after that.

The first birds to start trouble were a pair of robins who'd built their nest in a pear tree in our yard. They were kind of smug and snooty, the way robins sometimes are. If they'd been humans, they probably would have spent their time minding other people's business and worrying over the kind of neighbors moving in down the block. They puffed up their chests, ruffled their feathers, and started screaming and clucking over the commotion Sam made as he taxied back and forth across the lawn while trying to struggle into the air. Their complaining attracted a flock of grackles and jays. After that, a mob of starlings and sparrows flew in.

Most birds hate crows the way kids hate fried liver and onions, and these birds were no exception to that. They roosted on the roof and in the trees and on the telephone lines until there was a regular bird convention overhead. They flew back and forth, holding rallies and making speeches and starting indignation meetings along the top of the cyclone fence. They jabbered and scree-scrawed until you could have sworn old Sam Katzman was making one of his jungle movies in our backyard.

I got to feeling really irksome and flung dirt clods into the trees. But it didn't do any good. The birds flew back in about half a minute, screeching and cussing even louder than before. The result of their convention was that they passed a bird-ordinance that Sam couldn't be allowed to fly. As long as he sat on the lawn or in his fir tree, they'd hold themselves back to a few dive-bombing raids, or maybe a couple of pecks on the head. But every time Sam took a stab at flying, that bird mob worked itself into the most awful kind of fit.

Poor Sam. Those outraged birds zoomed at him in mass bombing raids and low-level torpedo runs. They split into squadrons and roared in to make strafing runs and kamikaze strikes. They even tried a sort of bird version of napalm and rocket attacks.

Through all that pecking and screaming, Sam kept right on flapping his wings and trying to jack himself off the ground. But those rotten birds roared in out of the sun in wave after screeching wave. They did barrel rolls, half loops, and some really fancy stuff that I think you'd call Immelman turns. They rammed and sideswiped poor Sam until he nosed over and cart wheeled across the lawn.

Each time he crashed, those crummy birds whooped and jeered and did all kinds of Apache war dances along the cyclone fence.

But old Sam kept at it, even though it seemed like he was losing feathers at a pretty alarming rate. And before long, he was sputtering from tree to tree with a whole bird air force screaming after him from all sides. I swore like a ditch digger and flung at least half a ton of rocks and dirt clods overhead.

But those rotten birds just wouldn't give it up. Whatever tree they roosted in seemed to turn black and sag halfway to the ground.

Wally and Arvey came to help, and between the three of us, we must have zinged another ton and a half of rocks and dirt clods and slingshot ammunition through the trees. Dad gimped out on his sore foot and helped too. But those birds got more worked up with every round we fired into the sky.

"Sheeeeooooot!" Arvey waved his arms and squirted licorice spit while he and I prayed to God for a Daisy pump.

Then Wally shagged on home and came back with about a dozen cherry bombs. "I've got an idea," said Dad. "Light it when I say three." He fitted a cherry bomb in my slingshot and pulled the rubbers back.

"Yaaaaahoooo!"

"Zoweeeee!" Arvey's cherry bomb rattled through the trees, and when it blew up, that bird army took off in about nine hundred squawking directions at once. Sam stayed in the tree and screamed like he'd been blasted out of his mind. Most of the birds landed in an elm tree next to Wally's garage, so Dad let them have it with another round. This one bounced off a branch and whizzed back, hissing and trailing blue smoke. All of us scattered like chickens, with Dad out in front, gimping and swearing on account of his bandaged toe.

"What in the name of . . ." Mom ran out on the back porch screeching like ten trees full of birds. "Theodore! March right in here this minute," she yelled at Dad. "Your toe is bleeding all over again."

That was that. The great bird war ended in a draw.

Chapter 14

Now it was summer for real, with Lake Michigan warm enough for us to ride our bikes to the beach at Twenty-ninth Street and dive off the end of the old sewer pipe without turning goose-pimply and blue. Jumbo perch crowded around the mouth of the sewer pipe, and Wally and Arvey and I'd catch a half dozen each with bamboo poles, along with a herring or two. Then we'd get out our Boy Scout frying pans, some butter, and corn meal and have a fish fry on the beach.

Over the Fourth of July weekend, the Mangione Brothers carnival rolled into town—all sorts of lumbering red trucks with pictures of lions, gorillas, and bearded ladies splashed on their sides. And there were roustabouts cussing and laughing and swinging sledgehammers and raising tents so fast it was like mushrooms sprouting overnight.

"Hey, kids," a guy with a straw hat and a cane yelled out. "Just ten cents—one thin dime. See the world's smallest horse and the world's largest dog!"

"Right here ta see the fat lady. Five hundred pounds of Jello jiggles when she laughs."

With money saved up from pop bottle returns, Wally and I bought each of us two cones of cotton candy, three hot dogs, a candy apple, a five-cent root beer, and a ride on the Tilt-a-Whirl.

"Oh," Arvey said. "I don't feel so good."

"Me neither," I groaned.

We went behind the fat lady's tent and threw up everything we'd eaten since Thanksgiving and tried another ride on the Tilt-a-Whirl. It worked. Our stomachs gave up the ghost and completely shut down.

Meanwhile, Sam had taught himself to fly from his fir tree to the poplar trees along Thirty-third Street. From there, he flapped into the oak grove along the railroad tracks and then into the elm trees next to Galilee Avenue. Old Sam could fly everywhere. Everywhere but down.

Now I had me a problem because Sam hadn't quite learned to feed himself yet.

"He's gonna starve," I groaned.

Screeeeee aaaaaah. Sam flapped overhead, sort of staggering from tree to tree, trying to get near the ground. It seemed as though he had a fear of heights; and each time he started to glide downward, he'd start screaming, then flap his wings and gain altitude again.

"Stay where you are, dummy!" I yelled. Running to the basement, I got my jar full of bugs and dumped them into a paper sack. Mostly grasshoppers and crickets, they made a popcorn-popping sound while jumping around inside the sack. I ran to the tree Sam was in and started to climb. It was easy at first, because I'd been climbing since almost before I could walk. Then it started to get hard because Sam was thrashing and complaining way out on the end of some skinny branches swaying even higher than our chimney top.

"Here, Sham," I said, holding the bug bag between my teeth.

Screeeegle eeeeegle eeeeee. Sam was screeching so loud his voice sounded rusty and worn-out.

"Come on. Come on." I took a night crawler out of the sack, and it made juicy wiggles while trying to squirm loose.

Yow yow yow. Sam spread his wings for balance and wobbled toward me along the branch. Then he stopped.

"Come on, mule head. Come on."

But Sam was paying attention to something else: a fat green caterpillar tractoring along a twig. It was a real beauty, with about a hundred stumpy legs and a line of yellow dots rippling along its fat sides as it humped along.

Ahhaaoooooaaah. Sam opened his mouth like a suitcase and let out a scorching screech. The caterpillar stopped, shifted into reverse, and backed up a couple of ripply steps.

Sam screeched again. Here was a bird that could gobble bugs by the quart. But he hadn't yet learned how to catch them with his beak.

Yaaaw. Sam stretched out his neck, just begging the caterpillar to crawl down his throat.

Kind of near-sighted and smug, the caterpillar stretched out its rubbery body and gave out what looked like a caterpillar yawn. Then it reached out, grabbed the top of Sam's beak, chinned itself on top of it, then kept right on crawling between Sam's bugged-out eyes, then along the top of his head.

Eeeeee! Sam yelled as the caterpillar reared again and hoisted itself onto another branch.

Yow yow yow. Sam edged after the caterpillar with his wide-open mouth just inches away as it trundled along.

"C'mon, Sham. C'mon." I finally got Sam's attention with the night crawler, so he lurched toward me again. After swallowing it, he jumped up on top of my Chicago White Sox baseball cap and tried to eat the button off the top. After that, he hopped back down on the branch and made strangling noises while

I fed him more bugs. When lunch was over, he clawed his way up my T-shirt front, love-pecked my nose, then gargled in my ear.

Pretty soon, this strange, tingly feeling ran through me while Sam and I sat in the cottonwood tree, like maybe he was part human and I was part crow. I started giggling as he danced a little jig on my shoulder and jabbered what sounded like nineteen different languages in my ear.

Then came the sound of crows cawing way off along the railroad tracks. Sam cocked his head and hunched his wings. And then for the first time, I heard him reach deep inside and fling out the cry of a grown-up crow. *Caw caw caw.* It wasn't much, sort of squeaky and shrill. But it was a start. *Caw caw caw.* Sam jerked his head forward each time he called.

Caw caw caw. The crows answered back. Squinting, I could see black specks in the sky.

Caw caw caw. I cupped my hands around my mouth.

Caw caw caw. Sam raised the feathers on top of his head until they stuck out in a little crest. He did a crow dance too, bobbing up and down and hopping back and forth from my head to my shoulder several times. I laughed because his voice sounded like a toy whistle half filled with spit.

Now we had a conversation going—Sam, the wild crows, and me. Just by listening to Sam and the wild crows, you could understand them—not in words maybe, but in the feelings that rang out in the shrill, raspy sounds they made.

Sam was saying he was a young crow just learning how to fly. And the wild crows congratulated him and invited him to join them in the woods as soon as he was able to fly that far.

All of a sudden, I looked down to see Alice and Shirley crossing the railroad tracks and heading for the green station house. "Caw caw caw," I screamed, a wild sensation fizzing up inside me, then tingling up and down the back of my neck. It was the same feeling Wally and I got one night while hiking in the woods and hearing foxes yap-yurring along Third Park ravine. Wally and I listened to the foxes, then started yapping ourselves, "Yap yap yurrr," until our throats hurt and we couldn't howl anymore. We walked home, feeling wild and shivery in the cool night air.

Yuk yuk yuk. Sam chuckled as he flew over to a dead limb about fifteen feet away. He rubbed his beak back and forth on the branch, scraping away bits of dry bark. "Woof woof," he said.

Below us, Sparky and two other dogs trotted up the alley, their tails wagging and their noses sniffing up the ripe garbage smells dogs enjoy.

"Hey, Ma!" I yelled down to Mom who'd come out on the back porch. "Listen to Sam. He thinks he's a dog."

"That's nothing," Mom answered, cupping her hands and hollering up through the silver-green cottonwood leaves. "A certain boy I know thinks he's a crow."

Chapter 15

It was a hot, sluggish afternoon. The radio was blaring news of Japanese torpedo planes attacking U.S. carriers somewhere in the South Pacific. On the home front, the great bird war screeched and fluttered overhead, then faded off to the big oak trees along the railroad tracks. I'd set up a lemonade stand, but nobody stopped, so I drank up my inventory and went into the house for an empty mayonnaise jar. I took it outside and caught a bumblebee that was buzzing against the screen door on the back porch. Then I went into the backyard, stirred up a red anthill the size of a bushel basket, then set the jar on it, upside down. "Eeeeyerrroooow." I made an airplane noise as the bumblebee butted against the jar, then dived down and crashed into the ant nest.

"Dow dow dow." Now the ants were swarming all over the bumblebee. It shook them off, buzzed, and bumped around inside the jar, then crashed again.

All at once, the hot afternoon air slid away from my face, sort of like a window opening to let cold air blow through. The lilac and honeysuckle bushes near the fence started to shake, and the sweat on my forehead ran cold. I looked up and saw blackish purple clouds rolling in. There was a funny churning way about them as they came.

Something whooshed by in the wind. "Sam?" I called. "Sam?" It was only a branch and some loose leaves chased by the wind.

I ran. And by the time I got around to the front of the house, the first raindrops hit—big splashy ones that cooled my face and hammered steamy splotches on the sidewalk next to the front porch. With my mouth open and my tongue stuck out, I tasted the rain while giant clouds boiled overhead.

Another wind gust whisked a paper bag across Galilee Street and pressed it against our cyclone fence. I started up the front steps, then thought of Sam. He'd been out in the rain before but never in anything like this.

"Sam? Here, Sam." I ran to his fir tree. No Sam. I looked in the big cottonwood tree but saw only branches sawing and creaking back and forth. The rain made me blink as I ran through the gate and looked across Galilee toward the big oak grove along the railroad tracks. Squiggly steam wisps drifted up from the pavement as I ran across the street. And the rain was spattering and jumping hard, sort of like the water droplets Mom would flick into her frying pan to see if it was pancake-cooking hot. And the wind howled, blowing like it was inside my head. The rain slanted sideways and splattered against my face.

"Here, Sam!" The wind shook the big oaks, seeming to rip my words loose and whisk them off like paper before you could hear what I said.

I didn't hear Mom yelling until she was about twenty feet away. She was leaning against the wind and holding her apron overhead. "Get in the house!"

But, Ma. I gotta find Sam."

"Git." She bent over and picked up a stick. The sting of it bit me where my blue jeans were tight and wet against my rump. The wind snapped and fluttered Mom's apron as we ran across the street.

The rest of the storm was so confusing I don't recollect all of what went on. But the parts I do remember are icy clear and will probably never melt away. For one thing, cottonwood branches clawed against the side of the house as I ran upstairs to change clothes.

"Be sure to put on clean underwear," Mom yelled.

Leave it to Mom to worry about clean underwear when a storm is about to blow your house away.

Now the wind was prying and twisting, like some kind of monster trying to rip its way inside. Came a feathery thump against the windowpane. Right away, I thought of Sam as I stood there with one leg shoved halfway into a pair of dry jeans. Saying his name half aloud, I squirmed the rest of the way into my pants while hobbling to the window to get a better look at the storm.

Not much to see except tree branches wrenching back and forth while all sorts of ragged odds and ends shagged past in the wind. Everything looked wavy and out of focus because of all the water gushing down the windowpane.

It was a dumb thing to do, but I pried open the window and screamed Sam's name into the storm. Rain gushed in like water squirting out of a fire hose while an achy feeling twisted my insides. After changing my clothes again, I used my wet pants and T-shirt to sop up the water before flopping on the bed and wrapping a pillow around my ears. Still I heard the wind. And the branches. And the rain. A picture of Sam, all broken and tattered, kept tumbling and flopping around in my head. His wings and legs were twisted. His neck was broken too.

"Come downstairs," Mom called. "Hurry up."

I lugged my wet clothes with me and hurried down to the living room. Then Mom and Carson John and I stood by the living room window and looked toward the southwest, which is usually the direction you can expect a tornado to be coming from.

"Dorfy? Toto?" Carson John was sucking his thumb while hugging a ratty old teddy bear and pointing out the window like he expected all the Wizard of Oz characters to come sailing by. Hailstones the size of mothballs rattled down and piled up on the lawn.

"Dorfy? Toto?" Carson John tugged at Mom's dress until she picked him up and gave both him and the teddy bear a kiss. For about the hundredth time, she started telling about Dorothy and Toto getting carried off by the wind.

"Eeeeeeooow!" Carson John put his head down, crying and hugging his teddy bear. Mom stopped telling the story and shushed into his ear.

"Dorfy? Toto?" But Carson John whined at her to tell the story again. Sometimes you can't win with a kid like that.

Well, there we stood, waiting for the tornado that never quite came. A big bundle of thundery, lightning-streaked clouds did roll past. Also, a sheet of plywood wobbled down from the sky and tumbled across the lawn.

"We were lucky," Mom said. Then she told about this tornado in Iowa and how it blew her grandpa Anderson's barn to smithereens and sucked the water from his cattle pond. "Then it knocked the back door to the house off its hinges, blew Grandma Anderson down into the basement and sucked her back up into the kitchen again. Not a scratch on her," Mom said. Meanwhile, Carson John stuck his thumb in his mouth and whimpered while I stared out the window and thought about Sam out there with all those leaves and branches, plywood and paper whooshing around in the wind.

Leave it to a mom to know how to read her kid's thoughts. "Don't worry about Sam." Her voice was honey-soft as she reached out and pulled me close. "They know how to get along in weather like this—animals and birds."

"Yeah, but not in a tornado," I moaned.

"Well, it wasn't quite a tornado." Mom put Carson John down and went to answer the phone. Carson John toddled after her, his thumb in his mouth and one grubby hand reaching out. You could see peanut butter fingerprints where he'd hung on to Mom's dress.

A curved staircase winds up from our living room, and I remember Mom sitting at the foot of it, her mouth open and one hand twisting and untwisting the telephone cord while listening to Dad on the other end of the line. Tornado or not, the storm had ripped an awning from Dad's storefront, twisted it into a wad of canvas and pretzeled pipe, then blown it right through the front window. Not satisfied with that kind of mischief, it scattered slivers of glass along with cereal boxes, toilet paper rolls, paper plates, and paper cups up and down the aisles.

"Get into your raincoat and galoshes," Mom said. "Dad's coming to get you to help clean up the mess."

The rain had let up, so I went outside and squished around in the yard, picking up the plywood along with some cardboard boxes and dumping them next to our garbage cans still standing next to the back fence. Then I saw something black fluttering around in the alley. "Sam?" I ran toward it while puddle water squished up from my boots. It was just a piece of cloth torn from an old umbrella, but it reminded me of the dead crows lying out in the field after the big crow hunt last year.

"Did you find Sam?" Mom was standing on the back porch, her shoulders hunched against the wind. Just then, Dad walked around the corner of the house.

"No," I yelled, feeling twisted up inside. "Can't I stay here and look?"

Dad shook his head. "Sorry. There's a god-awful mess we got to clean up."

"Don't fret." Mom came off the porch and tugged my yellow raincoat collar up around my ears. "When the wind dies down a little more, Carson John and I'll come out and look for Sam."

Good old Dad. He did his darndest to cheer me up on the way to the store. There he was driving along with his hat squashed down over his eyes, so he had to tilt his head way back to peek out from under the brim. Dad had big shoulders from lugging halves and quarters of beef around in his butcher shop. He hunched them up and screwed his face all around until he looked like a gorilla trying to drive a car. Then he cut down a couple of back alleys, weaving back and forth, pretending he couldn't see all the garbage cans and telephone poles he almost collided with. His voice cracked and wandered around all out of tune while he sang this goofy song. Even though I didn't feel like it at first, I started to laugh and then joined in.

> There was an old man named Michael Finnigan
> Grew some whiskers on his chinny-chin
> Along came the wind and blew them in again
> Poor old Michael Finnigan
> Begin again . . .

So there I was, trying to laugh and have a good time while Dad swerved past branches lying in the road. The wind still gusted and roared, only not so hard as before. But there were still runaway garbage cans rolling down the street while sheets of paper and cardboard boxes tumbled along. Shingles, too—ripped off roofs and scattered everywhere. And a dead chicken—run over flat in the middle of the street.

I'm sure I'd have gotten a kick out of everything if I hadn't been thinking so much about Sam. It's just like a kid to enjoy a good fire or flood or tornado, or some other disaster like a train wreck or a landslide. Just so it doesn't hit too close to home.

After we got done singing and joking, Dad said that the wind had blown the roof of the Zion Theater clean off. And a whole mob of religious fundamentalists, "funnymentalists," Dad called them, were praying and singing in the streets because they figured God had sent the storm to punish Zion City for having become such an evil place.

Sure enough, we got to the store and saw this skinny, little bitsy old guy with a beard and a cane marching up and down in the street, right in front of our broken window. "Hallelujah!" He laughed and waved his arms. "Praise the Lord!"

It's funny how the most thunderous voices sometimes bellow out of the scrawniest people you've ever seen. The Lord could have been deaf as a toadstool and had his hearing aid turned off and still could have heard that old geezer's voice.

"The Lord's holy wrath has spoken!" he whooped. "All ye purveyors of filthy swine's have broke b'neath His wrath!" He shook his wooden cane at us when we got out of the car. "Gaze ye, I say, gaze ye upon the wrath of the Lord!" He laughed like a loon and whacked his cane against the ground. Then he swished it like a sword around his head.

You can be sure I kept Dad between me and that old guy when we walked past him and into the store. "Wh-wh-wh-what's a purveyor of filthy swine's flesh?" I asked.

"That's us," Dad laughed. "It used to be illegal for anyone in Zion to sell or eat pork." He smiled. "Cripes, that was thirty years ago. Now all the butcher shops in town sell pork. Even the one in the Zion Department Store. And it had originally belonged to the old Zion Church."

Anyway, that crazy old coot whooped and hollered through the broken window as if he was a coon hound that had chased us up a tree. "Satan! Beelzebub!" He spit at us, only the wind blew the spit right back at him and plastered it on his sleeve. Shutting his eyes and flinging his head back, he yelled out some other Biblical names. He looked like he was praying, except the words sounded more like swearing to me.

Seems to me there's not much difference between praying and swearing sometimes. I've heard preachers string together a whole fiery necklace of hells and damns the same way that the gandy dancers along the North Shore railroad used cuss words while hammering spikes. About the only difference I can see is that preachers wear suits and ties and hold Bibles in their hands. If a guy shaves twice a day, uses lotion afterward, and looks to heaven when he cuts loose with a "hell" or a "damn," that's prayer, I guess. But if you don't shave every day, and you eat garlic sandwiches for lunch, say "hell" and "damn," then spit on the ground and kick stones, that's swearing for sure.

Anyway, the funny old guy with the beard got to crowing about the Zion Theater, calling it "that abominable house of sin and lust, broke to ruin by God's stormy hand!" Real poetical, even for a preacher, if you ask me.

The old guy kept at it and kept at it, and pretty soon, you could see the Old Testament was making a comeback that day. The old geezer even looked like Moses or some of those other Bible guys. You know, with his long beard and all.

Instead of robes, though, he had on an old coat—dirty gray, long, ragged—with a piece of rope for a belt. Like I said before, even though he was scrunched up and puny looking, his voice could blast loud enough to split the clouds and bring more rain. I was scared of him at first, but Dad told me he was no harm to anyone and that I shouldn't pay him any mind.

So I'm sweeping broken glass off the sidewalk in front of the store when the old man marches up to me and starts glaring with his crazy, fired-up eyes.

"Peace to thee," he says. That was the greeting they used in the old days if you belonged to the Zion Church. My grandma Hoover told me that. She used to belong to the church until she got mad and quit—something about its leader, John Alexander Dowie, wanting to have vestal virgins to take care of his every need.

"Peace on thee," I muttered down my raincoat front.

The old guy smiled, probably because he was hard of hearing and thought I'd come back with the right words. He whapped me on the back like we were lodge brothers and said, "Well, boy, what thinkest thou of the Lord's work?"

"Pretty good job. But my pet crow. I'm worried about him."

"Thy pet crow?"

"Yeah. He's just a baby and can't hardly fly. He got left out in the storm." I felt my lower lip start to tremble a little bit.

The old man frowned and stroked his beard like it was a pet rat. Then he straightened up and said, "Glory, boy. Nothing will befall thy pet. He is a creature of the fields and one of God's creations. He is without sin."

"Without sin?"

"Indeed, boy. Indeed. Animals do not sin as people do. Why, in the Lord's Holy Kingdom the lion shall lie down with the lamb. The good Lord protects the beasts of the field but brings his wrath down against mankind because we do not follow the Holy Word."

He pointed with his cane. "Behold."

I sighted down his raggedy coat sleeve and along his cane until a flock of starlings roosting in the trees across Sheridan Road fluttered into view.

"They are safe in the Lord's bosom, and thy crow will be safe too."

I felt a lot better after that and began to think the old man was okay, even if he carried on about the Philistines, Sodom and Gomorrah, and Dad getting turned into a pillar of salt.

"Yes, yes!" He danced a little jig. "Elijah the Prophet will soon return and run all the damnable swine peddlers into the lake."

"Yes, sir," I agreed.

The old man swished his cane around so hard I ducked through the broken window to keep out of his way. His shoelaces were untied, and he jigged around so spryly. I was afraid he'd do like Wally's grandpa and fall down and break his hip.

"Come to the great tabernacle. Come and be saved!"

"Yes, sir," I said again.

Poor old man. The Zion Tabernacle got burned down by some crazy guy the year after I was born. A pile of rocks, that's all it was. Sometimes a bum camped out in the ruins until the cops shagged him off. High school kids went there at night, and the next day, you could throw rocks and cement chunks at all the beer bottles and funny balloons left lying around.

I didn't have the heart to tell him there was no tabernacle anymore. Besides, listening to the old man talk was like being in Mrs. McFarlan's shed all over again.

"Oh, my boy," he said. "On the Sabbath, the tabernacle is most wondrous to behold." His eyes sparkled, and he spread his arms wide, like he was getting ready to hug the whole world. "The organ is so huge. And the choir. Oh, the choir. It's a hundred strong."

The way that old guy talked stoked up my imagination until I could almost hear the organ honking away like sixty while the choir boomed out a good old soul-saving song. A guy doesn't have to be much on religion to get a bang out of that.

"Lord God above!" the old man whooped. He reached into his coat pocket, which was as big as a gunny sack, and pulled out a card that said:

Fenton A. Marquand
Apostle of the Lord

"Take my hand, son. Take my hand."

I did. It was about twice the size of mine, even though he was all skinny and shriveled up. It was strong too, with big knuckles and blue veins bulging up beneath papery brown skin.

Then old Mr. Marquand left, holding his cane under one arm and teetering off on a bicycle with a cardboard sign on its rear fender that read: Trust in the Lord.

"Peace to thee!" he hollered out.

"Peace to thee," I answered back. And I really meant it that time. But I had to grin because his bicycle handlebars were twisted so that he looked like he was riding sideways down the street.

Dad came out of the store and stood next to me while old Mr. Marquand wobbled off to do more of the Lord's work.

"What a funny old guy," I said. "Looks kind of raggedy and poor to me."

"Yep." Dad grinned and wiped his hands on his butcher's apron. "He sure does. But one thing about him is that he's got more than his share of faith, which is sometimes the most important thing you can own." He picked up a box of Wheaties and flipped it through the broken window.

"What's so good about faith?" I started sweeping broken glass again.

Dad took off his hat and scratched his bald spot for a while. "Well, look. He's more than ninety years old, Mr. Marquand is. And if he didn't have faith in the return of Elijah the Prophet, he'd probably have kicked the bucket a long time ago."

Then Dad told me about another funny old guy named Don Quixote that galloped around on a sway-backed horse. Rocinante was its name. While telling the story, Dad took my push broom, straddled it like it was a horse, and hopped up and down. "Everybody should have a little Don Quixote in them," he said. "Don Quixote's life was full of adventure because he believed in knights in armor, magic spells, and fair maidens in distress."

I burst out laughing when Dad put his hat on upside down and did this imitation of Don Quixote galloping around after windmills with a really long spear called a lance. All a guy had to do was shut his eyes and imagine Mr. Marquand peddling like crazy on his wobbly old bike while waving his cane at the windmill out behind Anderson's barn.

"Then a sad thing happened." Dad poked me in the ribs with the broom handle, then put his hat on right side up. "Don Quixote found out the things he believed in weren't real. There were no knights in armor anymore. And certainly, no maidens imprisoned by magic spells."

"Sort of like finding out there's no Santa Claus," I said.

"Yes," Dad agreed. "Anyway, Don Quixote's life didn't mean anything to him anymore, so he got sick and went to bed. He just withered up and died."

"That really is kind of sad," I said. "I sure hope that Mr. Marquand keeps on believing in Zion the way it used to be."

Dad gave me back the broom. "I don't think you'll have to worry about Mr. Marquand on that score."

Then I told Dad what Mr. Marquand said about Sam and the beasts of the field being in the bosom of the Lord.

"He's probably right," Dad agreed.

Sure enough, when we went home, there was Sam out in the yard fighting a bird war with about nine million robins and jays. They all looked like they hadn't been rained on in a month, Sam and those birds. They had their feathers fluffed up and were pecking and wing-beating each other so hard that puffs of bird down floated all over the place.

I sure was proud of Sam. He piled on a robin and snatched out enough feathers to stuff a pillow with. Then he flew into his fir tree and swore nonstop. You could tell he was growing up because in the last few days, he'd added a whole dictionary of crow swear words to his list. Hooting and scrawing and cawing and skreeking, he sounded like a whole convention of crows.

Dad and I, we sat on the front porch and laughed until it hurt. Old Sam was so alive and busy and noisy, we just had to bust a gut, especially after worrying so much during the storm.

Mom came out to investigate the ruckus and started laughing too. Then Sam must have figured out he had an audience because he spread his wings and sputtered in crow talk for about a minute and a half without repeating himself or catching his breath. He flapped and war-danced in his fir tree until the whole top half of it shook.

Then he flew down on the front porch, and his claws went tickity-tick as he tap danced back and forth. Hopping up to each of us, he said howdy in that special gargling language that a crow or a starling speaks. Then he spread his wings and let them droop until they were like a velvet cape all spread out in the sun. His eyes shone joyful and shiny black. The feathers on his head stood up like a little cap.

"What a dandy you are," Mom said. She was admiring Sam but at the same time keeping an eye on Carson John who had a paper sack over his head and was running around bumping into stuff on the front porch.

"Hee-yaw." Sam bowed to Mom, then cut loose with what had to be a celebration of bubbling-over joy. Anybody who says animals can't talk has never listened seriously to a crow.

Yuk yuk yuk yuk. Sam flew to my shoulder and gave me a soft tug on my ear. That was his way of saying "I love you" in crow talk, so I gave him a kiss when he put his beak against my mouth. The air tasted cool and sweet after the storm. All of us, Sam included, started to laugh.

Chapter 16

It was a late June morning, all sunny and green and chockfull of flower smells. I jumped off the front porch and stopped as if I'd run into a wall. A giant yellow-and-black butterfly was circling one of the honeysuckle bushes next to Sam's fir tree.

"Oooooh!" Pasted right on my eyeballs was the biggest tiger swallowtail I'd ever seen in my whole life.

Of course, my bug net was exactly where it would do the most good: in my room. As Dad would have said, "The things you see when you haven't got a gun."

Our old house shook like it was ready to fall apart as I charged back inside and pounded two steps at a time up to my room. Bird nests and comic books flew like dirt flung out of a badger hole as I dug under my bed and hauled my bug net out.

Outside again in three shakes of a lamb's tail, I almost tripped over Carson John who was making car engine noises while rolling an apple core down the front steps.

It was still there. The tiger swallowtail. The only guy I knew of who had one in his collection was a kid named Billy Peal. But it wasn't a very good specimen because part of one wing had been chewed off by Billy's pet rat.

"Yawk." Sam flew from his fir tree and landed on my head.

"Scram." I gave him a back-handed swat. He slid flapping and complaining down the back of my neck, then hooked his claws into my T-shirt and hung upside down screaming, "Wa-wa-wa-wa!"

Meanwhile, the swallowtail landed on some honeysuckle blossoms and rested there, its black-and-gold wings pumping up and down. Even during the crow shoot, I don't think I was as excited as I was just then.

Beeeble beeble. Sam had climbed up on my shoulder and was love-biting my ear.

"Crud." All I could do was just stand there waiting for Sam to quiet down while the swallowtail's wings trembled in the sun. Boy. If I could catch it, I'd never need to catch another butterfly. Not ever again. Sam stopped moving around and snuggled against my neck, so I started sneaking across the lawn.

Sure enough, I had only about ten feet to go when Sam got restless again. First, he stretched. Then he scratched. And then I felt those clammy little feet of his as he edged down my arm, heading for the net to see if there was anything good to eat inside.

"Sheeeooot!" I grabbed the net handle with both hands, shook Sam loose, and charged the honeysuckle bush. For a second or two, it seemed like nine dozen swallowtails were dancing around my head while I swung the butterfly net back and forth so hard it sounded like when Mom shook out a wet sheet before hanging it on the line.

Then the swallowtail was gone. And Sam was cackling at me from the top of his fir tree along the fence.

I ripped off a couple of cuss words that Mom would have spanked me for saying, then grabbed my net like it was a spear and reared back to throw it at Sam. But the swallowtail flew back, swooped around my head, then flitted over the top of the roof. After it I ran, lickety-split, tearing around the corner of the house, then tripping over my shoelaces while the swallowtail kited over some lilac bushes along the fence and disappeared into the weed lot next door.

"Fart." I got up and ran out from under Sam who'd glided down for another landing on top of my head. He screeched like a police whistle behind me as I scooted out the gate and down the alley as fast as I could rip.

I heard a gate bang shut and saw Wally and Sparky coming out of their yard as I ran by. You know how dogs are. They'll chase just about anything, even if they don't know what it is. Sparky's tail shot up like a flag, and he let out a string of rabbit-hunting *yip yip yip*s. He raced ahead of me with his nose sniffing along the ground.

From behind me, I could hear the marbles in Wally's pockets chinking up and down as he ran.

At the end of the weed lot, we saw a yellow-and-black flag fluttering above Mrs. McFarlan's shed.

"There it is!" Wally pointed with the Tom Mix cap pistol he had in his hand.

We dived into a jungly patch of ragweed and goldenrod that was so high you could barely see over its top. "Ouch!" Weeds were snagging the rubber straps of the slingshot in my back pocket, pulling them out, and snapping them against my rear end. Cawing, Sam flew up behind me and tried to land on my head again. But I was bobbing up and down too fast through the weeds.

That old swallowtail glided like a golden dream, leading Wally and me past the cherry tree we used as a sniper's hideout, then through Mrs. Powell's tomato patch. A blue jay swiped at it as it circled over Mrs. Powell's front porch. Then it slid into a long glide and flew low over Galilee.

"Hey," Wally yelled. "Look out!" Came the screech of tires locking up and squalling against pavement as I tore across the street.

"Damn stooopid kid!" A wavery out-of-focus red face yelled at me through a car windshield, but I kept pounding across the street, through the oak grove, then down the slope leading to the railroad tracks.

I splashed through a muddy ditch, climbed a slope of clattery, white rocks and staggered up on the railroad tracks. Somebody giggled. It was Alice Croft and fat Shirley Baldini pointing at me from the station house. Dumb old girls. What did they know about wanting a tiger swallowtail.

It's dancing right in front of me now, and I take about a hundred swipes at it while charging across the tracks and jumping over the ditch on the other side of the tracks. "Sheeeeooot. Crud." Now there's a steep slope I've got to climb. So I claw and pant my way up about twenty feet of crumbling dirt, my knees wobbling like they're a hundred years old. They give out when I stagger to the top.

"There! Over there!" Wally is yelling and aiming his cap pistol while clattering below me across the railroad tracks.

Sure enough—tiger isn't through with me yet. He's flitting easy as pie along the edge of Mr. Gushowski's grape vineyard. I crutch myself up with my net handle and run again.

"Shoooot! Fart poop!" There isn't a butterfly anywhere that can match a big yellow tiger swallowtail for running the pants off a kid. It loped ahead of me, then all at once seemed to turn itself inside out, charge back toward me, dive under my net and through my legs. I fell, staggered up, then raced along the vineyard edge. Red, pink, white, and yellow blotches flashed everywhere while soft dirt mashed underfoot. The swallowtail slowed down, sort of dancing in circles like a prize on the end of a string. I remember swinging my net hard enough to chop down about half an acre of weeds.

"Oh my god!" All at once, a white face popped over the top of a peony bush. There was this awful moan, the kind you'd expect to hear in a funeral home. "My peonies!"

I stopped dead, like a stake hammered into the ground. I'm smack in the middle of Mrs. Fenner's flowerbed.

"My peonies," she groaned again.

I looked down at my net. About five hundred pounds of peony blossoms were bunched up like chopped lettuce inside the bag.

I know you're supposed to apologize to grown-ups when you've done a bad thing. But by the time Mrs. Fenner whacked my shins with her hoe handle a couple of times, I was on the run—no apologies said. I slid back down the dirt slope so fast the seat of my blue jeans got warm.

"Ya got him! Ya got him." Old Wally was laughing and waving his cap pistol around as we ran back across the tracks.

"Huh?"

"There. In yer net."

Sure enough, the swallowtail was struggling around all crumpled up in a salad bowl of pink and white peonies.

I reached in, sort of tweezering it between my thumb and forefinger, then pulling it out. Part of one hind wing was gone. The rest of it looked like Carson John had run over it with his fire truck.

"Gosh," Wally said. "It sure was a beaut."

"Yeah," I agreed. It was trying to fly, its wing muscles throbbing between my fingertips like a little heart.

Braaack. Yuk yuk yuk. Sam landed on my shoulder again, then danced down my arm. *Waaaa,* he screamed when he saw what I had in my hand.

"Why don't ya go ahead and feed it to him," Wally said. "It ain't any good no more."

"Yeah," I agreed, holding it out for Sam. All tattered and smudged, it was still big and yellow and trying really hard to fly. All at once, I thought of the crow shoot again, and a funny feeling slid over me, like a cold fog or something like that. Opening my fingers, I let it go. At first, it staggered in the air just a bit. But then it flew fast and strong down the railroad tracks.

Yow yow yow! Sam screamed.

"Wudja do that for?" Wally asked.

"Dunno. Just felt like it, I guess."

"Yeah," Wally agreed.

We climbed back up the slope on the other side of the tracks with old Sparky trotting ahead of us, his tail wagging back and forth. Sam shifted his position and rode the rest of the way home, all puffed up and indignant on top of my head.

Chapter 17

"Eeeeya! Eeeeeya!" Sam and I were looking for crayfish in the frog ditch along the railroad tracks when Richie Baldini's Tarzan yell echoed like dynamite up and down Thirty-third Street. "Oh jeez," I groaned. Lots of times, while climbing trees or running around in the woods, I imagined I was Tarzan of the Apes. Only I knew better. I really did. With those gorilla muscles and that foghorn voice of his, old Richie Baldini really was Tarzan of the Apes.

"Eeeeeeyah! Eeeeeeya!" Another blast. Loud enough to make every kid for five miles around feel like he'd had snow crammed down the back of his neck. Sam gave a nervous flit of his wings and looked up from the dead crayfish he was pecking at along the edge of the ditch. A red-winged blackbird flew off screeching when a rock clanged against the stop sign at the corner of Thirty-third and Galilee.

"C'mon, Sam." I ran hunkered down along the edge of the ditch below the railroad bed. Sam cawed behind me as Richie's yell squeezed my insides again. After running a hundred feet or so, I cut left and scooted like a gopher into the goldenrod and milkweed growing along the railroad right of way. Ahead of me was a wire fence. Scared Richie would see me climbing over it, I snaked underneath and eased up on the other side.

I rose up, peeking just over the tops of some purple thistles blossoming along the fence. It was Richie all right, strutting along the embankment and hooting his Tarzan yell again. He looked right at me, so I scrunched down in the weeds. Even from way off, I could see his arm muscles bulge as he scooped rocks from the railroad bed and flung them into the ditch. "Dow!" he yelled. "Dow dow!" Then he ripped off another Tarzan yell, jumped off the embankment, and landed at the edge of the ditch.

He was after the frogs again, flinging rocks in the water so hard you could see muddy geysers pooching up.

Caw caw caw! Sam dive-bombed Richie's head a few times while barking his danger call, then flew down the tracks about a hundred feet behind me and perched on a power line pole.

I turned away from watching Sam and looked in the direction of my house. It was just a hundred yards away, but to get there, I'd have to sneak close by the ditch where Richie was bombing frogs. Of course, I could up my chances of staying alive by cutting across Mr. Johnson's garden on the way home. Not much of a choice, especially after Mr. Johnson told me he'd kick my fanny up between my ears if he caught me cutting through his garden again.

"Eeeeeeyooo!" Richie tossed something high in the air. It trailed blue smoke before blowing up with a wet *bang*. That was something only a kid like Richie would do—catch a frog, stick a firecracker in its mouth, and throw it like a hand grenade.

Picking up a rock, I squeezed it in my fist, hating Richie like one of those canker sores you sometimes get in your mouth. And I sort of hated myself too for not having the gumption to run right up to him and bash him on the head for being so mean. But it wasn't any use. What can a kid do against a guy who smokes cigars and has hands the size of baseball mitts? It's awful to be mad and scared at the same time—like freezing and scalding all at once. The only thing I could do was to drop the rock back down in the weeds.

Meanie Baldini, that's what us kids called him—only not to his face. The first time I met him, I was only five years old. That was the day he strutted into my yard and peed in my sandpile and all. I'd never had anyone do that before, so I just stood there gawking while warm pee spattered off my red dump truck and on my bare legs.

Then Richie got down on his knees and peed as hard as he could on my toy soldiers until they fell over in the wet sand. After that, he climbed the big cottonwood tree and tried to pee on my head. Only he was almost out by then, so the pee just made a few dribble marks down the trunk of the tree.

"Hey!" Mom came out of the house just in time to see old Richie getting ready to slide his pants down and do bombs away out of the tree. "Don't you think it's time for you to go home?" she asked.

"Aaaa, screw you." Richie gave Mom the finger and tipped over our garbage can as he swaggered out the back gate.

A couple of months later, Dad brought home a little gray-and-white kitten he found by the smokehouse in the back of his butcher shop. It was the first kitten I can remember having, and I gave it rides up and down the alley in a red Radio Flyer wagon Mom and Dad gave me for my birthday. Well, you know what kittens are like. It batted a marble I put in the wagon back and forth, then reared up and jumped on it like it was a mouse.

Down the alley we went, bumpity-bump, the marble jiggling like it was alive. I remember laughing and running while the kitten nearly turned itself inside out chasing its marble around and around. The game was so much fun I forgot where I was. We ended up several blocks away, in the alley behind Richie's house.

I didn't know it was Richie's house until something hit in the alley beside me and exploded in a cloud of brown dust. There was Richie about fifty feet away, standing on a pile of dry dirt. "Eeeeeya!" He picked up another dirt clod and flung it hard. My wagon clanged and vibrated as the dirt clod exploded against its metal side.

"Hey!" Richie jumped off the dirt pile and ran toward me along with a dirt-smeared mob of kids who must have been his brothers and sisters. I tried to run, but it was too late.

There must have been seven or eight Baldini kids, all of them tough. They gouged, bit, and swore, and they had muscles and calluses from working with their old man who collected junk in an old green dump truck that didn't have any doors on both sides of its cab. When they weren't fighting each other, they beat up other kids. They had bad breath and rotten teeth. Most of the time, they smelled like dried-up pee.

Anyway, one of Richie's older brothers grabbed my kitten out of the wagon, and then he and Richie tossed it back and forth. It mewed and clawed at the air until it scratched Richie's brother on the wrist.

"Ouch! Hey!" Richie's brother had a weaselly look in his eyes. He threw the kitten like a baseball, high in the air.

It thumped and bounced a little when it hit the ground.

I was so little and so scared, I don't remember all the things Richie and his brother did to my kitten after that. But I do remember how they tied a piece of string around its neck and hung it from a clothesline wire. I remember screaming, "Here, kitty . . . Here, kitty," while trying to reach up and pull the kitten down. But it was dangling too high over my head, even though I climbed inside my wagon and jumped as high as I could. It kept spinning around and around, clawing at the place where the string bit into its neck. Once, it reached up with its front paws and started to pull itself up the string.

"No ya don't." Richie hit the string with a stick.

The kitten fell, thrashing and spinning and making little gagging sounds. I was crying really hard by this time, so they cut the kitten down. "Aw, quit yer bawling," Richie's brother said. "It's dead anyways." Then he and Richie ran up and down the alley, swinging it on the end of the string. "Swish . . . swish . . . swish." The kitten flew around and around until they got tired of playing with it and went back to their big pile of dirt. I picked the kitten up, crying so hard it hurt way deep inside. Then I picked some dandelion blossoms and put them in the wagon with the kitten. After that, I went home.

When I got to be older, some of the neighborhood kids told me that Richie was mean like that because his real dad was an older brother who'd run off and joined the marines. I think it was Wally who started that story going around. He said Richie was "inbred" or something. His mom and dad talked about it one night after they thought he was in bed.

There was another story about Richie messing around with his sister Shirley in Mr. Gushowki's grape vineyard. Richie bragged about it all over the neighborhood, and once, he invited the older kids to come along and watch. He even bragged about messing with his old lady at least once a day when his old man was out collecting trash in his junk truck.

Most of the kids didn't believe that story because Richie was scared to death of his mom and dad. Whenever he got caught stealing, they'd pull his pants off and whip him with a belt until he got big welts all over his rear end.

Notice how I said they whipped him when he got caught. Richie's folks weren't against his stealing. It was the getting caught they couldn't stand. I know that for the truth because one day Arvey was walking by the Baldini house and heard Richie's mom yelling at Richie to sneak next door and swipe some vegetables from the neighbor's garden. Arvey told on Richie, and that night, Mr. Baldini whipped Richie and made him sleep outside in the back of the junk truck.

Richie found out Arvey snitched on him, so he caught him on the way from school and beat him up. Then he held him down and peed on his face. He said he was going to get me too because I was Arvey's friend.

"Blam!" I was still thinking about Richie when another frog blew up above the railroad tracks. Still hunkered over, I scrunched along the fence toward Thirty-third Street.

"Blam!" Old Richie sure was a one-man-judgment-day for those poor frogs.

Erp erp. Just then Sam glided down and dug his claws into the top of my head.

"Sssst." I stopped running and tried to brush him off. No sign of Richie through the yellow goldenrod. But then, a rock the size of a pumpkin whistled over my head. "Oh jeez." I took off running again while Sam cackled and hooted and did his crow dance on top of my head.

"Hey, kid. Wait up!"

I slowed down, then lit out running again.

"I said wait up!"

Richie's voice yanked me to a stop like a rope looped around my neck. Squawking, Sam slid down the back of my neck and dug his claws into my T-shirt as I stood up and looked toward the railroad tracks. With his legs apart, Richie was standing on the railroad bed, a bunch of cattail stalks in his fist.

"Ooooooo aaaaah! Ooooooo aaaaaah!" Richie threw one of the stalks like a spear. It sailed high in the air toward me, some of the cattail fuzz flying off and drifting away as it glanced off the top wire of the fence. "Hey! Izzat yer crow?"

"Y-y-y-yes." I was trying hard not to sound like somebody being strapped into an electric chair.

"Well, wait up a minute. I wanna see 'im up close." Richie jumped off the embankment and sailed all the way over the ditch. He was the only kid I knew of who could do that.

"Shoo." I brushed Sam off my shoulder, and he flew off and landed on a telephone pole. The goldenrod swished apart as Richie pushed through with his big hands and arms.

"Hey! How come he flew off?" Richie grinned at me as he leaned against the other side of the fence. He was about four years older than me—really big for his age. Ratty-looking red hair. Scraggly fuzz sprouting out of his chin.

I started stammering, hating myself for being so chicken. And hating Richie for making me feel that way. "H-h-h-he's not r-really all that t-t-tame."

"Oughta put 'im ina cage." Every time Richie breathed in and out, there was this greenish yellow snot bubble hanging from his nose that got bigger, then smaller again.

"Y-yeah," I agreed.

"How much?"

"Huh?"

"How much?" Richie nodded toward Sam who was laughing and bobbing his head. A queasy feeling boiled up in my stomach, like when you swallow smoke from wet, burning leaves. Sam was getting ready to glide down and land on me again.

"H-h-he ain't for sale," I said as Sam came to me in a long sort of feathery glide. His wings swished, and then he was chuckling in my ear and rubbing his beak against my neck.

"Wow! Le'me hold 'im fer a second." The fence creaked as Richie climbed partway over and pawed at Sam and me with a big scabby-knuckled hand.

Caw caw caw! Sam edged away from him and hopped on to my head.

"Y-y-yuh can't hold on to him 'cause he'll get scared an' peck your hands."

"Oh yeah. Well, if he pecks me, I'll wring his neck. Give 'im here."

I backed away as Richie swung one leg over the fence. Breathing hard, I had my hands knuckled into fists and my feet spread wide apart. Sam squawked and flew back up on the telephone pole.

"Told ya he ain't very tame," I said.

The grin that always seemed to be smeared all over Richie's face got even wider as he looked down at me from the top of the fence. He had on a ragged T-shirt and was scratching his stomach and picking belly button lint through one of the places where it was torn. Across his T-shirt front were big black letters. Blatz Beer, they said. "Hey!" Richie blew his nose with his fingers, then wiped them on his pants. "If he ain't so tame, then maybe he ain't really yer crow."

I didn't say a word; just looked back at Richie, trying to muster up a friendly smile.

"An' if a guy wuz ta catch 'im an' put 'im in a cage, then he'd belong ta that guy. Right!"

Now I'm shaking, feeling runty and ashamed.

"Right?" Richie's voice hammered at me, big and bullying, more like a man's voice than a kid's. He swung his other leg over and sat on top of the fence. It swayed back and forth from his weight.

"Guess so," I mumbled while backing away.

"Well, I know so," Richie snarled.

I turned around and walked along the fence, then across the street. If I'd been a dog, my tail would have been between my legs.

"Hey," Richie called. "Wanna come an' blast some frogs?"

"No thanks," I said, turning partway around. Richie jumped off the fence with that crummy grin still on his face. Picking up a rock, he chucked it hard along the surface of Thirty-third Street. It skipped and hummed, and I jumped out of its way.

"Crows ain't no good!" Richie yelled. "Maybe I'll go an' blast his rotten head off with my old man's .22."

I didn't say anything. I just slunk through the front gate and into the yard. After that, I went into the house, got a bag of Blue Star potato chips and came back outside. The branches of Sam's fir tree shook as he flew out of it and landed on my arm.

Yaw yaw yaw. He started begging, just like a little kid. And when I put a potato chip in my mouth, he reached around and took it in his beak. I fed him some more potato chips and scratched his head while he ate.

Glooo gloooo. He bubbled happy noises while wiping his beak against my neck. When I petted him, his feathers ran soft under my hand.

"Don't you worry none. Don't worry at all." My voice was trembling, and I felt dumb and girlish, ready to cry. But there was another feeling, too—a kind of sharp-toothed, squinty-eyed feeling that was kind of scary and exciting at the same time because I couldn't remember feeling that way before. Every so often, Richie's Tarzan yell or the soggy bang of another frog blowing up echoed from the direction of the railroad tracks.

Chapter 18

*C*aw caw caw! I stopped riding my bike down the alley behind our house and squinted up in the sky to where Sam was tracing excited circles and swoops. The sky was an easy place for Sam now, and it was fun to watch him soar and dive, or maybe just hang on the wind. Just watching him made me feel so light and airy inside that I wanted to climb the highest tree for miles around.

Caaaaaw caaaaaaw! Sam banked over until he was sort of balanced on one wing tip. Then he folded up and dived toward the ground. Instead of coming to me, he swooped into an apple tree in Mrs. Klammers backyard. Grinning, I took a bite out of my raspberry Popsicle and leaned against the handlebars of my bike while Sam flung a lung full of crow swear words at the ground.

Sam was yelling at Tiger, no doubt, Mrs. Klammer's big brown-and-black-striped tomcat, who was the neighborhood champ now that the Weed Lot Bum was gone. *Braaaaack.* Sam screeched. *Haw haw haw.*

I could imagine old Tiger scowling up at Sam while gimping on the sore paw he'd mashed in a rat trap a couple of weeks ago. Mashed paw or not, Tiger was meaner than spit. He could shred more fur off another cat in two seconds than you could clip off in five minutes with a pair of shears. Even with a sore paw, Tiger could jump over the Klammers' fence without scraping his belly across the top. Every other time you saw him, he had a dead rat or a dead robin hanging from his mouth.

Just then, Sam dive-bombed from the apple tree into the Klammers' backyard. "Sam," I yelled. "Sam!" The loose fenders on my bike rattled like tin cans as I jolted down the alley as fast as I could pump. Of all the cats for a smart-alecky crow to mess with, Tiger wasn't the one. Only I was about to find out that Sam was not your ordinary crow.

"Here, Sam. Here, Sam." I bailed off my bike, ran hard, then climbed partway over Mrs. Klammer's wire fence. Then I took another bite of my Popsicle and dropped back to the ground. Sam was strutting around in the

Klammers' chicken pen, scratching and pecking with a flock of white bantams and some Rhode Island reds.

You should have seen Sam swaggering around as if he was part-owner of the joint. Even though Tiger could climb inside the pen, that silly crow couldn't have been safer if he'd been locked in a bank. That's because Tiger had been paddled and no-no'd since kittenhood each time he even thought about sneaking near that pen. The barest whiff of a chicken was enough to send him slouching off with his belly dragging on the ground.

I went back and picked up my bike, then wheeled it over and leaned it against the fence. "Hey, Sam. How d'ya like chicken feed?"

But Sam was no longer in the chicken pen. *Er erk erk*. He was near the Klammers' back porch, jabbering at Tiger who wasn't more than ten feet away and hunched over a bowl of table scraps.

"Hey!" I yelled, taking the Popsicle out of my mouth. Sam just looked at me, chuckled in crow talk, then turned around and bobbed his head in Tiger's direction, sort of mumbling and nodding and cocking his head this way and that, like some old lady squinting at her sewing over a pair of rimless glasses. What Sam was interested in was the way Tiger's tail kept curling and straightening out, curling and straightening out. Pretty soon, Sam started edging forward, jigging up and down and jabbering like he was going to have a fit. Me, I was already having a fit because Tiger was big enough and mean enough to munch Sam down with one bite, then blow feathers and leftover bones out of one corner of his mouth.

"Shoo! Hey, shoo!" I flung my Popsicle at Sam, hoping to scare him off. Then I took a jump at the top of Mrs. Klammer's fence as the Popsicle made a big raspberry splat about five feet from Sam. *Haw haw haw*. Sam wasn't fazed. He hopped, flitted his wings, then gobbled up the tip of Tiger's tail and took off with it about the same time I hooked one foot on top of the Klammers' fence and fell into their backyard. An electric-sounding screech shivered the air as Tiger spun around with his fur sticking out as if he'd been plugged into a wall socket. He sure was mad.

Then he saw Sam. "Oh jeez," I groaned. But what a surprise it was to see Tiger let out a puny hiss and back away. *Buck buck buck*, Sam clucked. He hopped after Tiger who kept backing off.

Craw craw craw. Sam stopped and stood on one leg for a second before charging right at Tiger and pecking him on the nose.

Tiger hissed, took a feeble swipe at Sam, and edged around the other side of his bowl. He was whipped.

Brrrruck brrrrruck. What a crow. A regular bird psychologist, that's what he was. He looked and sounded like a little banty hen as he fluffed his feathers and pecked Tiger's nose again. After that, he paraded back and forth the way a chicken does, stopping every once in a while and standing on one foot like they do when scratching for food.

Poor Tiger. He figured that something wasn't quite right. No chicken had ever treated him like that before, so part of him wanted to step up to his food bowl and make a meal of Sam along with a pile of leftover pork chop fat. But another part of him probably remembered the *thwap thwap* of a rolled-up copy of the *Zion Benton News* swatting his rump every time he even thought about fresh chicken meat.

Sam knew he had Tiger's number, so he pecked another dent in Tiger's nose and chased him behind a sheet of plywood leaning against the house. After that, he strutted back to Tiger's food bowl and stood there congratulating himself. *Haw yuck. Eeble beep.* It was crow talk, the kind of noise a crow makes when he knows he's just about the smartest bird there is.

After congratulating himself, Sam ate some pork chop fat, then swaggered around with his little eleven-inch chest puffed out as far as it would go.

Oh, the kick my crow was getting out of life. He whooped and screeched and ran back to give that bone-headed cat's tail an extra tug, just to prove one more time who was boss. Sam was so excited and happy he went back and did a little war dance around the rest of Tiger's food. After that, he spread his wings and gave a deep bow, as if thanking everyone in the audience for their applause. Finally, he flew up on the Klammers' garage roof, where he put on a one-bird crow parade that strutted back and forth. I sure was proud, probably because when you've got a really smart pet, it makes you feel smart yourself. And when I climbed back over the fence and got on my bike, Sam landed on my shoulders and rode along with his wings spread out. His feathers sure were pretty—a deep greenish blue-black.

When Sam wasn't teasing cats, he kept busy scrounging all the shiny things he could find. He collected glass bits and tinfoil wads, pop bottle caps, paper clips, hairpins, tin can lids, marbles, safety pins, and the little doodads you dig around for in the bottom of Cracker Jacks boxes. He found money too, along with old buttons, nuts, bolts, washers, and screws. He got all worked up over car hubcaps and mirrors but couldn't figure out how to fly off with anything that size.

Anything he could pry loose and fly away with he'd bury in the pea gravel in our driveway and along the edge of the road. What a miser he was too. He squawked and scolded and fluffed his feathers and skipped back and forth between all his gravel piles. Get too close, and he'd run over and camp right on top of the most favorite thing he'd buried that day. He was so bullheaded about standing on a nail or a strip of foil from a pack of chewing gum you could just about dump a bushel basket over his head before he'd fly off.

Sam would crank up to a screeching fit if someone messed around too long next to his favorite stuff. He'd dig up his penny or his paper clip and hop away with it to another part of the driveway. After burying it as deep as he could, he'd look up and see someone standing next to the old belt buckle he'd stashed the day before. So he'd rescue it and run off to bury it before skittering back to dig up the bottle cap he figured you were getting ready to steal. He swore at Dad's car a lot because it was usually parked on top of his favorite button or paper clip.

Sam kept adding to his collection because he was never satisfied with what he had. The newest tinfoil wad had had more shine on it than the one found the day before. My silly, nonstop crow got so excited over collecting things he was as bad as Wally and Arvey and me haggling over baseball cards. To hear him screeching and yelling over the junk we teased him with, you had to figure he'd trade most of his feathers for a door hinge or the lid of an old Mason jar. But the one thing he ached to own most in all the world was my watch.

It really wasn't much of a watch. Old and tired, it got dug out of a Lake Michigan sand dune when Arvey and I were playing pirate earlier that spring. Depending on its mood, it ran at two or three different speeds. And it ticked so loud I buried it in my underwear drawer at night.

But oh, how Sam wanted that watch. According to Sam, it had a little heart you could hear beating away when you put your ear up close.

After finding out how much Sam wanted that watch, I'd unstrap it and hold it up when I wanted him to land on my arm. He'd be all over me before I could blink, his eyes sparkling like wet stones as he clucked and haw-hawed and stuck his ear next to its face. Screaming and gurgling in crow talk, he brought stuff like maybe an old zipper or a paper clip from his gravel pile, begging me to take them in trade. When I wouldn't cooperate, he might give my ear a tug and fly off to run screaming back and forth along the roof.

One day, Sam couldn't stand it anymore. There was that watch, dangling and ticking above the crook of my arm as he swooped, caw-cawing, off the roof. The instant he hit my arm, he snatched that watch just like it was a tomcat's tail.

"Hey," I yelled.

Haw haw, Sam jeered as he flew away with my watch and landed on top of Mrs. McFarlan's shed. *Yow yow yow! Skreeeet!* What a joyful crow—all worked up and whooping like some old prospector who's stubbed his toe on a chunk of gold. His feet went tickity-tick as he danced across the roof, circling the watch with his wings spread and every feather he owned standing straight up.

Gloooooo. Scraw eeee. He stuck his ear next to it and listened for signs of life. Then he stood on its strap and hammered at it with his beak. After that, he jumped up and down on it for a while. And when that didn't kill it, he picked it up by its strap and tried to beat it to pieces against the roof.

Old Sam really wanted that watch to be dead. He whang-banged it so much I was sure that all the cogs and wheels and springs and whatever else is in a watch would come flying loose. When it still wouldn't stop ticking, he flew to the top of a telephone pole and dropped it on the ground. From there, he carried it back to Mrs. McFarlan's shed where he took up swearing and hammering again.

I sure had new respect for that old watch. No matter how hard Sam jumped on it and flailed it against the roof, that old thing kept chugging away. It wore Sam out. With his tail feathers and wing feathers limp and dragging on the roof, Sam edged around the watch a couple more times. And when he put his ear against it and heard it still ticking, he shook himself several times, then sat on it as if it was an egg.

Now was my chance, I figured. With a running start, I tried to vault up on the shed roof and grab the watch, all in one leap. But the edge of the roof hit me in the chest. I bit my lip and fell down in the weeds.

"Sheeeoot!" I lay in a patch of thistles, sucking my bloody lip and rubbing my chest while the watch flew away, hanging from Sam's beak like a dead mouse.

By golly, no crow was going to get the best of me. I ran home, got a rake, and started raiding Sam's gravel piles. With Sam hopping and squawking behind me, I uncovered an earring, a handful of bottle caps, three nickels, a dime, and four cents. Besides that, I dug up the knob off a radio, a bottle opener, one of Mom's thimbles, a St. Christopher's medal, a charm bracelet with most of the charms still on it, a tie pin with a big red stone in it, and Joan Hubble's roller skate key that she said I'd swiped from her last week. Also, I dredged up the axle and wheels off a toy car, plus a roll of copper wire stolen from the back of Mr. Hubble's pickup truck. I even found my Marine Band harmonica, which was last seen lying next to my baseball mitt in the backyard. But no watch. With Sam burying me under a landslide of crow cuss words, I put the rake away, thinking that once again I was playing straight man for a smart aleck crow.

A few days later, I was on the roof of Mrs. McFarlan's shed reading *Captain Marvel* comic books when Sam commenced gargling and twittering nearby. Sure enough, there he was, prancing around on the Klammers' garage roof visiting with Mrs. Klammer while she was hanging up clothes in her backyard.

Sam was a natural born visitor. He sat on the station house and visited with people waiting for the North Shore train. He visited with the gandy dancers while they hammered spikes or sat eating salami and garlic sandwiches along the tracks. He jabbered away at old Mrs. Powel, gurgling at her from the top of her cherry tree while she worked hunched over in her tomato patch. "Howdy do, Mr. Sam." Laughter would spread all over her wrinkled brown face as she called his name. Sometimes she sang Negro gospel songs with Sam twittering and gurgling right along with her as she sang.

Sam even visited with things that didn't visit back. He could argue politics with his own reflection in a hubcap or a rear view mirror. He was also partial to scarecrows. And once, I even saw him laughing and bowing at an old jacket draped over a post.

This morning, it was Mrs. Klammer Sam was interested in. Mostly, he seemed to be jabbering the kind of crow talk he used after locating something shiny he would like to own.

Old Mrs. Klammer was talking right back to Sam, and in German too. Dad laughed one time and told me that she liked Sam so much because he could speak and understand German really well.

"Aw, Dad. You're joking," I said.

"No, I'm not. Not at all. Sam speaks English when he's arguing with you, and he jabbers in Polish and Italian when he's bumming salami from the gandy dancers over by the railroad tracks."

Dad went on to explain that if an animal likes a person, it can understand whatever language it is that that person speaks.

So anyway, Sam and Mrs. Klammer were yakking in German, and pretty soon, Sam flew down from the garage and landed on a clothesline pole. Screeing and squawking, he teetered along the clothesline and pulled some clothespins loose. A pair of Mr. Klammer's underpants fell on the ground, and Mrs. Klammer laughed and flapped a pillowcase at Sam. Her face was all flushed and happy, and she had her grayish blonde hair tied up in a bun. She was singing this little German tune, and every once in a while, she'd turn partway around, give Sam a nod, and imitate some of the funny German-sounding noises that gargled out of Sam's throat.

Mrs. Klammer was a tall, broomstick of a lady with hollow cheeks and a long skinny nose. Even though she was kind of sour looking, she baked cookies and gave them to all of us kids in the neighborhood. In the fall, she let us climb up and pick big crunchy apples from her apple trees.

Even though Mrs. Klammer was nice to Wally and Arvey and me, we did a really mean thing to her one Halloween. We rang her doorbell, then hid out in the vacant lot across the street. When she came to the door with a bunch of candy and stuff, we yelled, "Nazi!" and ran away. I felt really crummy and finally told Mom what I'd done. She smiled and ruffled the hair on top of my head. "You're a good boy for sharing this with me." Then she grabbed me gently but firmly by the ear and steered me toward the back door. "Go next door and apologize. Right now. You can have a cookie when you get back."

At first, Mrs. Klammer looked really mad and tight-lipped while I was saying how sorry I was. But then she smiled. "Kommen se," she said. Or something like that.

Her house was a big old place, a lot like ours. Only it had these terrific bakery smells when I went into the kitchen. Another thing in her kitchen was a collection of wooden clocks, about eight or ten of them at least. And as I was standing there, telling Mrs. Klammer how sorry I was, they all went off. Pigeons and cuckoos, owls and elves, along with lots of other neat things, started popping out. One clock had a little gnome in it that jumped out and started tipping his hat each time a gong went off.

"Bong."

"Cuckoo!"

"Tweet!"

It was just like Santa's workshop at the North Pole. And the best clock of all was one that had this little door open up, and then a little old lady popped out and ran around and around, chasing a little boy and bonking him on the head with a stick.

Mrs. Klammer pointed at the old lady and the little boy. "Das iss us. Ya?"

I grinned. "I guess so," I said.

"Goot boy." Mrs. Klammer hugged me against her bony chest, then went to a big jar and pulled out a cookie that must have been as big as a plate. "Tell friends to come und I giff dem cookies too. Ya?"

I nodded and grinned again. The cookie had a vanilla flavor and turned buttery in my mouth.

Just then, another clock went off. Out popped a little bird that said, "Cuckoo-cuckoo," until a little man with a gun popped out. The bird fell over like it was dead. Then it and the little man ducked back inside.

Mrs. Klammer laughed and set the hands of the clock back just a hair, then gave me another cookie and another hug. She was just about the nicest person there was, even though she did talk with an accent that made her hard to understand.

Anyway, there I was on Mrs. McFarlan's shed watching old Sam parade around on top of Mrs. Klammer's garage while making all sorts of I-want-to-trade-for-something sounds. And when Mrs. Klammer turned her back, he flew down to her clothes hamper and edged around it, clucking and exclaiming over something that had grabbed his eye. *Eeeeeek. Zeeeeeeeek.*

Mrs. Klammer turned around. "Shoo!" she yelled.

Quick as a card trick, Sam dived inside the hamper and grabbed a shiny thing that turned out to be the metal snap on Mr. Klammer's pajama bottoms. Mrs. Klammer yelled something in German and swiped at Sam with a wet towel. But it was too late.

Right out of the clothes hamper those pajama bottoms jumped, just as if they had an invisible man inside. And old Sam was hanging on to that metal snap and flapping like a vulture while the pajama bottoms ran beneath him across the ground. For a second, it looked like Mr. Klammer's bottoms might run into the fence. But then they made a graceful leap and came loping across the alley toward Mrs. McFarlan's shed.

Sam was going to land on the shed at first. But he saw me and veered away, his wings going *whump whump*, and me almost grabbing Mr. Klammer's bottoms as they ran past. They were white and covered all over with pictures of big red ants, if I remember right.

Poor Mrs. Klammer; she didn't know whether to laugh or frown. When she saw me on the roof, she waved and pointed at the pajamas, which were disappearing into the oak grove by the railroad tracks.

I jumped off the shed, ran cussing and laughing through weeds, then crossed the street to where Sam was congratulating himself.

"Now look what ya done!" I gawked up through crisscrossed branches to see him pecking at the bottoms, which were wedged in the crotch of a big oak about fifty feet overhead.

Haw haw. Skreeeeek. Sam cocked his head and looked down at me, then started pecking and worrying the bottoms again.

"Get down here! Right away!" I had to laugh at myself on account of I was sounding just like Mom.

Of course, Sam didn't pay me any mind. Getting him to do what you wanted him to do was about as hard as teaching the wind how to behave. Sam just laughed and started imitating the sound a screen door hinge makes when it's opened and closed.

Well, I started climbing while muttering to myself about all the times I'd nearly broke my neck on account of Sam. Of course, he tried to fly off with the bottoms again, but they snagged on some branches, and he couldn't pull them loose.

Caw caw caw! Sam barked his danger signal while circling overhead. Then he sat on a limb and swore at me while I shinned and hauled and did a fair amount of swearing myself.

That oak sure seemed like the Mount Everest of all oaks, so it took ages to get up to where Mr. Klammer's bottoms were stashed. After getting there, I found out that Sam had more than one hiding place for all of his stuff. In the crotch beneath Mr. Klammer's bottoms were several wadded-up cigarette packages, some gum wrappers, the lid off a jar of Kraft's mustard, more bottle caps, a two-headed coin, a police whistle, and the mate to the earring I'd found in the driveway two days ago. Most important of all, there was my watch.

Chapter 19

"Eeeeeeyah eeeeeeeeyah!" There it was again, Richie's Tarzan yells raising goose bumps on the back of my neck. Sam dug his claws into my T-shirt and scrambled to stay on my shoulder while I scooted for cover behind an oak tree along the edge of Thirty-third Street.

I peeked from behind the tree and saw the top of Richie's head bobbing above the top of the railroad bed. He was between me and home, so I hunkered down to think.

Glooooo gloooo. Sam fluffed his feathers and cooed in my ear, sort of like giving me advice.

Richie must have come swaggering on down to the frog ditch while I was at Mr. Gushowski's buying a sack of fresh spinach for Mom. He hadn't seen me yet, but I still had to figure out how to get home. Maybe I could tear like mad down Thirty-third Street in hopes that he'd be so busy killing frogs he wouldn't see me until it would be too late for him to catch me and pee on my face like he'd been threatening to do. The safest bet would be to circle about ten miles out along Green Bay Road, hike down Twenty-fifth Street, wallow about half a mile through the Twenty-ninth Street Slough, then crawl on my belly down the tracks and sneak home after dark.

"Pow pow pow!" Richie kept heaving rocks at the little green leopard frogs when they came up for air. Monster explosions of water and frog guts pooched up, then sifted down in a dribbly mist as I squeezed the spinach bag under my arm and swore deep down inside. My frog ditch. My frogs.

Caw caw caw caaaaaw! Sam barked his danger signal as he sprang from my shoulder, then swooped past Richie's head and landed on a power line above the ditch. *Braaaack screeee! Yah yah yah!*

Caw caw! Richie croaked. He climbed on top of the railroad bed and pitched a rock at Sam.

Yuk yuk! Haw poot! Sam made an insulting remark about Richie's aim as the rock sailed way above his perch.

"Dow dow." Richie aimed and fired an imaginary gun.

"Errrr." I felt a weaselly growl grind in my throat as I edged from behind the tree, dug through some gravel, and found a smooth, marble-sized stone. Then I whipped out my slingshot with its new red inner tube rubbers, took aim, and let fly.

Ever done something, then changed your mind almost before the deed was done? I mean, as soon as that rock was on its way, I wanted to race after it and catch it before it plinked off Richie's freckled hide. Puny rock; it wouldn't even break the snot bubble on old Richie's nose. But it would make him mad. And anybody Richie got mad at had as much chance of survival as a toad squatting in front of a road-grading machine.

Came a dinky little pinging sound as the pebble glanced off a rail no more than five feet from where Richie stood with his arm reared back to fling another rock. Slowly, like the gun turret on a battleship, Richie's head started to turn around.

"Oh jeeez. Oh jeeeez. Oh jeeez." I flung myself behind the oak tree, rolled into a ball, and laid there groaning while knobby acorns gouged my ribs.

Paralyzed, that's what I was. Nothing worked, except for my sweat glands, which were oozing like a wrung-out sponge. With the last breath I would ever take wedged sideways in my throat, I heard Sam cawing from the other side of the tracks. Old Richie was coming for sure, rock-hard fists and a crazy snot-nosed grin spread all over his face. Clodhopper shoes scuffing gravel along the road, and then a sticky snot bubble swelling in front of my face. Soon, hot, yellow pee would be dribbling down the back of my neck, or even worse, spattering on my face. Then I remembered when Richie beat Arvey up, kneeing him in the crotch and punching him in the stomach so hard he puked all over himself.

That did it. Wheezing hard, I ran, cold sweat freezing against my face while my breath was all raspy like sandpaper against the back of my throat. I didn't stop until I reached the big maple tree next to Mr. Gushowski's front gate. Only when I turned around and looked back, old Richie—the King Kong of my worst nightmares—was throwing rocks at the frogs as if nothing had happened at all.

"Aw jeeez. Ohh fer cryin' out loud. Poop!" There was my bag of spinach, back along the side of the road. I slunk into Mr. Gushowski's yard, thinking I might ask him for more spinach, on credit this time. But I felt too ashamed, so I just sneaked through his vineyard, figuring to take a long way home. Of course, I'd have to creep past Mrs. Fenner's flower bed too, checking first to make sure she wasn't in her backyard. My tail was between my legs, and a cowardly feeling hung all over me like flies buzzing around a dead skunk.

A couple of minutes later, I crept up on the railroad bed and peeked at Richie from behind a power line pole. He wasn't looking, so I started crossing the tracks.

Caw caw caw. Only here came old tattletale Sam, swooping down to land on my shoulder and let the whole world know where I was.

"Aw, crud," I said, running fast. Then I had to laugh at the way Sam reached around and tried to peck at my teeth. He liked the sound his bill made when he pecked your teeth. Arvey said that Sam could work in a dentist's office checking teeth, just by the sound they made.

Meanwhile, Old Richie was still bombing frogs. I was home free.

I heard a whistle, looked across the tracks toward my house, and saw a couple of kids coming through the oaks. It was Wally and a shirt-tailed cousin of his, a kid named Frank Murray who rode his Whizzer motorbike up from North Chicago and hung out around our neighborhood every once in a while.

Frank was about Richie's age, maybe a little older, but not as big. He was really tough, though—most North Chicago kids are. He chucked rotten fruit at cop cars and shot out streetlights with his pellet gun. He took girls out to movies and bragged about making out in the dark. He smoked Camel cigarettes without getting sick, and he carried a switchblade he cleaned his fingers with.

"Hey, Teedo, what's up?" Frank was playing catch with a rock as he and Wally slid down the slope toward the railroad bed.

"Oh, nothin'." I caught the rock Frank threw at me with an underhanded toss.

"'Nothin',' hey. You hidin' from that big dumb kid over there? The one with the stupid grin on his face?"

"Naw. Just takin' a shortcut across the tracks."

"Don't look like no shortcut to me. Wally and I seen you comin' down Thirty-third Street a little while back." Frank grinned and gave me a little punch on the arm. You could see where he'd taken an ink pen and drawn a swastika on the back of his hand. "Come on. Let's go back down along the tracks."

"This way's shorter." Wally's German army helmet swiveled and rattled on his head as he nodded in the direction of my house.

"Hey, what's up? Both you guys scared?" Frank reached out and petted Sam who was now perched on my head.

"Well, he is kind of tough." Wally kept looking at Richie while chewing on one of his fingernails.

"The heck he is." Frank didn't bother to look back as he started walking in Richie's direction along the tracks.

Trading sick grins, Wally and I hurried to catch up.

Frank had some marbles with him, so we took turns shooting my slingshot at glass insulators on the power line poles. After knocking a chip out of an insulator, Frank winked at Wally and me, then sailed a marble about five feet over Richie's head.

"Oh gosh," Wally groaned. "Look out."

"Look out for what?" Frank squinted over the fork of my slingshot and bounced a marble off a power line pole about five feet from where Richie was blasting rocks into the ditch.

It was probably my imagination, but all at once, the weather seemed to turn cold. Sam leaped up from my head and flew screaming into the oak grove.

Richie turned around, his yellowish green eyes zeroing in on Frank who just stood there grinning and twirling the slingshot at the end of its rubber straps. "Hey, ya jerk. Shoot that thing at me one more time, an' I'll knock yer teeth down yer throat."

"Yeah? You and who else?"

"Me, myself, an' I." A rock the size of Australia hummed past our heads. Richie bent over and picked up another one in his knobby-knuckled fist.

"That does it, turd face." Frank stuffed my slingshot in his back pocket and motioned for us to spread out along the railroad tracks.

"Oh, cripes," Wally groaned.

"C'mon." Frank reared back and threw a rock.

In unison, Wally and I made little whimpering sounds. No one—I mean, no one—had ever thrown a rock at Richie and lived. But there we were, throwing white limestone rocks at a guy who reminded me of a warthog I'd seen last week at the Racine Zoo.

Funny thing, though. Besides being scared of Richie, I was madder than spit at Frank for what he'd done. He could jump back on his Whizzer and make a getaway back to North Chicago after the rock fight was done. Wally and me, we had to keep living in the same neighborhood with a kid who could do one-handed pushups and who once ate a cockroach, just to show how tough he was.

Meantime, you could tell old Richie wasn't scared. He was strutting around yelling, "Eeeeee yah! Eeee yah" while letting the rocks we threw at him come close without bothering to duck.

"Ah, ya throw like a girl!" He caught one of Wally's rocks and zinged it back. It took a cock-eyed bounce off a railroad tie and popped Wally in the knee.

"Ohhhhhh." Wally turned the color of library paste. "I wanna go home."

"Y-yeah," I agreed.

But there was Frank, a regular General Patton, still throwing rocks at Richie who kept calling Wally a crybaby in between Tarzan yells. He was beating his chest too. And you could see his arm muscles bulging up below his dirty T-shirt sleeves.

"Chickenshits! Crybaby chickenshits! Can't hit the broad side of a barn, even if yer inside it." Richie turned his back on us and leaned against a power line pole.

Frank got a sly smile on his face when Richie did that. He picked up a really big rock and instead of throwing it hard, he just lobed it at Richie as if they were playing catch. It took a while for the rock to get there, but it couldn't have been a better throw. Richie had just turned back around when it hit him with a big watermelon thump, right where it said Blatz Beer on his T-shirt front.

"Okay!" Frank yelled. "When I say 'Now,' everybody throw."

I couldn't tell if Richie was really hurt or just scared. But after a couple of volleys, he had no more fight left. He just stood there bawling and yelling, "You dirty guys! Leave me alone. Leave me alone." Big tears streaked down his dirty face.

Frank charged right at Richie, head down. Even though Richie was about twenty pounds heavier, Frank butted him in the stomach and knocked him down.

Richie let out a warthog grunt, sat on his rump, then did this really incredible, slow motion, backward summersault through the cattails and into the frog ditch.

Sam cheered, *Caw caw caaaaw!*

I war whooped and flung a rock that splashed in front of Richie and exploded water in his face.

"Yaaaa! Chickenshit Dago chickenshit!" Frank was jumping up and down, flapping his arms. "Buck buck buck. Now look who's the chickenshit. Get out of that ditch or I'll bash ya with a rock."

When Richie got up and started to climb out of the ditch, Frank punched him in the mouth. Richie didn't fall, or even stagger. He just stood there yelling, "Leave me alone. Leave me alone."

"Dago chickenshit." Frank braced one foot behind Richie and tried to trip him up. Instead, he lost his own balance and sat down on the slope of the ditch. Frank looked tight-faced when he rolled over and got up. I guess he thought old Richie was going to jump on him the way Wally and I thought he would. But Richie just stood there with his hair all plastered with mud and blood oozing out of his nose.

"Come on, you guys." Frank punched Richie, and Richie fell back down in the ditch. Frank waded partway into the ditch and pushed Richie's face in the mud. "Come on!" he yelled again.

My knees felt all rubbery when Wally and I ran down to the ditch, and I just stood there shaking while Frank straddled Richie's back and worked his face back and forth in the mud. Both Wally and I expected Richie to bunch up those big Tarzan muscles of his and pitch Frank out of the ditch. But he didn't. He just kept bawling, "Le'me alone! Le'me me alone!"

Frank got off Richie's back, kicked him in the side, and climbed out of the ditch. His eyes looked wild—kind of like animal eyes. "Get up," he said.

Richie got up, sobbing and spitting mud out of his mouth.

"Okay," Frank told Wally and me. "Push him back down."

"Naw." Wally was shaking. "He's had enough."

Now Frank was really yelling. And his lips were pulled back, showing his teeth. "Do it! Push him back down!"

Together, Wally and I gave Richie a shove. His chest felt hard under his wet T-shirt, almost like it was carved out of wood. He stepped backward but didn't go down.

"Harder!" Frank yelled.

This time, Richie went down, almost before we pushed. He sat there, grinning that stupid grin at us from down in the ditch.

"Hey, look." Frank held up a rusty tin can. "Turd face has been catchin' crabs out of your ditch." He handed the can to me. In it two bluish green crayfish were circling like two wrestlers with their pinchers locked.

Frank said, "You know what we're gonna do? We're gonna depants him and let the crabs pinch him where it'll do the most good."

Wally and I looked at each other, and then at Frank's wildish-looking eyes. I got a tight, uncomfortable feeling between my legs. We didn't say a word.

By this time, Richie was trying to get up, but Frank pushed him down and started tugging at his pants. This time, Richie fought hard, his arm and back muscles bulging, his chest pumping really hard in and out.

Now Sam's shadow was flickering over the frog ditch. *Caaaaaw caaaaaw! Caaaaaaaaaaaaaw!* It was a crow war cry, the same war cry I heard on a day when shotguns blasted and the sky was all swarmy and black with crows.

All at once, a fierce, hot feeling churned my insides. I grabbed Richie's leg and tugged at his pants.

"You dirty guys! You dirty guys!" He kicked and twisted, but I hung on to his leg and bit him as hard as I could. Mud felt gritty but at the same time kind of oily in my mouth. I spit it out and gnawed on him again.

"Ow ow owww!" Richie made big bawling noises, like a calf. Then he kicked loose and heaved around on his stomach. Frank was on him, piggyback. Muddy water made this sucking and slopping noise each time they moved.

"C'mon, you guys! Gimmie a hand!" Frank had Richie's arm twisted in a hammerlock.

Still bawling, Richie heaved up on his knees. He propped himself with one hand and tried to crawl out of the ditch. Frank was shoving his twisted arm so far between his shoulder blades I thought something might snap.

All at once, I wanted Frank to stop. Only I couldn't say a word. I just stood there listening to Richie bawl while he and Frank swilled around in the mud. Old Sam kept screaming like some kind of death angel overhead.

I sure was scared—not of Richie anymore, but of Frank and Wally and me, and of what we were trying to do. And I remembered other times when I was sort of like in a gang and had done mean things I'd never have done if I'd been by myself. Like the time I chased poor old scabby-legged Angie Smith with a rotten bullhead and shoved it down the back of her neck. And Wally and Arvey and a bunch of other kids were laughing and cheering me on.

And there was this other time when I hid in the weed lot with Wally and Arvey giggling behind me while I waited for old Mrs. Powel to come by on her way home from shopping at Marshall's store. And when she shuffled down the alley with a shopping bag full of stale bread and produce scraps Mr. Marshall had given her, I yelled, "Hey, you old jigaboo," feeling really mean and dirty even before the words blurted out of my mouth. And I watched her pull inside of herself and grow even older and more tired than before as she reached up with a skinny, black hand and pulled her ragged brown coat tight around her neck.

Now it was going to happen all over again. Only I didn't want it to, even if Richie was a dirty, rotten kid who'd killed my kitten and done a gazillion other rotten things. It was like I'd started running downhill, and it was fun at first, but then I didn't want to run anymore, only I couldn't stop.

"Hey. Jiggers." Wally gave me a poke and nodded in the direction of my house. It was Mom. She was running hard and pulling loose the red-and-white-checked apron coming untied from around her waist. I looked back to where Frank was still pushing Richie's face in the mud.

"Hey, look out," I said.

Frank heard me and stood up. When he saw Mom running, he started talking to Richie in a loud voice. "Okay. I'm gonna let you go this time. But don't you come around here pickin' on anyone else again." He grabbed Richie's arm and helped him out of the ditch.

By this time, Mom was standing at the edge of the road, scowling down at us in the ditch. Her hair was mussed up from running, and she stared at us for what seemed like forever. Finally, she brushed some hair from in front of her eyes and said, "Richie, maybe you'd better go on home."

Richie stopped bawling. He was breathing in little sobs—the kind you can't stop, like hiccups that hurt when they jump out of your insides. He looked at Mom with his stupid grin, then tried to use his T-shirt sleeve to wipe mud and snot off his face. All he did was smear it from one place to the next. Mud was clogged up in his hair too, and his clothes made wet, hissing sounds when he climbed out of the ditch.

"Here." Frank gave him the crayfish can. Richie took it, then sucked in a deep breath before bawling again.

Scary big loud sounds, they flung themselves out of his chest—like maybe he was crying for all the times his old man had whipped him and he hadn't opened his mouth. "You dirty guys! You dirty guys!" And then he sloshed off down Thirty-third Street. His voice rang loud in my ears, even after he was gone.

"Get on home!" Mom's fingernails dug half-moon marks in my arm. "And it's time for the two of you to go home too." Her voice sounded like iron when she spoke to Wally and Frank. Then she started leading me toward the house.

"The spinach," I said. "It's on the other side of the tracks."

"Leave it," Mom said.

I was sure Mom was going to give me a good licking, but she didn't say another word about what we were doing to Richie in the frog ditch that day. She did make me take a long nap and stay in the house for the rest of the day. And every so often, she gave me a frowning, almost-fearful look, as if she'd turned over a rock and seen all kinds of scary-looking bugs and beetles and centipedes crawling and wriggling around underneath.

Chapter 20

"Land sakes! What have we got here?" Grandma Hoover came out on her back porch and sort of squinted over her rimless glasses at Sam and me. She was a feisty little lady with warmish brown eyes and happy wrinkles that turned up when she smiled. She was quick, sort of like a bird, even though she was more than eighty years old. Ever since I could remember, she'd been more than eighty years old.

In those eighty years, Grandma had seen and done most everything, just about. She'd seen real, wild Indians living in real tepees when she was a little girl out west. She'd lived through blizzards and tornadoes, dust storms and floods, ridden in a stagecoach, flown in a biplane and driven an ostrich cart. She claimed to have seen a real western gunfight, got her skirts singed in the Chicago fire, and seen old Teddy Roosevelt at the Bull Moose Convention in 1912. When she told me stories, my mind crammed itself full of zinging bullets and buffalo stampedes, wrecked ships smashing against rocks, and tornadoes spinning down out of the sky. Grandma Hoover was just about the best grandma a kid like me could wish for on a star.

When she wasn't churning out stories, she was doing nine million interesting things. For example, she had this antique sewing machine, the kind that works with foot power instead of electricity.

Buffalo gals won't you come out tonight
Come out tonight
Come out tonight . . .

Laughing and singing, her skinny legs pumping, she made me my first butterfly net.

One summer, she caught a praying mantis and put it in her window. "I want you to meet Reverend Dowie," she said. Then she put me to work catching flies for the reverend who held them in his front legs and munched on them like you'd eat vanilla cookies.

I remember one time when Mom and Dad took a week-long trip to Lake Geneva so as to escape parenthood for a while. In swooped Grandma, saying, "Land sakes. This place looks like the wreck of the Hesperis." So then she bustled around, dusting everything that didn't move and putting Mom's books right side up in the bookshelves.

"What kind of cookies do you like?" she asked, heading toward the kitchen.

"Chawkit chimp," Carson John yelled. He spun around and around and fell on his rump.

While cookie smells seeped out of the oven, Grandma plunked a big black purse down on the kitchen table. She reached in elbow deep and fished out all the stuff needed to make a bunch of homemade toys. With an empty thread spool, a rubber band, a couple of toothpicks, and a button, she made a little machine that raced across the kitchen floor faster than the windup car Carson John got for his birthday.

A little later, she took some tinfoil, a needle, and matches and made a rocket that spurted smoke and flew halfway across the room. "Eeeeeyow!" Carson John spun around and fell on his rump again. After Dad and Mom got back from Lake Geneva, Dad said that the two of them could have stayed away another week. Maybe even a year.

Anyway, Sam and I were on Grandma's back porch, and when she came out, he flew from my shoulder to the top of her head. *Ooooogle ooooo*, he gurgled. Grandma was the lady who gave cookies to hungry crows.

Grandma shrieked in a high, rusty voice while Sam pecked and worried at the place where her hair was knotted in a bun. "Tom fool crow." Then she frowned into the bucket I'd lugged up and set down on her back porch. "Been to the lagoon again, I suppose."

I grinned and wiped mud from my hands on to my blue jeans. The lagoon was this two or three acre-sized pond right smack in the middle of town. It just sat there, surrounded by cattails and willows and filled with all kinds of wiggly, creepy-crawly beasts. Most everybody called it the Zion Pond, and some folks said it was an eyesore that ought to be cleaned up. Isn't it a shame that some people can't stand to see a weed patch or a swamp without wanting to chop it down or fill it up? People like that are the natural born enemies of most ten-year-old kids.

Eyesore or not, to Sam and me, the Zion Pond was heaven, and we wouldn't have traded it for anything, not even a Ferris wheel or a merry go 'round. Its mucky water was all ripply with tadpoles, minnows, water striders, and whirligig water bugs. If a guy didn't mind getting a little muddy, he could sneak up on frogs—little spotted green ones you could hypnotize by stroking under the chin. There were water snakes and snapping turtles, too: big ones that bit like alligators if you didn't grab them just right.

Besides that, I could catch baby bullheads and sunfish with an old coffee strainer while Sam argued with the redwing blackbirds that nested in the cattail reeds. And sometimes I might catch a crayfish to feed Sam for lunch.

The good old Zion Pond. That place was so wild and swampy it had to be left over from when thunder lizards and duck-billed dinosaurs sloshed and stomped through the muck.

"Well, land sakes," Grandma was saying. "What tom fool creatures have you caught this time around?" Her glasses slid down her nose when she bent over to look in the bucket of greenish pond water slopping back and forth and spilling all over my P.F. Flyer tennis shoes.

"Land o' Goshen! What's that?"

"A bullhead."

"What! With all those feelers and things?"

"Yeah, Gran'ma. An' look at this." I tilted the bucket and drained some water out so she could see all the way down.

"Mercy sakes!" Grandma's eyes popped wide open while she jerked her hands up and covered her mouth. "Enough crawdads and hoptoads to fill Noah's Ark. Don't you let them get away, or a body won't be safe in her own house."

Ga do, ga do, Sam agreed, sort of doing a little polka on top of her head.

I grinned while putting a board over the bucket and weighing it down with a flowerpot. Grandma and I were playing the game we always played when Sam and I stopped by her house on the way home from the pond. Somehow the day seemed a lot more exciting if she pretended to be scared to death of what I caught. But of course, it was just a game. In her day, Grandma'd been chased by just about everything, including a forty-pound turkey that got insulted when she tried to turn it into Thanksgiving dinner and knocked her down the cellar steps. She sure as heck wasn't fearful of no little green frog.

"Well, mercy sakes. Come on in." Grandma gently swiped Sam off her head. "But old Sammy Crow and all those animal friends of yours will have to stay outside." Bent over and smiling, she tilted the board up just a crack. "Goshen!" she shrieked when a leopard frog tried to jump out. "The good Lord surely did make enough creatures that crawl and hop."

I went ahead of Grandma as she reached over my head and pulled open the screen door. "Now listen," she whispered, sort of herding me inside. "Let's not get to talking any more about frogs, snakes, and such. Poor Mrs. Funk is out of sorts."

Poor Mrs. Funk. She was a sour old soul who'd been staying with Grandma for almost a year. When she talked, her voice reminded me of scouring pads, and she was skinny and stringy haired and all wrinkled up. Where the wrinkles in Grandma's face turned up, Mrs. Funk's turned down. And where Grandma had fizz water bubbling through her veins, Mrs. Funk had lemon juice. The old lady was in the kitchen when Grandma opened the door. She scooted away like a scared lizard when the two of us went inside.

After skittering out of the kitchen, Mrs. Funk turned around to scowl at me over a pair of rimless glasses and down this really long carrot of a nose. She was tall and gloomy and stood hunched over, sort of like a question mark. "The word of God," she rasped. "Teach him the word of God." I could tell she was still upset from the last time when a frog jumped at her out of a paper bag I was holding in my hand.

Poor old Mrs. Funk. She had to be a bigger strain on Grandma than me or any frog or snake that might get loose in the house. To say it politely, the poor old soul had sort of fallen off her perch. The cause of it all was Mr. Funk.

I didn't hear the whole story when I was ten, probably because a kid can be dirty behind the ears, but between them he's got to stay pure. How they expect a guy to grow up, get married, and "beget offspring" like it says in the Bible is more than I can figure out. I guess grown-ups figure everything a kid needs to know about stuff like that will seep in through his pores. Eavesdropping helps.

The Funks, I learned mostly at the top of the stairs when Mom and Dad thought I was asleep, were religious folks. "Fundamentalist fanatics," was what Dad said several times. Anyway, Mr. Funk was one of those self-appointed soul savers you see standing on street corners every once in a while. A couple of times, Arvey and Wally and me saw him in the parking lot of Shorty's Tavern when we rode our bikes south of town. He was this tall, bony old guy, and his voice rasped a lot like dry bark or sandpaper while he read out of the Bible and preached against something he called "the bedevilment of John Barleycorn."

"That's whiskey," Dad later explained. Dad also said that Mr. Funk spent a lot of his time praying for the souls of wayward young girls. You know, girls that have run away from home.

Only there was a funny thing we noticed about this particular wayward young girl we saw him with one time. She looked to be about thirty years old, had bright orange lipstick and frizzy blonde hair. She had on a clingy, green dress that shimmered and rustled like tinfoil when she walked.

Mr. Funk was yelling and praying and thumping an open Bible with his fist. And the wayward young girl had one arm around his waist and kept saying, "Tell it to 'em, preacher man." She winked at Arvey and me and gave Mr. Funk a bump with her hip.

There were several of these wayward young girls in the area, and one day, Mr. Funk went home from Shorty's with one of them in his 1932 Dodge. He told Mrs. Funk something about anointing her with the love of God and providing her with a decent Christian home. The fact that the wayward young girl wore her hair piled in curlicues, had purple eyelids and fire engine red lips didn't bother Mrs. Funk. She was so worked up over doing missionary work she allowed Mr. Funk and his wayward young girl to have private prayer meetings down in the fruit cellar for quite a while before figuring out what was going on. But when she did find out, the shock of her revelation nearly drove Mrs. Funk crazy, and Grandma took her in.

Mr. Funk? He ran off with the wayward young girl and never came back. Arvey said he heard something about them joining a traveling revival meeting of some kind. You know—where a mob of people sing and pray inside a big tent. And then some crippled people jump out of wheelchairs and holler, "Dear Lord! I've been cured." Afterward, the crippled people that have been cured come by all teary-eyed and ask you to put money in a hat or on a tin plate.

Anyway, now that Grandma was taking care of Mrs. Funk, I began to add to the education I'd been getting while talking to Arvey about girls' underpants and looking at the picture book before it got stuck in the handlebars of his bike. Of all people, my best teacher was Mrs. Funk. She didn't educate me on purpose. But I got educated just the same.

Like the time Mrs. Funk was in the parlor with Grandma, knitting and sipping tea and talking about the bake sale at the Grace Missionary Church. All of a sudden, Mrs. Funk started to squirm, then to moan: "Ohhhh, Lordy . . . Oooooh, Lord."

Came a deep breath. Then a scream: "Ohhhh, Satan! Oh, Jesus Christ!" Boy, when she did that, her voice prickled my skin like fingernails scratching a slate. Right after that, her teacup and knitting frog hopped straight into the air, and she started ripping her clothes off and tossing them all over the place—just like a gopher flinging sand out of a hole.

Of course, I didn't know as much then as I do now. So I was really more interested in all her twists and moans and her big old plaster-cracking whoops of, "Lord save me! Old Satan's got me!" than I was in the parts of her being shown off.

Later on, Arvey and I crawled under a carnival tent south of town and peeked at a strip tease show before they shagged us out. It sure was exciting, but I took off on my bike, thinking I'd seen it done before, only with a lot more style. Poor Mrs. Funk. Maybe she kind of missed her calling somewhere along the line.

Anyway, while Mrs. Funk was undressing in the parlor, Grandma went scratching and clucking through her purse until she fished out two quarters and a dime. "Mercy sakes," she gasped. "It certainly is hot. Why don't you run on down to Bicket's drug store and get yourself a malt."

It sure would be interesting to figure out why old Mrs. Funk acted the way she did. Maybe she was getting back at the religion she probably figured had let her down. And then there's that old saying—something about hell and fury and a woman scorned. I've mulled it over quite a bit because I guess you could say I was the one who accidentally unscrewed the last couple of bolts that held together what was left of poor Mrs. Funk's brain.

It happened like this. After I left my bucket on the porch and got in the kitchen, Grandma decided I needed a bath. Either that or a good hosing down. "Which is it going to be?" she asked, sort of grinning and frowning at the same time.

"I really ain't very dirty," I said. "But I guess I'll take a bath just the same."

"Hog wash," Grandma snorted. "Don't forget your ears." She reached out and fingered them as if they'd been dead for quite some time and left to rot in the sun.

If you want to know the honest truth of it, I'd been looking forward all day to Grandma's tub. It was a big-bellied monster, sort of squatting on a set of legs that looked as if they'd been swiped off a dinosaur. There was so much fanciness about it, and Grandma kept it so clean and white you could have put wheels on it and driven it to church without feeling ashamed. Besides that, it was so long and deep a kid my size could stretch out and glug around underwater without touching its slick porcelain finish at either end. It had brass faucets too. Turn them on and it was like water thundering out of a fire hose.

Anyway, I had the water gushing full force as soon as Grandma shut the door. Her old tub rumbled and bubbled like a waterfall while I shucked my clothes off and climbed inside. Along with me, I brought the garter snake I'd hidden in a paper bag tucked down inside my pants.

Let me tell you, there isn't anything quite like the tickly feeling of a garter snake slithering across your bare stomach and squirming between your legs. I snorted and gurgled around underwater, coming up every half minute or so while that poor, yellow-striped snake raced around making squiggly tracks in the soap suds. I bet I was in that tub half an hour at least—the longest time by twenty minutes I'd ever spent taking a bath. I didn't get out until Grandma pounded on the door and hollered that lunch had been ready so long that the bread was getting stale. "Land sakes," she yelled. "I thought you might have drowned in there."

I got dressed, but left the snake in the bathtub. The plan was to smuggle a frog in the house after lunch and see if the snake would eat it underwater.

Meanwhile, Mrs. Funk was shuffling around complaining that the floppy, oversized slippers she had on were cramping her feet. Poor old lady. I can still picture the sad sight of her as I came out of the bathroom. She had her teeth out, and her lips were sucked up inside her mouth. Yellowish gray hair dangled, all forlorn and stringy, in front of her eyes. A yellow bathrobe hung from her bony body, kind of like a gunnysack nailed over an empty widow frame. She'd taken a pair of scissors from Grandma's sewing basket and was snicking them around in midair. When she went by me, I heard those paddle-sized slippers of hers flapping against the soles of her feet.

"Lord," she groaned. "Lord, Lord, Lord."

Into the living room she went, moaning and complaining something about it being the Lord's will that she should bear such a cross. From where I was sitting in the kitchen, you could see her gnawing away with those scissors across the toes of her slippers while muttering something about Satan doing the best to squeeze the breath out of her soul.

"Dear me," Grandma sighed. She commenced bustling around the kitchen, watering her African violets and muttering something about it being, "another one of Edna's bad days."

All of a sudden, Mrs. Funk got up and headed in the direction of the kitchen. But then she made a right turn halfway down the hall and shuffled into the bathroom, moaning like a whole hospital full of sick people as she went inside.

My whole body froze up when that bathroom door slammed shut and the lock clicked into place. I'd just taken a big bite of my peanut butter and jelly sandwich, and when I swallowed everything, it felt like a gob of mud had been dumped down my insides.

"You sick?" Grandma asked.

"N-n-no."

She gave me the eagle eye over the top of her glasses and pressed the back of her hand against my cheek.

Now I'm listening to the toilet seat coming down. It gets quiet. Then there is a whole bunch of bathroom noises that polite people aren't supposed to hear.

"You sure you're all right?"

"N-n-n . . . I mean yes."

I blew out a little sigh as I heard the toilet being flushed.

"Come on," Grandma said. "Stick out your tongue." I did, and she grabbed it like it was a slab of meat, then twisted it around so as to get a good look at it from all sides. "How are you feeling?" she asked again.

"Ogay," I said, trying to peek around her in the direction of the bathroom door.

All at once, Grandma let go of my tongue as the most monstrous, plaster-cracking shriek echoed up and down the hall.

"Dear Lord above," Grandma said. "What was that?"

Came another shriek, all shrill and gargly and half-strangulated with spit: "Eeeeeeeooooooguh!" And then a whole string of out-of-breath *yip yip yip*s commenced keeping time with whatever was banging against the bathroom door.

Jiggling and rattling like mad, the door sort of bulged in the middle, then flew open and banged against the wall.

Out skipped old Mrs. Funk, one hand jacking up her underpants. They were pink. Some of the elastic had pulled loose and was hanging down her leg. "There," she wheezed. "In there."

"Dear Moses in the wilderness!" Grandma started after her, but Mrs. Funk backed off and skittered halfway into the living room.

"Oh, Lord," she moaned. "The devil's come. He's here! In this very house!"

Her eyes goggled up to the ceiling, then dropped down and zeroed in on me while I sat there as if the seat of my pants was nailed to the chair. Something soft and mushy was oozing out of my fist. It was the squished remains of my peanut butter and jelly sandwich bleeding these giant glops of grape jelly all over Grandma's lace tablecloth.

"Save him!" Mrs. Funk screeched. "He brought the devil into this house! Save his soul!"

The sleeves of her robe flapped against her skinny arms as she scooted into the living room and snatched the scissors up. "Kill the devil! Cut the devil out of the boy!"

Grandma tried to fling herself between the two of us, but that crazy old lady shot past her in half a flash. She moved so fast that one of her slippers flew off. And then I could hear that one bare foot of hers slapping against the linoleum as she paddled toward me across the kitchen floor.

I didn't need to hear or see any more. Butcher knives—that's what those scissor blades were. And Mrs. Funk was going to slice me in half with one snicker-snack.

I bailed out of my chair so fast it squealed and spun across the floor. What was left of my sandwich landed like a wounded animal on the linoleum as I started running around the table with Mrs. Funk baying like a whole pack of coon hounds at my heels. "Satan!" she screamed. "Devil's child!" Each time she took a swipe at me, the sleeves of her robe made these flapping, bat-wing sounds.

Well, Mrs. Funk didn't stay behind me for very long. I ran so fast that after about three or four trips around the table I nearly lapped Grandma who'd grabbed the hem of Mrs. Funk's robe. Then Mrs. Funk slipped on a wad of peanut butter and jelly, banged her hip against the table, and spun it halfway around. Grandma and I were going too fast to stop, so all three of us piled into each other and slammed against the kitchen sink.

"Satan!" Mrs. Funk's howling, wrinkled face loomed so close I could see the crinkly hairs sprouting out of her nose.

"Good Lord above." Grandma moaned as Mrs. Funk lunged at me with the scissors in a kind of wild, sidearm swipe. I ducked. Everything went black. I was dead for sure. I had to be dead. Only if I was dead, how come I had to go to the bathroom so bad? Then I found out that my head was stuck halfway up the sleeve of Mrs. Funk's robe.

I was only inside Mrs. Funk's robe for a little while, but it sure enough seemed like a day and a half. Every time she wound up to stab me, my head got yanked back and forth. Then she stopped swinging, and I knew right away she was changing those scissors over to her other hand. Sucking in a deep breath that smelled musty, like the inside of Mrs. McFarlan's shed, I dropped to my knees, slid out of Mrs. Funk's robe, scooted under the table, and popped up on the other side. The old lady took one more good swipe at me before I shagged off for the bathroom with her war-whooping behind. In one move I slammed the door, flicked the lock, and dived for cover between the bathtub and the toilet bowl.

"Oh jeez, oh jeez," I moaned. Old lady Funk was going to get me for sure. There I was, hunkered down, shaking all over and waiting for her to come crashing through solid oak.

But I didn't need a lock, or even a closed door. Mrs. Funk might have been crazy, but she wasn't dumb enough to bang her way inside a room that had both the devil and his disciple in it at the same time. The old lady didn't even touch the knob, but her voice howled like a regular blizzard just outside the door.

Well, you've got to give credit where credit is due. No one, not even Mr. Marquand, could lay into the devil like Mrs. Funk. "Oh, Jesus! Oh, Jesus Christ!" There wasn't any doubt in her mind that she had Satan holed up and was going to keep him cornered until the Second Coming. Maybe longer than that. From my hideout, I could hear her one naked foot and her one giant slipper slapping, then flapping up and down the hall. "Cut the devil out of the boy!" she whooped. "Save his soul!" Even though I'd gone to the bathroom a little while ago, I still did a fair to middling good job of wetting my pants.

Then Grandma joined in. "Oh, Lord," she sang in her best prayer meeting voice. "Give us strength and come to the aid and deliverance of thy humble flock."

For half a minute, I thought Grandma had switched sides, and I was going to have to dive through the bathroom window and run off in a shower of broken glass. Or maybe I could use the snake to hold them off with if they came crashing through the door.

But then a dim understanding of what Grandma was up to started to soak in. She'd lived in Zion long enough to know that an old devil chaser like Mrs. Funk couldn't stand to hear someone pray without joining in herself.

"Hallelujah!" yodeled Mrs. Funk. Down on the floor she went, rolling and blubbering and praying until she sounded like a whole revival meeting all by herself. "Light thy holy light, oh Lord, and wash away our sins."

Too bad I missed the first part of Mrs. Funk's act. But for a while, I was too petrified to move. Besides that, I was wedged behind the toilet so tight it would have taken a truckload of firemen with hoses and ladders, axes and crowbars, and all kinds of fireman tools to pry me loose. After a while, though, I got an itch to see what was going on. Creeping to the door, I opened it just a crack.

Just about that time, old Mrs. Funk came up with the best part of her act. Making a sort of whinnying sound, she got up from where she'd been thrashing around on the floor and asked Grandma to pray while she sang and prayed for my soul. And about halfway through "The Old Rugged Cross," she set about shucking her clothes off like they were full of ants.

What came after that was just about the most bodacious performance a kid my age could ever hope to see—better even than the Fourth of July fireworks at Shiloh Park or the *King Kong* movie Arvey and I sat through twice in one day. Not satisfied with just tearing off her clothes, Mrs. Funk started ripping them to shreds until they flew like shredded cat fur all around the room. She was a regular windmill of salvation—poor old thing, praying and chanting until that sandpapery voice of hers must have woken up every spirit in the universe.

In my imagination, that crazy old lady did the rain dance, the corn dance, a voodoo dance, and maybe even some kind of belly dance too. She also recited the Ojibway death chant and went through a bunch of Aztec fertility rites.

For just a second, I shut my eyes and saw angels and dragons come fluttering down to earth. The waters of the Zion Pond parted, and thundershowers fell on drought-struck Navajo cornfields two thousand miles away. Through it all, poor Grandma kept banging at the piano without looking up from the keys. And outside somewhere, old Sam kept cawing and cawing as if Armageddon was on its way for sure.

A little later, Mrs. Funk said a screechy "Amen," folded up on the sofa, and fell asleep. Poor old lady—without her dander up, she was just a pile of worn-out, knobby bones, sort of snoring and shivering and whimpering all at the same time.

Grandma looked tired too. Her bun hung partway undone, and her lower lip trembled, as if she was getting ready to cry. I felt really bad, like sour milk; and while Grandma covered up Mrs. Funk with what seemed to be the right kind of blanket—a crazy quilt—and wiped her face with a damp cloth, I fished the snake out of the bathtub and turned it loose outside. Then I got some Old Dutch cleaning powder and started scrubbing up the ring I'd left in the tub.

After a while, Grandma came in the bathroom, leaned against the wall, and looked at me while I scrubbed away.

"You all right?" she asked.

"Yes, Gran'ma." I kept quiet for a while, thinking maybe I'd get a good licking for what I'd done, even though I hadn't meant any harm. Then when I saw Grandma wasn't going to spank me, I felt worse than I had before. Funny thing about spankings. Sometimes they make you feel good afterward, even though they hurt some at the time.

All at once, I got up and hugged Grandma as tight as I could. "I'm sorry, Gra'ma. Really I am."

Grandma sighed. When she did that, I could feel how little and skinny she was. And old too, a lot older than Mrs. Funk. Then I thought of old Mrs. McFarlan and how pretty she was in an old picture I'd found of her inside her shed. Only now she was in an old folk's home. I started to sniffle and wiped my nose on the back of my hand.

"Oh, Lordy me." Grandma patted my head. "That's all right—even if you did a thoughtless thing, especially since you knew how fearful poor Edna is of frogs and snakes." She sighed again. "But if it hadn't been that fool snake, it would have been some other darn thing."

Grandma had been talking in a trembling voice, but all at once, she sounded strong again. And when I looked up at her, I saw how her jaw was set, and there was even a little smile on her face. Her eyes were like Mom's eyes—big and brown. Kind of warm.

"I think a part of Mrs. Funk has given up," she went on. "And when that happens, there sometimes isn't anything a person can do except have faith in the good Lord to help see things through. Life goes on," she said, almost as if talking to herself. "People die or run off. A body grows old."

All at once, I realized something I'd sort of known but never really thought about before. Grandma'd been a widow for years and years. Grandpa Hoover was only a picture in a scrapbook—the way Mrs. McFarlan was.

Grandma was kind of surprised when I asked about Grandpa and wanted to see his picture in the album again. "Well, land sakes. Of course, you can see his pictures. But I can't imagine why you want to look at them now."

She got out an old leather-covered album and told me about Grandpa Hoover while I looked at some pictures of a sort of stern but half-smiling man. He had a big walrus moustache and a strong-looking chin—like maybe a boxer or a football player might have.

"Your grandpa was a riverboat captain on the Columbia River for a while." Grandma's skinny fingers stroked one of the pages while she spoke. "Then he was a Pinkerton detective and a policeman after that. He died of heart attack," she said kind of wistfully, "in a train station in Kenosha, a long time ago."

All at once, I felt scared again. "A heart attack. Could I die of one of those?"

"Well, mercy me. No one knows for sure how they're going to die." Grandma laughed and gave me a hug. "But I guarantee at the rate you're going, you'll be causing a lot of heart attacks before it comes time for you to have one of your own."

Grandma put away the picture album and helped me clean the tub that had a ring in it about a foot wide. Then she took me into the kitchen and gave me some cookies and a glass of milk. "Well," she said after I'd eaten, "I guess it's about time you went on home."

Before leaving, I slipped into the living room and looked at Mrs. Funk. She had her eyes open, but it was like she really didn't know where she was.

Her eyes jerked back and forth, kind of scared, sort of like bird's eyes when it has a broken wing.

I was scared too, and even though I wanted to say I was sorry, I shagged out the front door instead. Next day, an ambulance came and took poor Mrs. Funk to a place where she wasn't likely to find Satan in the bathtub. Unless she dreamed him up on her own.

Another sad thing happened a couple of weeks after Mrs. Funk went away. A bunch of workmen, all shouting and waving their hands, showed up when Wally and I were fishing at the Zion Pond. "Hey, you kids are gonna have to move." Then a guy in a bulldozer drove up and started uprooting most of the willow trees shading the pond. For some reason, I'll never forget that bulldozer guy. He was smoking a stumpy cigar and had a round reddish face that looked kind of like a pumpkin pie. After uprooting the willow trees, he drove his bulldozer right in the pond and dredged most of the mud out on the shore. Bullheads and tadpoles and crawdads flopped and crawled around, just dying in the sun.

"Please, Mr. Gee whiz! Don't!" Wally and I tried to scoop some of them up and throw them back in the pond.

"Hey there! You kids." The bulldozer guy spit his cigar stub out and yelled at us to stop. Red-winged blackbirds screeched and flew in circles while the rest of the workmen mowed down what was left of the cattails and the high weeds.

Next day, the workmen brought in several truckloads of clean sand and dumped them in the pond. They laid down sod where all the weeds had been and poured an asphalt sidewalk all around the pond. Then they set up park benches and some whitewashed rocks. A week later, they brought in a whole navy of ducks and geese that cruised around wiggling their hind ends and gobbling up bread that people threw in the pond.

Instead of throwing bread, Wally and I threw rocks. Old pie-face, the Bulldozer Guy was the new park custodian, and he told us if he ever caught the two of us hanging around the pond again, he'd kick our hind ends up between our ears.

Chapter 21

*S*kr*aaaaaack . . . Purrrrrr ooooot. Ge-daw, ge daw.*
    I yawned, rolled over in a hog wallow of twisted bed sheets and saw Sam perched on my outside window ledge.

"Hi, Sam." I knuckled sand grains of sleep out of my eyes.

"Wow!" Sam cranked his head back and forth while gladness sparkled in his eyes. *Screeeee. Gloo gloo gloooo. Braaaaaack.* If you're a crow, windowsills are made for strutting. And that's what Sam did, bobbing his head up and down while reciting the speech he'd made up in crow talk.

The speech ended the way it had started up, with Sam bowing and gurgling like a bottle of soda pop emptied on the ground. After that, Sam did imitations and cracked jokes. I sat on my bed and laughed while he made noises like a rusty screen door rasping shut, a lawn mower clicking, a dog barking, a cat meowing, a jay scolding, and a chicken clucking over a handful of corn.

Sam was jabbering at me as well, inviting me outside to see if I could find the Boy Scout knife he'd stolen and hidden in his gravel pile, or maybe in a tree. Maybe I could help him catch crayfish in the frog ditch, or laugh while he screamed at the last place he'd seen a little green frog plop into the water, stick its goggle eyes above the surface, then duck back out of sight. How about a bike ride, or maybe a game of dive-bomb the cat? Sam was asking me to be his friend, and he was asking the only way he knew how, by imitating the sounds we both listened to every day.

What a crow. I bounced out of bed and scrooched into my blue jeans while old Sam haw-hawed and bowed to the imaginary audience that was applauding the whiz-bang minstrel show he was putting on. "Here, Sam. Here, Sam." Now he was pounding on the screen and punching holes in it with his beak. Then he cocked his head back and made a noise that sounded like a handful of pennies falling one at a time into a jar. It was one of his happiest noises, the one he saved for warm, bug-filled mornings when the grass was all sweet and wet.

I went to the window screen, opened it, and let Sam inside. He hopped on my shoulder and gurgled directions about how to brush your teeth and comb your hair while I finished getting dressed and went on downstairs.

Carson John was bouncing and wiggle-worming in his high chair, and as soon as he saw Sam, he stuck his cereal spoon in his mouth and shook his head back and forth.

Here was a challenge no self-respecting crow could pass up. Letting out a Comanche war cry, he flung himself at Carson John, landed on the high chair top, and grabbed the other end of the spoon.

You can't imagine how strong a pound and a half of cussing crow feathers can be. Carson John's cereal bowl flipped about two feet in the air, spilling Cheerios all over Sam, Carson John, the high chair, then the floor. Then Sam stepped on a piece of strawberry jam and peanut butter toast that stuck to one of his feet.

None of this fazed old Sam. He hung on to that spoon and screeched like the Wicked Witch of the West, his wings flapping and his feet digging for traction on Carson John's high chair top. Trouble is, it's hard to get traction in a swamp of milk and cereal with one foot glued to a slice of peanut butter and jelly toast.

"Oh, for God's sake!" The war got bigger as Mom charged into the middle of it. She whapped her dish towel back and forth and gave the cereal bowl an accidental kick across the floor.

Sam hung on for a few seconds, then squawked and flapped over to the countertop next to the kitchen sink. The milk and Cheerios that had landed on him flipped off when he flapped his wings. The peanut butter and jelly toast fell off too and landed jelly side down on the new copy of *Ladies Home Journal* Mom had just started to read.

"Out!" That is the one word that, when screeched in the right tone of voice by an outraged mom, will send a kid flying to save his neck. As a matter of fact, I was already moving before Mom could draw breath. Running to the sink, I grabbed Sam who was making peanut butter and jelly tracks across the countertop. Then I ducked under a damp, whistling towel and scooted through the back door. I didn't slow down until I was off the porch and in the middle of the backyard.

Caw caw caw. I let Sam go, then stood waiting to see and hear what was going to happen next.

Moms are like hand grenades. When they go off, the closest you can be to them is about fifty yards away. Me, I gave Mom about an extra ten feet, kind of flinching and moaning at the shrapnel of yells and threats blasting through the screen door. There was really fearful stuff like: "Gonna disown the whole messy tribe of you and move as far off as I can get by plane, then oxcart and finally by foot!"

"Aw, Mom," I whined back at her. "I'll clean it up. Honest, I will."

"Big talk smarty pants," a hidden voice yelled through the open door. "Who forgot to empty the garbage yesterday? Huh? Get on out of here and leave me alone!"

"Gee, Ma. I fergot. But I'll clean everything up. Honest ta God."

"Don't 'honest to God' me. This lady's had enough."

Now there's a dead, kind of scary silence inside, except for little whimpers leaking out of Carson John. All at once, I had this picture of Mom upstairs flinging shoes and stockings and dresses and underwear in a suitcase while Carson John is hanging on to her, whimpering and leaving jellied finger prints on her dress.

"C'mon, Ma," I yelled. "Gee, Ma! Awww . . . Geeee!"

Still no sounds. By now, she was probably lugging her suitcase down the stairs with Carson John blubbering along behind.

"Ma? Ma? Maaaa?"

By this time, she'd called a cab. With her face white and her jaw set, she'd pushed Carson John away and stomped out the front door.

"C'mon, Ma. I'll clean up the whole mess an' do the dishes besides."

Now I could hear a car coming up Thirty-third Street. I shut my eyes and started to sweat. Mom's cab was almost here.

"Gosh, Ma. Aw gee. Hey, Ma. I'll do the dishes fer a whole week. Honest, Ma . . . Huh, Ma. Huh?" Now I was picturing myself at an orphanage, all bony and ragged and shivering and sitting at a long silvery table with a mob of bony, raggedy kids. Our porridge bowls sat in front of us, empty and licked clean. At the head of the table stood this orphanage lady, really big and fat and having arms the size of stovepipes folded over her chest. Beside her stood a hawk-nosed guy wearing a black frock coat. He was laughing, and he had a whip coiled up in his fist.

"Ma! Hey Ma?"

All at once came the blessed whine of the screen door opening up again. Mom stepped out on the back porch, and I let out a big sigh when I saw she still had her apron on. She grabbed a mop leaning next to the back door and held it out. "Come," she said.

This will probably surprise you, but after I swabbed up the mess and sat down to breakfast, Mom forgave Sam and let him in when he landed on the windowsill and pecked on the glass. Maybe she believed what I told her about old Mr. Marquand saying Sam was a beast of the field and was without sin. Anyway, there he was on her shoulder while she fried bacon and eggs. She even laughed as he cooed and gurgled in her ear.

As soon as Sam figured he'd been forgiven, he hopped over to the sink, landed on the drain board, and started bobbing his head up and down.

"Hmmmmm." He commented on the shiny silverware. One at a time he picked up knives, forks, and spoons and dropped them on the floor, haw-hawing over the clatter they made.

I sort of cringed. "Don't worry, Ma. I'll clean 'em up when I do the dishes and all."

"You bet your life." Mom's voice sounded kind of frosty. But then she smiled, broke off a piece of bacon, and tossed it to Sam who caught it, then flew to the table and broke into little chunks. When I started eating, he hopped up on my shoulder and pestered me for a share of bacon and toast. I gave him some, and that made him thirsty, so he dipped his beak in my milk glass, tilted his head back and let some milk trickle down his throat.

Then Mom came and sat at the table too. Figuring he hadn't got in enough trouble already, Sam walked through the butter dish, across Mom's *Lady's Home Journal* and swiped a piece of toast out of her hand.

Instead of eating it, he tap danced back to me and climbed up my arm to my shoulder, leaving buttery footprints as he went. *Cloo cloo.* With his neck stretched out, he shut his eyes while I scratched his head. After a minute or so, he reached around and stuck some toast between my lips.

"That's a love offering." Mom was smiling over the top of her magazine.

"Wuv offing," said Carson John.

Mom reached out and slapped his hands when he tried to pour orange juice into his fresh bowl of Cheerios.

"A love offering?" I stroked Sam under his chin.

"Certainly. When a grown-up bird feeds another grown-up bird, that's a sign of affection. Maybe Sam thinks you're another crow."

"Gosh." I laughed and jabbered at Sam, imitating his crow talk. Jabbering back at me, he took another piece of toast from me and shoved it in my ear.

"Whee." Of course, old Carson John had to stick a piece of toast in Mom's ear too.

"Well, thanks," Mom said, looking a bit frazzled. "But don't I get a kiss?" Laughing, she screwed up her face when Carson John left a strawberry jam kiss mark on her cheek. "Well now. I guess my day is complete."

After breakfast, I washed the dishes, emptied the garbage, then cleaned up my room besides. "I need to take your temperature," Mom said. "You must be sick."

Then I went outside and rode my bike around the neighborhood while Sam cawed and circled overhead. I'd just given my bike a new coat of blue paint, plus I'd stuck pop bottle caps in all the spokes, so it looked pretty good. Besides that, I'd fastened a piece of cardboard to the front fork. When the tire spokes hit the cardboard, they made a whirring, airplane sound.

Shying away from the new sound at first, Sam swooped down and landed on my head. From there, he hopped to the handlebars and perched there with his wings spread out. *Gleep gleep.* He gurgled, me pumping as fast as I could. A furry, black-and-gold bumblebee flew beside us, then darted off. The sun glittered off the spinning bottle caps while white puffy clouds reminded me of blimps and whales drifting across the sky. My cardboard engine purred.

Raaa ooom! Lickity split we raced, charging down the hill to Sharon Park Ravine while I pretended I was flying a Corsair fighter plane, hot on a Jap Zero's tail.

Arrooom. Dow dow dow.

Gleep gleep. Caw caw caw.

Braaaaaaap.

After diving to the bottom of the hill, we swooped left on to Sharon Place and zoomed through a cool, maple-tree tunnel while my imaginary Zero crashed and made this big flaming cartwheel along the ground. The road made a sharp bend, and we turned off it to go bumping along a path leading past wild raspberry bushes and down to the creek. The water ran all fresh and ripply, and you could see minnows darting through the reflection of clouds and trees. Old Sam bobbed up and down on my shoulder, yelling at his reflection while I tried to catch minnows with my hands.

A blue jay screamed. Sam flew off while a squirrel chuckled overhead. After a while, I gave up on the minnows but kept wading in the creek, keeping an eye peeled for brown wood frogs on the bank. Water striders made dimples on the water. Wood frogs plopped off the bank.

All at once, Sam was back. I'd been splashing around after frogs so hard I didn't hear him until he landed on my head. I laughed and turned loose the frog I'd just caught.

Sam hopped down on to my wrist, then danced up my arm, clucking and cooing like mad. It seemed like there was a motherly tone to his voice, and something long and pink and kind of rotten was dangling from his beak.

"Yaack!" I turned away. Whatever it was, it had been dead a long time.

Ever get a present you didn't really want? Like the time your great Aunt Lilly gives you a sissy shirt with ruffles down the front. Or Aunt Jane knits you a sweater with the arms about three feet too long. That's the way it was with the love offering Sam had dangling and stinking in front of my nose. I took it from him and held it out between my fingertips.

"Oh boy. Num num." When I thought he wasn't looking I dropped it on the ground.

Half a minute later, it was back where I didn't want it, all pink and smelly and being lowered down between my eyes from the top of my head.

"Hey. Cut it out."

Erg erg erg. But old Sam was making me an offer I couldn't refuse.

So there I was, laughing and almost throwing up at the same time while Sam jumped from my head to my shoulder, then back to my head again while trying to stick what looked like rotten mouse guts in my mouth. Finally, he let out a disgusted squawk and flew off, swearing as he went. I stood in the creek and laughed while Sam hooted down at me from a maple tree. Then I reached up and pulled his present out of my ear.

A couple of hours later, this really strange, cold breeze swooped down from the north, dropping the temperature maybe as much as thirty degrees.

"It's a summer cold snap," Mom explained when I went in the house. "Once when I was a little girl, we even had snow on the first day of summer."

I put on my new blue windbreaker jacket, the one with Chicago White Sox in big letters on the back. Going outside, I saw little wisps of my own breath as I called for Sam. He dropped out of the cottonwood tree onto my shoulder, then started fussing over the newness of my jacket, probably because he figured I'd grown myself some brand-new skin.

After a lot of cooing and jabbering and head scratching, I finally got old Sam calmed down. Then we piled on my bike again and went cruising past the woods and fields along Thirty-third Street out to Green Bay Road. The cool air tingled my ears and nose and sort of splashed like gulps of ice water down my throat.

Sam stuck to my shoulder, making noises that sounded like a hundred Apaches war-whooping after a wagon train. Each time a car passed us, it would slow way down and sometimes come close to driving into a ditch.

After a couple of hours, the weather warmed up a bit, so we went home and I took my jacket off and dumped it on the lawn. Hungry from all that riding, I went in the house to get Sam and me some potato chips. Only when I came back outside, there he was, running back and forth in front of my jacket while talking to himself.

Oooooogle scraaaak. Puroooot puroooot. You could see he thought I was still inside that jacket and had shriveled up and maybe died right there on the lawn. *Ooooooop ooooooooooop.* Now he was yo-yoing his head up and down so fast you'd swear he had a little motor inside.

Ga ga ga. Bent over and imitating some of Carson John's baby talk, he laid his head and neck out along the ground. *Erp?* he asked the jacket. Then he edged forward and stuck his head up its sleeve. *Ong ong.* "Hello."

When Sam didn't get an answer, he backed out of the jacket sleeve and tried to do everything a crow could think of to bring a human creature back to life. He screamed. He gurgled. He flapped. He jumped up and down on that jacket as if I was inside and needed some air pumped into my lungs. Finally, he pecked at it, tugged at it, then put one ear to it, checking for signs of life.

I sat on the porch and laughed until it hurt. But then I saw how worried he was. And then I thought I was doing to him what I'd done to poor old Mrs. Funk—being careless and not thinking about other people's feelings. By this time, Sam's wings had drooped all the way to the ground. He was screeching. *Eeeee eeeee.* And he was hopping back and forth.

I yelled, "Hey, Sam. Over here!"

Sam looked up and cocked his head back and forth to make sure it was really me. *Caw caw caw.* He screamed at me, then screamed at the jacket. He couldn't have been more excited if he'd seen another crow climb out of its feathers and hop naked across the lawn.

Caaaaw aaaaaw! He sure was glad to see me—but really mad too. The way moms and dads are when you hike through the swamp and lose your brand-new jacket and get muddy and don't come back until after dark, and about five hundred policemen and deputies are out combing the woods with flashlights and dogs.

Yeeeek! Sam flew over to me, landed on my shoulder, gave my ear a good yank, then flew off again, screeching like a dozen police whistles. He didn't stop until I put the jacket on again.

"What in the name of glory is going on now?" Mom flung open the back door and ran out on the back porch. She'd been jump roping in the living room and was breathing hard.

When I told her about Sam and the jacket, she got a warm, soft look in her eyes and reached out to scratch Sam on the top of his head. Then she gave me a little swat on the back of the neck. "That little bird sure loves you. I hope you've got enough sense to realize that."

Chapter 22

It was morning. With my eyes shut, I rolled over and listened for Sam's crow parade on the windowsill. But it was quiet, except for robins clucking on the lawn. Maybe it was raining, I thought. But when I opened my eyes, there were dust specks swirling in the sunlight spreading into my room.

I got up, went to the window, then jerked it open and called for Sam: *Caw caw.* But it was still quiet, and no shadow slid across the porch roof.

"Here, Sam." I hollered. The only answer I got was the whining and burping of Mr. Hubble's old pickup truck backing out of the Hubbles' garage. Sparky ran beside it, barking, wagging his tail, and biting at its wheels. Mr. Hubble chugged away, and it got quiet again.

I got dressed and ran downstairs, zipping up my jeans as I went. "Hey, Ma. You seen Sam?"

Mom was in the kitchen, fixing breakfast and doing her ballet exercises at the same time. If I hadn't been worried about Sam, I might have laughed to see her do a pirouette, take a slice of toast out of the toaster, then make a pointy-toed leap to where Carson John was in his high chair jigging up and down.

"Not since yesterday, sometime in the afternoon." Mom did another pirouette as she wiped jam off Carson John's face.

"Sammy crow." Carson John took a drink of milk, tilted his head back, and made a gargling sound.

Mom grabbed Carson John by the back of his neck and made him swallow his milk while she bobbed up and down on her toes. "Dad called for him this morning. But no luck."

A jagged, kind of nervous feeling started gnawing down in my stomach. I pushed hard against the screen door and ran out on the back porch. The screen door banged hard against the side of the porch, then its rusty spring twanged behind me when it slammed shut. Mom usually scolded me when I let the screen door bang. But this morning, she just came out and wiped her hands on her apron while I dragged my bike from under the porch. "Don't you want breakfast?"

"No, Ma. I ain't hungry," I yelled over my shoulder while riding out the back gate.

"Aw, jeez." My pant leg got snagged between the bicycle chain and the front spoke, so I had to stop and work it loose. After rolling my pant leg up, I took off down Thirty-third Street, yelling, "Here, Sam," as I went. It was a hot day already, and sweat trickled down my face.

"Hey, Beaner. What's up?" Arvey rode his bike out of the gravel parking lot at Marshall's store. He had a sack of groceries balanced on his handlebars, and a rope of black licorice candy hung out of his mouth. You could see a fresh scab on his arm from where he'd fallen off his bike. Old Arvey wanted to be a race car driver like Barny Oldfield, so he did Kamikaze stunts on his bike. Like riding backward down Sharon Park Hill and crashing into the creek.

Turning into the parking lot, I tore up dust when I hit the brakes. "Jeez, Arv. I can't find Sam."

Arvey frowned and squirted licorice spit. "Wait up an' I'll help ya go look." Arvey lived in a big old house with a maple tree and a rope swing in the backyard, so I swung on the rope, making gorilla noises and Tarzan yells while he took the groceries inside. When he came out, we rode slow down Gabriel Street calling Sam's name.

Like some sort of scab on the landscape, old Richie's house came into view. It was a big gray box, like a giant chicken coop with more than a dozen people crammed inside. You could see broken windows, and there was no step going up to the front porch. The yard seemed to be strangled by weeds, and there were empty tin cans all around. Six or seven old cars were hunkered down in the weeds, including a Packard Super Eight without any wheels or doors.

We were riding fast, and by the way Arvey looked at me, you could tell we were thinking the same thing—like maybe poor Sam was lying there in the weeds, or strung up somewhere, the way my kitten had been.

Came the sound of glass breaking, and we saw Richie and one of his little brothers flinging rocks at some beer bottles lined up in the alley behind their house. The sun was blazing down on a million bits of glass in the alley and in Richie's yard. Sort of a diamond mine of trash.

"Hey, Richie," I yelled. "Ya seen my crow?"

"Maybe I have an' maybe I ain't. My old man says he's gonna shoot him if he don't stop pullin' letters outta our mailbox."

We sped up. Then Arvey looked back and let fly with one of his famous licorice spit bombs. "Yer old man's too drunk to hit the broad side of a barn if he's inside it," he yelled.

Richie bent over and picked up a rock. But we were too far away, even for him. "Go soak yer head," he yelled back.

After circling the block, we rode down the alley between my house and Wally's house and met Wally coming out his back gate. He had on his German army helmet, and a Buck Rogers ray gun was stuck down inside his army belt. "I hear yer lookin' fer Sam. I ain't seen him since yesterday."

"Could be he's over at Anderson's barn." Arvey ripped a chaw out of his licorice stick.

"Wait up. I'll get my bike." Whipping out his ray gun, Wally aimed it at Arvey's crotch. It went *Guuuzzzzork!* as it cranked out a shower of red sparks.

A couple of minutes later, car brakes screeched and a horn blasted at us as we raced out of the alley and turned west on Thirty-third Street. "Dawgone stooopid kids. Gonna getcherselves killed!"

"Here, Sam! Here, Sam!" We rattled across the tracks, then stood up and pumped hard toward Anderson's barn. Wild crows cawed above some alfalfa fields as we turned in to a long driveway and rode up to the barn. We leaned our bikes against it and stepped into a place that was cool and dark and smelled of hay.

The barn was big and empty, but filled with the rustle of pigeon wings. "Here, Sam!" My voice echoed as I climbed a ladder to the loft. On an overhead beam, there was another hiding place for some of Sam's stuff. Underneath it, you could see where paper clips, wadded gum wrappers, and bottle caps had fallen down into the straw. But no sign of Sam.

"Hey," Wally said. "Maybe if we got on our bikes and just rode around."

Wally and I waited while Arvey took a leak out the hayloft window. Then we rode out to Lewis Avenue, checking the woods and fields on both sides. A hot wind started blowing as we headed back into town along Twenty-ninth Street and stopped at Graff's Corner Store. We bought grape Popsicles and sucked on them while leaning against our bikes.

"I bet somebody shot him," Arvey said.

"Naw." Wally frowned. "Ain't nobody'd do that. He's a pet."

Arvey threw his Popsicle wrapper on the ground. "Don't make no difference. Not to some guys anyhow."

I just stood there, looking at all the cigarette butts and Popsicle sticks and bottle caps along with all the other little bits of trash littering the cinder parking lot. The cold Popsicle made my teeth ache. Maybe I'd made a mistake. Maybe I should have kept Sam in a cage. Or maybe I shouldn't have stolen him out of his nest to begin with.

"If I find out some guy has shot him, I'll go get Uncle Floyd's twelve gauge." Wally scowled, looking cross-eyed at his grape-colored tongue.

We finished our Popsicles, then flicked cinders and pea gravel at each other with our Popsicle sticks. After that, we rode around some more, calling for Sam. A couple of times I thought I heard Sam cawing and told Wally and Arvey to pipe down for a second. But there was only the sound of wild crows cawing along the edge of the Twenty-ninth Street slough.

We rode toward the slough until we got to Hannah Ponder's house. Hannah was this idiot girl about eighteen years old who spent most of her time sweeping the sidewalk in front of her parents' house. She always had a funny look on her face—kind of drooly and open-mouthed. She usually wore a red sweater that was always crooked because of the buttons being in the wrong holes.

It was really strange, watching Hannah sweep. You know, with her drooly smile, and her humming a funny song that didn't have any real words. Kind of like a train whistle—low, lonesome, and far away.

"I wonder if she ever gets unhappy," I blurted out all at once.

"Who? Hannah?" Arvey was making stupid faces while groaning and slobbering the way Hannah did whenever she tried to talk. I didn't feel very good when he did that.

"Naw," Wally said. "She's too dumb."

I felt funny when Wally said that. He was probably right. I felt funny about it just the same.

We got back on our bikes and rode toward the slough. Might as well go frog hunting since we'd come this far. Only when we got there we saw a gang of kids throwing rocks at some cans lined up in the ditch along Gilboa Avenue. Just as we got alongside them, one of the kids looked up. "Hey, you." He pointed at me.

He was big and fat with thick glasses and squinty eyes. He wore a Captain Midnight decoder ring, and he had on a pair of old army pants—the kind with ginormous pockets bulging all over the place. Each pocket was crammed so full of rocks I was sure his pants were going to fall down each time he took a step. I slowed down a little but kept ready to peel out if he came after me out of the ditch.

"Hey. Wait up, will ya. Ain't you the kid that owns a pet crow?"

"Yeah." I stopped peddling and got off my bike.

"Well, this guy caught a crow yesterday on the other side of the slough. He's got it in a cage."

"Where at?" Wally and Arvey turned their bikes around, came back, and stopped.

"C'mon. I'll show ya where." The fat kid grunted while climbing out of the ditch. When he swung his leg up to get on his bike, several rocks fell out of his army pants pockets and clattered on the ground. I came near to laughing because the rear tire on his bike nearly went flat when he took off down the street. "I was lookin' for ya yesterday," he yelled over his shoulder. "But I didn't know where about ya lived."

We kept riding while the fat kid told us how this guy who lived down the street from him had taken his coon hounds out for a run in the slough. "And when he gets back to his pickup truck, there's this crow inside, just sitting on the steering wheel and pecking at the rearview mirror."

"Hey, that's old Sam, all right." Wally laughed and did a wheely on his bike.

"Well, anyways," the fat kid went on. "It ain't right to go an' put no bird in no cage. An' besides, he says he's gonna clip its wings an' slit its tongue so as he can teach it how to talk." The fat kid turned his head and blew a wad of gum into the ditch. "Anybody that knows anything about crows should know that slittin' their tongues ain't gonna make 'em talk." He was riding fast, with rocks tumbling out of his pockets and bouncing along the road. Right then, I liked him—even if he did wear glasses and was fat.

We turned down an alley and rode halfway down it before the fat kid stopped, grunted, and got off his bike. "Over there." He pointed to a white house with a fence around it and a big chicken wire pen in its backyard. Three floppy-eared dogs ran back and forth inside the pen. "They're huntin' dogs," the fat kid explained. "If they ever get out an' yer in their yard, they'll rip ya ta shreds."

I looked toward the pen. Against it leaned a beat up shed. On top of the shed sat a tiny cage about three feet long and a couple of feet wide.

"He's in there." The fat kid was wheezing from riding his bike so fast.

"Here, Sam," I yelled.

Something dark and miserable flopped inside the cage.

"Sam," I yelled again.

Caaaaaaw caaaaaaaw. Sam's voice came cracking and sawing through the heat.

The dogs started barking and howling, *Argh argh, aroooooo*, while jumping against the side of their pen.

My knees shaking, I got off my bike. "I'm gonna turn him loose."

I could hear the fat kid wheezing behind me as I walked up to the back gate. "Careful. That guy'll sic his dogs on ya if ya go into his yard."

I grabbed hold of the gate and tried to yank it open, but it was locked with a big padlock from the inside. "Maybe ya ought to go get yer folks." The fat kid yanked on the gate too.

I started to climb the gate, then let go and stepped back.

Now Sam was beating himself against the wire sides of the cage, and there was this really desperate, twanging noise. Loose feathers spurted out of the cage and blew across the shed roof. Sam made a strangled cry I'd never heard before.

"Oh jeez." I climbed back on the gate and sat on it with one leg on each side. My throat felt tight, and there wasn't any spit in my mouth.

"Ya gotta do it," Arvey said.

"Hurry up." The fat kid kept looking at me and then at the dogs that were making the wire pen bulge each time they jumped against its sides. They showed their teeth and threw their heads back each time they barked.

Now a screen door slammed shut. A man stood on the back porch of the white house, a bag of garbage in one arm. "Hey, you kids. Get off my gate."

I bit my lip but stayed with one leg over the gate. "Please, mister. That's my crow you got over there."

The man clumped down from his porch and walked to about ten feet from where I still sat on his gate. He bent over and dumped his garbage into an empty oil drum. His arms were thick and sunburned where he had his blue shirtsleeves rolled up. "Sorry, kid. That crow's mine. Caught him in my pickup truck."

"He ain't yours. He ain't! My mom and me, we raised him from when he was just a chick."

The man lit a match and threw it in the drum. "Well, that's too bad. If he was yours, you should have kept him caged up."

"Don't want to keep him in no cage." I felt my teeth biting hard against my lower lip.

The man shrugged his shoulders. "Well, that's too bad."

"Hey!" The gate creaked and wobbled as the fat kid heaved himself up beside me and leaned over the top. "How come ya ain't gonna let this kid have his pet crow?"

Wally and Arvey climbed on the gate too. It creaked louder, as if it was going to break in half.

Red-faced now, the man gave the drum a kick. "Damn it to hell! I told you to get off my gate!"

Like a rock crashing through a window, this funny feeling bashed into me, and without thinking, I just jumped off the gate and walked toward the shed without looking to see if the man was coming after me or not. It was like he was breathing right down my neck. But I didn't turn around. It didn't matter if that guy was ten times Richie's size. Sam was flopping around in that cage, and I was going to turn him loose. Or else.

I got close and saw Sam fluttering twice as hard as before. Some of his wing feathers were broken, and blood oozed out of his beak from where he'd pecked at the wire cage. "It's okay, Sam," I said.

Now the dogs were flinging themselves against the wire pen so hard it made a ringing sound. Their ears flopped while slobber flew out of their mouths. Looking at those dogs reminded me of Grandma Hoover telling about these people in Siberia, and how they got chased through the snow and were eaten up by wolves.

"Damn it to hell!" That was the man's snarly voice.

The back of my neck prickled, but I didn't turn around. I just climbed on top of an empty nail keg and propped my arms across the shed roof. Pressed against the shed, I felt my heart thumping against its rotten boards.

The fat kid was hollering again. "Ya better leave him be. Or I'll get my dad ta call the cops!"

The guy had to be coming after me now. But I didn't look. The cage door was wired shut, and the stiff wire hurt my fingers while I was twisting it loose. Sam panted inside the cage. Like one of those wounded crows out in the field, he flopped up and down, then flung himself against the side of the cage. "Shhh," I said. But he wouldn't stop. It was almost as if he didn't know who I was.

By this time, the breath was wheezing in and out of my throat so hard I couldn't have heard the man with the sunburned arms, even if he was right behind me, ready to bash me with his fist. But I didn't care. If I was going to get beaten up, then I was going to get beaten up.

Now Wally was yelling, "Ya better let him turn his crow loose or I'll go get my dad. An' I'll get my uncle too. He's a policeman an'—"

"I'll get my dad too!" Arvey yelled. That made me start crying again because Arvey didn't have a dad. He'd died of stroke when Arvey was a little kid.

I got the cage open and grabbed Sam. He screamed and pecked and beat his wings against my arms. I let go, then grabbed him again, and pressed his wings against his sides. Then I pulled him out of the cage. His mouth hung open, and he was panting like a dog. I heard Arvey groaning, "Aw, jeez," from on top of the gate.

"Only a stinker'd put a crow in a cage!" the fat kid yelled.

I jumped off the nail keg, landed crooked, and twisted my ankle when I fell. But I kind of turned as I did so as not to hurt Sam. I rolled over, propped myself on my elbows, and got up.

The man with the sunburned arms hadn't moved more than a couple of steps. He just stood there with his jaw set tight and his red arms folded over the front of his blue shirt. As I limped past him toward the gate, a woman's voice called out, "Sonny, is that your crow?" A little dark-haired lady stood on the back porch. She had a dish towel flung over one shoulder, and her hands were propped against her hips.

"Yes, ma'am," I said.

"See," she said softly. "I told you that bird was somebody's pet."

"Ahhh." The man made a disgusted movement with his arms, like he was throwing something on the ground. "All right then. All right. Take your damn crow and get outta my yard."

I held Sam out to the fat kid, who took him carefully in his pudgy hands. *Eeeee!* Sam dug in with his claws, screeched, and bit the fat kid on the back of his hands. The fat kid winced. But he didn't let go.

The man was laughing behind me now. "That sure is a tame crow you got there, all right."

The gate wobbled when I climbed on it. And when I jumped off and landed in the alley, my ankle hurt a little where I'd twisted it. But I didn't care.

"He is too tame, he is too!" the fat kid yelled. He handed Sam down to me and yelled some more at the man with the sunburned arms. "He is so tame! He is so! He'd ride around on yer shoulder and . . . and everything! He is so!"

For some stupid reason, I started crying again. I guess I was laughing a little bit too. That fat kid was mad all over—he certainly was. The way he hung over the gate made his T-shirt peel up so you could see the pink fat on his sides tremble when he shook his fist. He sure was fat. But if he was a girl, I might have kissed him right on the spot.

A couple of crab apples and a yo-yo tumbled out of the fat kid's pockets as he shook his fist and hollered again the man with the sunburned arms. "And if he ain't tame no more, then it's all your fault. Ain't nobody but a stinker'd put no crow in no cage!"

He heaved himself off the gate and lumbered over to where the rest of us stood in the alley, his breath kind of wheezy as he reached out and scratched the top of Sam's head. Sam stabbed at the fat kid's fingers, and the fat kid pulled them away. "Whillikers. He sure is scared."

"We ought to cover him up with a T-shirt or something." Arvey back-handed streaks of sweat off his forehead and the tip of his nose. "My ma says if ya can keep a bird in the dark a while, it'll quiet down. She fixed this bird once when it flew against our window last spring."

With Sam still under my arm, I bent over and picked up my bike. Sam screeched. I could feel his heart beating like it was going to explode. I dumped my bike back down and held him close to my face. "Sam?"

He kept making these awful, strangling sounds. And he jerked his head back and forth, trying to look everywhere at once. His eyes were wild, sort of like they were screaming inside his head.

"I gotta let him go," I said. Then I held him against my chest, feeling him trying to fly, just like the tiger swallowtail when it was between my fingertips not so very long ago.

"Might be you'll never see him again," the fat kid warned.

"I know. But I gotta turn him loose."

The fat kid thumbed his glasses higher up on his nose. It was a funny nose: little and round. "Okay. But when ya let him go, ya gotta toss him up in the air real good. I know this guy that bands birds an' then turns 'em loose. He says ya gotta toss 'em up real good."

Hugging Sam against my stomach, I petted the feathers on his back. Then just for a second, I pressed him up to my cheek. I didn't want to turn him loose, but I knew I had to because every part of him wanted to fly. With my eyes closed, I listened to the strangling sounds Sam made. A killdeer was crying out in the slough, and I felt the sun glancing off garbage cans and hard-packed alley dirt. I was standing near a telephone pole and could almost taste its hot, creosote smell. Flies buzzed back and forth, and they filled my ears with a kind of frying sound.

"Okay, Mule Head," I whispered to Sam. "I'll see you back at the house." Sucking in all the back alley smells, I tossed him high, as high as I could.

He tumbled and flopped at first—then caught the air with his wings. His feathers rustled, sort of like dry grass in the heat. Then he beat his way down the alley, wobbly and crooked at first.

At the end of the alley, he flew higher and steadier, then pounded out across the slough, aiming toward the railroad tracks. For a second, I shut my eyes because I couldn't stand to see him flying away like that. Finally, I opened them again and watched him until he was just a dot disappearing into some trees.

"C'mon." Arvey piled on his bike and took off. "We gotta find him again." Wally and the fat kid and me—we took off too. I was crying and having the hiccups, both at the same time. Dried tears and sweat made sticky streaks all down my face.

"He's gonna come back. You just wait and see," the fat kid kept saying over and over again.

Chapter 23

S am wasn't there when we got home. The fat kid came with us, and on the way, we whistled and cawed while shading our eyes and squinting up into all the big trees. "Ya done right," the fat kid kept saying. "Ya had to let him go on account of he was so scared. Only a stinker'd put a crow in a cage."

The fat kid was really nice, even though he was so fat. And smart too. He could name all the state capitals, and he knew the batting averages of all the big league ballplayers and how many home runs Babe Ruth had hit each year. Really important stuff. And he took a harmonica out of one of his pockets and played "Battle Hymn of the Republic" so good it sounded like music on the radio.

Anyway, after getting home, we clumped into the house, all sweaty and out of breath and talking all at once to Mom about the man with the sunburned arms.

"I betcha Sam's been scared off for good," Arvey groaned. His red mussy hair hung down in his eyes as he scuffed his U.S. Keds tennis shoes across the linoleum floor. You could see the hurt twisted around on his freckly face because he liked animals as much as I did. In his backyard, Arvey had an old horse trough sunk into a hole. He had chicken wire around the horse trough, with room inside the fence for a rock garden with neat plants and some box turtles clumping around. Bullheads and turtles swam around in the trough.

"Now now. Everything will be all right." Mom went to the refrigerator and pulled out a pitcher of lemonade. She smiled and bustled with the ice cube tray in one hand and the pitcher in the other. "Sam likes us all too much to fly away for good." She reached back and kicked the refrigerator door closed with her foot.

I wasn't sure Mom meant what she said, because she fixed a giant batch of peanut butter and jelly sandwiches and let us eat as many as we wanted. The only time she let me fill up like that was when she was worried about how I felt.

The fat kid, whose name was Buddy Ledford, ate three sandwiches all by himself, along with three glasses of lemonade. When Mom wasn't looking, he showed us how he could guzzle a whole glass of lemonade without swallowing even once.

"Do you want some more?" Mom turned around and saw Buddy's empty glass.

"Naw." Buddy grinned. "Don't want to spoil my supper. We're havin' pork chops an' black-eyed peas."

Afterward, we went outside and played army for a while, with Arvey pretending to be a Jap sniper hiding in one of the evergreen trees in the front yard. Buddy, Wally, and I ran to Wally's yard and picked a bunch of crab apples while Arvey yelled, "Rousy 'Mericans. Can't shoot straight."

"Kaboom! Kaboom!" We pretended the crab apples were hand grenades and pegged them at Arvey up in the tree.

But it wasn't that much fun, maybe because I was too worried about Sam to pay much attention to a stupid army game. I kept standing up while everyone was shooting, so I could look around at all the trees and power line poles.

"Jeez, Beaner," Arvey yelled. "If I'd of been a real sniper, ya'd have yer head blown off about fifty times already."

"Hey, I'm gittin' hungry. Think I'll head on home." Buddy Ledford put some crab apples in his pockets, then took one out again and bit a chunk out of it as he waddled over to his bike and picked it up.

The rest of us quit too. Wally and Arvey went home while I hiked off down the railroad tracks toward the woods.

I kept calling, "Here, Sam. Here, Sam," as I went. The hot sunlight screamed down like fire on the white rocks of the railroad bed. I kept squinting into the sky while sweat ran into my eyes and made silver streaks and bubbles in the light.

For a while, I pretended I was in the Sahara Desert and had my eyes burnt out by the sun. Eyes shut, I felt my way along the edge of the tracks with my feet, calling "Here, Sam," and hoping he'd fly down and land on my shoulder while I was stumbling around.

Hotter and hotter it got, the sun kind of like a red-hot saw rasping across the back of my neck. Heat glanced up off the ground, sucking the sweat out on my skin. Then I tripped and fell, skinning my hands and knees on the white rocks. With my eyes still shut, I sat at the edge of the tracks listening for Sam's gurgling voice and the swish of his wings.

The far-off wail of a train whistle seemed to stretch out like a thin wire in the heat. I lay down and pressed my ear to the ground, the way some Indians did in a movie Arvey and I'd seen about a month ago. I couldn't hear anything, but I pretended I did. "Iron horse come this way," I grunted, just like the Indian in the movie did.

The train wailed again, sad and hurt and lonesome while it crawled closer across the white rocks. For some reason, I thought about lying down in the middle of the tracks and letting the train rumble over me when it came. Arvey said you could do that—lie still and let the train roll right over you and not get hurt because it was high enough off the ground.

I got up, then sprawled out between the rails and pressed one ear against the railroad ties. You could smell the black creosote on the railroad ties, and the air felt so hot and thick it was like breathing in soup. I wondered how far away the train was and if I had the courage to stay flat and let the train roll over me the way Arvey said it would.

The train yowled again. *Eeeeeeyoooo.* What would the engineer do when he saw me lying there between the rails? Would he hit the brakes? Or would he just blow his whistle and keep barreling along because it would be too late to stop anyhow?

Now the sound of the train was vibrating "Clickity-click" up through the hot ground. What if it was so close now that if I sat up, I'd get splattered all over the white rocks? What if the only chance now was to lie still, so the train could roll over me with all that hot, clangy iron rushing just above my head?

Then I remembered when a car full of high school kids got hit by the train just a block away from my house. One kid had no legs left, but his dad kept holding a mirror up to his mouth and yelling, "He's alive, damnit! Can't you see his breath?"

And Richie Baldini came along and picked up somebody's boot. Only there was still a foot inside the boot. At least that's what Richie said. And then this lady named Mrs. Walker came down the tracks and said there was a piece of brain just lying there in the ditch and shouldn't someone bury it, or at least cover it up with some rocks. She led a bunch of us kids down the tracks and tossed a rock at something all pink and shiny lying in the ditch.

"It's terrible leaving something like that lying around." She took a hankie out of her pocket and held it up to her nose.

Wally and Arvey and I picked up some rocks and threw them at the piece of brain. Only we threw them hard, trying to mash it instead of just trying to cover it up. What a rotten thing to do—laughing and talking loud and flinging rocks until whatever it was lying in the ditch got pounded to nothing in the mud.

Just thinking about what we'd done made me afraid of dying and maybe going to hell. And it was hot—really hot. Then the train yowled again, so I sucked a gulp of that hot air, opened my eyes, and went rolling and crawling off the railroad tracks. Down into the ditch I went, right through this big jungle of thistles and goldenrod.

I sure felt stupid when I saw how far off the train really was. Several minutes later, it finally thundered past, the whole world shaking and the whistle climbing to a high pitch while the people in the windows flickered by. A little kid was looking out one of the windows, and even after the train was gone, it was like he was still there with his hands pressed against the dirty glass. I kept wondering if he'd seen me as I sat there listening to the train whistle drop back to a moan, then drag itself off, all hurt and lonesome as the train rushed away.

After the train left, I sat in the weeds thinking about Sam and the Weed Lot Bum and the kitten old Richie had killed when I was a little kid. And the bullheads and tadpoles, too—the ones dredged from the Zion Pond and left to die in the sun because no one would let me throw them back. For a while, the world was just too big to stand up in, so I stayed down in the weeds, hiding and watching little gray spiders and red ants climb up and down the goldenrod stems. Bugs—I wondered if they ever got scared, or if they worried about dying and stuff like that.

After a while, some crows started cawing down in the woods, so I got up and jogged along the tracks, cawing and whistling as I went. After running across the overpass crossing Wadsworth Road, I cut left, climbed a creaky wire fence, and jumped into a cornfield on the other side. The corn rustled, almost as high as my head, all smooth and cool as I pushed through it, sort of swimming with my arms. Through leaves and the beginning of tassels, I saw the chokecherry tree I'd shot the crow out of last spring.

The crows I'd heard earlier were in some trees further along the edge of the field. They took off and flew toward the big tree where Sam was born. I ran, cawing and whistling after them. But they disappeared, sort of melting away in the hot sky above Third Park Creek.

I stopped running and sort of lollygagged along until I got to the woods. The air felt cooler, and the green corn and dry weed smell faded as I slid down the slope of the ravine. My slingshot fell out of my back pocket, so I stopped and picked it up, then went on down to the creek. With my shoes off and my toes wiggling, I sat on the bank and dangled my feet in the creek.

The water ran cool while whirligig beetles traced squiggly lines across the reflection of trees and clouds. Pretty soon, some minnows came out and darted through the sunny patches trembling down in the deepest part of the creek.

The crows cawed again—they could have been Sam's brothers and sisters, I guessed. Maybe he was with them right now. Then I saw my reflection jiggling in the water and thought about old Mrs. McFarlan and how pretty her picture was—the one I found in her shed. I remembered her mirror too and how I'd thought about not looking in mirrors anymore so you wouldn't get old. But what would happen if you just sat around and stared in a mirror all the time? Would you see yourself get bigger, then start to shrivel up and get old? Or does that only happen when you're not looking—like when you're asleep?

Anyway, I stayed by the creek the rest of the day, just thinking and looking at my reflection and listening to the bird and animal sounds that got louder and nearer as the woods got used to me being there. First, some squirrels scolded and bent the tip ends of branches while jumping from one big maple tree to the next. Blue jays screamed and flashed their colors through the sunny places as they flew up and down the ravine.

When the sun dropped below the top of the ravine, a couple of rabbits hopped out of some underbrush and nibbled leaves near the creek. Two hen pheasants and a cock flew from the cornfield into the ravine. Pretty soon, the cock pheasant and the two rabbits started chasing each other—zigzagging through the dry underbrush. The cock kept letting out this wild, honking screech.

Noisy bird. Kind of like Sam was sometimes, he figured he was boss of the place and kept showing off for the two hens that stayed brown and quiet along the edge of the creek. Pretty soon, that old cock strutted so close to me I could see the ear tufts on his head and the white ring around his neck. About that time, the slingshot turned to a hard lump against my rear end. But I just watched the cock parade back and forth, then run back to the hens. Every once in a while, his wild call echoed up and down the ravine.

I was late getting home for supper that night, but Mom and Dad didn't seem to mind.

Chapter 24

After going to bed that night, I prayed for the first time in a long time, promising God I'd be good for the whole rest of my life, if only Sam would come back. I even promised to go to Sunday school almost every week and not swear or help Arvey write dirty words like "womb" and "uterus" on sidewalks or look at pictures of naked ladies or break power line insulators with my slingshot or slop around in the creek, get my pants wet, and then let them dry in the basement behind the furnace so Mom wouldn't find out.

After going to sleep, I had a terrible dream about the time when I was little and I went in the back room of Dad's store. Dad had bought several dozen chickens from a farmer and was butchering them himself. He reached in a big crate, grabbed a chicken by the hind leg, and hauled it out. It screeched and flopped, then gave up when Dad laid it on a wooden chopping block.

There was a meat cleaver on the chopping block. Dad picked it up and—wham—with a noise like a gun exploding, he cut the chicken's head clean off. Then with the cleaver blade, he brushed the head into a box and threw the headless chicken into a big barrel.

Came this wet, fluttering sound, and one of the headless chickens, maybe the one Dad had just thrown in, hopped up and perched on the edge of the barrel. I started to gag at the sight of that poor chicken sitting there and jerking its stump of a neck back and forth like it was looking around the room.

Then the chicken jumped on the floor and started flapping and skittering around, bumping into boxes and vegetable crates and table legs until it bounced off the wall and headed right at me. I was only about six years old, so I just stood there crying while Dad picked up the chicken and threw it back in the barrel.

Poor Dad: he wanted to hug me and tell me everything was all right. Only he couldn't at first because his hands were spattered with chicken blood.

And that's what ran through my dreams all night: Dad with his bloody hands, a barrel full of flopping, headless chickens, and crates of live chickens beating themselves crazy, like Sam had done when he was in that awful cage.

Finally, from somewhere I heard a crow calling, *Caw caw caw*, just as regular as a saw rasping through wood. The cawing got louder until my eyes popped open and blinked at the sunlight reflecting off my aquarium tank.

Caw caw caw.

Out from under a swamp of wet sheets I swam. Then I sat on the edge of the bed holding my breath. It was quiet now—just the usual sparrow fight out by the garbage cans. But then, sure enough, I heard Sam cawing as his shadow slid into the room and flickered across the aquarium tank.

"Sam!" I bounced off the bed, kicking over a stack of Batman comics as I ran to the window and looked out.

Caaaaaw caaaaaaaaw! The sound of his voice told me he was on the roof. Half a second later, he was in his favorite fir tree; and from there, he flew over the house and swooped down to land on Mrs. McFarlan's shed. *Caaaaaaaaw caaaaaw!*

By this time, I'd grabbed my wadded-up pants from off the floor and was tugging the pant legs right side out. Then off I charged down the stairs, sort of hopscotching along and stuffing myself into my pants at the same time.

The back door had been flung open, and a coffee puddle was seeping into Mom's red-and-white checked tablecloth.

"Caw caw," I yelled as I scooted out the back door, nearly trampling Carson John who was dancing around yelling, "Chickum, chickum," and waving his cereal spoon.

I was so happy and excited I picked him up, put him on my shoulders, and ran down the back steps.

"Horsey, horsey." He grabbed one of my ears and hit me over the head with his cereal spoon. But I was too happy to care.

Now Sam was in the big cottonwood tree, his feathers all fluffed up as if someone had used him to dust furniture with. He was bobbing his head up and down like a yo-yo or maybe a rubber ball.

"Here, Sam. Come on." Mom had her roller skates on and was wobbling around as she ran across the lawn. In one hand, she had a cup of coffee slopping over and spilling on the ground.

"Here, Sam." I yelled at Sam too. But he wouldn't pay me any mind. All he wanted to do was fly around and scream like a whistling teakettle boiling over on the stove.

Pretty soon, he flew across Galilee, flapping from one telephone pole to the next while screeching at the people waiting for the morning train inside the little green station house. Then he flew off again, making big circles and cawing at a kid named Jackie Lloyd who was riding his bike down Thirty-third Street.

Half a minute later, he swooped into Mrs. Klammer's backyard and landed on her clothesline post. Still screeching like sixty, he edged along the clothesline until he got to Mr. Klammer's pajama bottoms that were now hung up using big safety pins. He jabbered away at those bottoms like they were an old friend who he was telling about the gosh-awful experience he'd survived. Then he started pulling clothespins off the line until Mrs. Klammer ran after him, waving a dish towel and shagged him off. He perched on her apple tree and gave her what for—probably in German, I guess. Finally, he flew into our yard and landed on the porch roof.

All at once, it seemed like he saw Mom and Carson John and me for the first time since coming back. He flew down, landed on Carson John's head, and tried to swipe his cereal spoon. Then he flew to Mom's head, swiped his beak through her hair, laughed and gurgled, then flew off again.

Skreeeek skreeeeek. He circled above the yard before flying across Galilee Street and landing on the mail truck that had just pulled up.

Our mailman was a guy named Jim. He was sort of little, with happy-looking eyes and a big grin. Jim was a good friend of Dad's and he used to work for him in the butcher shop. Only one day, Jim got his right hand caught in the meat grinder and it ground all his fingers off, except for his thumb.

Jim was good natured most of the time, in spite of the accident in the butcher shop. And when he heard Sam dancing on top of his truck, he got out and stood in the middle of the street and started jabbering at Sam in crow talk, just as if the two of them were perched on the same tree. Jim could babble away in all the crow talk sounds—almost as good as me.

Old Sam nearly went crazy when Jim started talking to him like that. With his wings spread out, he stood on one foot, then on the other, his throat trembling and filled with gurgling sounds. Jim did the same thing, sort of spreading his arms out, gurgling and dancing in the middle of the street.

Bow wow wow. Sam started running in circles on top of the truck while Jim imitated him, right out in the middle of the street. He had to get out of the way when a blue Oldsmobile drove up and stopped beside the truck.

There was a lady in the car, and she got out and started laughing when Jim pointed to Sam on top of the truck. She had on a green dress and some silver bracelets that glittered when she laughed and clapped her hands. Jim said something to her that I couldn't quite hear, then pointed to my house and then at Sam. Of course, Sam knew that people were paying attention to him, so he stuck his chest out and paraded back and forth on top of the truck. *Geeble beeble. Guzzzork.* He was making his radio static sound.

I had to be part of the fun, so I started across the street with Carson John still on top of my shoulders. He'd dropped his cereal spoon and had his wet, wormy little fingers wrapped around my ears so hard it felt like he might pull them off.

"Hi, kiddo." Jim grinned. "We were just talking about your pet crow. Now watch this," Jim said to the lady as he walked around the truck to where the mailboxes were. You know how mailboxes have metal flags that you put up when you have a letter you want mailed. Jim went to each mailbox that had a flag up, took letters out of them, then put the flags back down. While he did that, Sam was running back and forth screaming *Yow yow yow* and going to the bathroom on top of the mail truck.

"Okay. Now get a load of this." As soon as Jim stepped back from the mailboxes, Sam flew down, landed on one of them, and made a mumbling sound. Then he reached down, and after a few seconds of tugging and swearing, pulled the flag back up.

"Whoop-yow." Sam cocked his head back and forth, then hopped to the next mailbox and pulled its flag up too.

"I've just plain old given up on those flags," Jim laughed. "When they're down he puts them up. When they're up he puts them down."

Sure enough, right while Jim was talking, Sam had finished standing the flags up and was knocking them down again. But the thing about those flags was that getting them back down was a trick that took a bird scientist to figure out. First, you had to lift the flag straight up, then swivel it backward to make it swing down. Anyone watching Sam at work would have to admit that he was a very scientific crow.

"Hey, kiddo. Why don't you and Sam show us the letter trick?" Jim went to our mailbox and slid some letters in it while Sam flew back to the top of the truck and hopped up and down.

Here was my chance to show how smart Sam really was. With Carson John still on my shoulders, I walked to the mailbox, opened it, and called for Sam.

Sam glided off the truck, landed on the mailbox lid, then stretched his neck out and looked inside. As soon as he saw a pile of letters, he got all excited and did a little dance on the lid. Of course, he was also a little scared because crows don't like to get inside anything that looks like it might be a trap. But in a little while, Sam's curiosity got the best of him, so he stuck his head inside the mailbox and began making his chicken-clucking sounds. Then he pulled a letter out. After giving it to me, he dived in after another one and pulled it out too. *Bow wow wow.*

Gronk. Glooop. Each time he grabbed another letter, he seemed to be making a new sound. You could probably send Sam to a dozen mailboxes and not hear the same noise twice.

I heard the lady laughing behind me, and her bracelets tinkled as she clapped her hands.

After Sam brought out the last letter, he crawled partway inside the mailbox to make sure there wasn't anything left. *Geensnorkle zaatze!* Then he jumped back out of the mailbox, all fluffed up and excited, probably because he figured he'd been yelled at by a monstrous crow. After that, he hopped up on Carson John's head and looked around for something else to do.

Crazy bird. He was so excited over all the attention he was getting that he just had to put on another show. His beady eyes skiddled back and forth, hoping to spot a dog to bark at, a pair of pajama bottoms to fly off with, or a cat's tail to yank. Finally, he had to satisfy himself with cracking jokes in crow talk and yanking Carson John's ear while I went over to the lady and asked her if she'd like to let him perch on her arm.

"Will he bite?" Her eyes were big and blue, and she gasped a little and put her fingertips against her lips.

"No, ma'am—not hard anyway. And only for fun. That's if you don't try to grab him or anything like that."

The lady was nervous at first—like lots of people who've never touched a frog or a bug, or any kind of wild thing before. But Sam made her giggle when he hopped right over to her arm and started pecking at the silver bracelets she wore. After that, he edged up to her shoulder and had a telephone conversation in her ear.

Jim grinned and whispered, "I sure hope he doesn't go doo-doo down the back of her neck." He got in the truck, beeped his horn, and drove off.

By this time, Sam and the lady were good friends, with her clucking and cooing while he edged back down her arm and started pecking at her bracelets again.

"What a wonderful pet. Did you teach him all those tricks?"

"Well—sort of. His name is Sam, and he's just naturally so smart and curious that he learns to do stuff all by himself."

"Do suf aw-aw-aw ba sef." Carson John kept pointing at Sam while huffing and stammering like crazy as he tried to talk grown-up talk.

The lady trilled a breathless little laugh, sort of like singing, and when Sam flew on top of her car, she reached over and hugged Carson John.

"Chikum poo-poo!" Carson John cheered.

Sure enough, Sam had gone to the bathroom on top of the lady's shiny, blue car. But she only smiled and asked more questions about what it was like to have a pet crow.

I sure was proud of Sam. And I felt important too. Here I was, just a kid, and a grown-up was asking me questions and was interested in what I had to say.

Carson John kept huffing and stammering and screwing his face up while saying things like "Chikum fry—Whee" and "Poo-poo."

After a while, the lady got in her car and drove off, honking and waving as she went. I remember how long and yellow her hair was, and how she kept pushing it away from her eyes. She was pretty, and very nice too.

Anyway, I took Carson John back home, then dragged my bike out from under the back porch and took off like crazy down Thirty-third Street. "Caw caw!" I yelled. "Here, Sam. C'mon."

In about half a minute, Sam landed on the back of my neck. Then he hopped on the bike handlebars, spread his wings, and stuck his neck straight out. Now the two of us were headed down the hill toward Sharon Park so fast it seemed like my bicycle wheels weren't even touching the ground. It was so sunny and the sky was so blue it was like I was sucking in drops of sweet soda pop each time I breathed. Harder and harder I pumped. And the faster Sam and I raced, the slower time seemed to slide by, like maybe we were in a picture surrounded by a shiny gold frame. And it was going to be summer forever.

And nothing would ever, ever change.

Chapter 25

School had started again. That meant arithmetic, geography, *Fun with Dick and Jane*—and Sam outside the schoolroom pecking on the windowpane.

"Wow!" someone yelled. "Look at the hawk!"

"That ain't no hawk. It's a crow." A kid named Ricky Saunders crumpled a piece of yellow tablet paper and threw it at the window so hard it made Sam jump. Ricky had big Dumbo ears, and I was thinking that after school, I might give them a yank.

Skreeeek. Sam put one eye against the glass. "Woof." His eyelid fluttered, then squinted, like peeking through a telescope.

The kids were laughing up a storm now, even pickle-faced June Morris, who never laughed at anything except when you fell down playing tag or crashed into a ditch while riding your bike.

Sam cranked out a rusty, screen-door sound, nodded, and said "Hello."

"Well," Miss Andrews said. "It must be someone's pet." Miss Andrews was my fifth grade teacher, the nicest teacher I'd ever had. She was young and pretty, with black hair that bounced when she walked. She had dark eyes too. Sometimes they reminded me of Sam's eyes when he was excited about something to eat or about something shiny to hide in his gravel pile. She'd spent a couple of years in England, so she talked with an accent and used words like "Marvelous" and "Good show."

The other kids liked Miss Andrews too. She was little and quick, and she filled the blackboard up with interesting drawings when she explained things about geography, history, and arithmetic. Sometimes she used up chalk so fast that little bits of it chipped off and fell on the floor. She had chalk marks on her hips from leaning against the blackboard when she talked.

Arvey raised his hand and told Miss Andrews that Sam was my crow. "He's raised him up and taught him to do all kinds of tricks," Arvey said.

I felt shy at first when Miss Andrews asked me to get up in front of the class and talk about Sam. But once I started talking, I wasn't bashful anymore because the kids were interested in what I had to say. I told them all about the work Mom and I and Wally and Arvey had to do at first, just to keep Sam fed.

"Yeah," Arvey agreed. "Baby birds have these monster appetites. In my bird book, it says that they eat five times their weight in bugs every day."

"Crows are bad." A kid named Corky Meyers was frowning and shaking his head. "They eat farmer's crops, and sometimes they eat hen's eggs and baby chicks."

"Yer full of it." Arvey made a sour face at Corky. "Just 'cause yer grampa owns a chicken ranch."

"Now, Arvard." Miss Andrews was smiling and sitting on the edge of her desk. "Remember there is a right way and a wrong way to disagree." Miss Andrews had on a pair of shiny red shoes and a white dress. She looked nice.

Arvey grinned and scrunched down in his desk. Miss Andrews was always making us be polite to each other. We didn't mind it, though, because we all liked her so much.

Then I told the class that people who study birds said that crows ate enough bugs to more than make up for the bad things they did.

"Yeah," Arvey agreed. "And I read about this farmer that would pay anybody fifty cents for any crow shot near his farm. Pretty soon, all the crows got killed or chased off. Only the grass his cows ate stopped growing 'cause their roots got ate up by grub worms and all. And that was because there weren't any crows around anymore." Arvey grinned and gave old Corky an evil-eye stare.

After that, I told everybody about how I'd learned some of the calls that crows use when they're talking back and forth.

Miss Andrews's eyes got big, and she leaned forward from the edge of her desk. "You mean you can understand what crows say to each other?"

"Yes, ma'am. Well, sort of. Like if a crow is screaming, 'Caw caw caw,' real fast, like a dog barking, it means danger and everyone in the flock should fly away. Or if a crow is going, 'Caw aaaaw, caw aaaaaaw,' kind of long and drawn out, it means he wants the other crows to come, because there's a hawk or an owl that needs to be chased away."

"Marvelous." Miss Andrews went to the blackboard and started drawing cartoons of owls and crows. The owls had on glasses and flat professor hats, while the crows wore turtle-necked sweaters and smoked cigars.

I was all warmed up by now—not afraid of the gap-toothed grins, freckled faces, and goggling eyeballs all around. "Hey," I said, "and if a crow gives just two or three quick caws, not too soft, not too loud, it means be on the alert. And if a crow is gurgling and chattering to himself, he's sort of contented but maybe a little lonesome and would like to make friends."

Miss Andrews put her chalk down and looked out the window where Sam was jabbering and strutting back and forth along the window ledge. "That kind of sound—is that it right now?"

"Yes, ma'am."

"Do you think he might like to come into the room?" Miss Andrews's red shoes clicked like they were making music as she walked over to the window and smiled at Sam.

Sam stopped strutting and pecked on the glass again.

"What do you say, old chap? Would you like to come inside?" Miss Andrews tapped a long red fingernail against the glass while Sam tilted his head back and made a gurgling sound in his throat.

"I think it would be okay if we let him in," I said. "Only we got to be careful and not scare him or he might fly into something and get hurt." I felt goose bumps on the back of my neck. It's not every day that the nicest, prettiest teacher there is invites a kid's pet crow into her room.

"Well, everyone." Miss Andrews smiled while her dark eyes danced around the room. "Can you all be silent for a while?"

"Yes! Yes!" There were whoops and cheers—and everybody bouncing up and down in their desks.

"And what about you, Arvard?" Miss Andrews smiled and frowned at Arvey at the same time.

Arvey grinned at her and scrunched down in his seat.

"Well, all right," Miss Andrews said.

You could hear everybody in the room suck in a deep breath when I went to the window. "Here, Sam." I held out my arm.

Eeeeerooop. Sam skipped along the window ledge and hopped on my arm.

Everyone tried not to laugh, but they couldn't help it when Sam climbed up on my shoulder and pecked at my ear. And when I turned my face toward him, he said, "Hmmm," and pecked at my teeth.

"He likes the sound he gets when he pecks hard shiny things," Arvey explained. Sam recognized Arvey sitting in the front row, so of course, he had to fly over and peck at his teeth too.

Miss Andrews's desk was next. Sam got there by hopping from one kid's head to the next, like crossing a creek on stepping stones. Everyone giggled, except for June Morris who screamed loud enough to crack glass and ducked under her desk when Sam tried to land on her head.

I was afraid but sort of hopeful at the same time that Sam might mess down the back of June's yellow dress. But he just squawked and flew to someone else's head while poor old June doubled up and crawled under her desk.

"Saw yer underpants," Arvey yelled. "Pink pants stink. Har-har."

"Arvard! That is quite enough!" Miss Andrews's eyes can turn hard and glittery when she gets mad, but then she couldn't help but smile when Sam skipped over to her desk and started oohing and aahing while doing an Apache war dance over a pile of paper clips she kept on a little plate.

"He likes metal stuff," Arvey explained. "That's 'cause they shine and tinkle when he drops them on the ground."

Still smiling, Miss Andrews got her purse and dumped everything out of it on her desk.

"Ooogle oooh." There it all was—a giant pile of everything Sam had ever wanted in all the world: nickels and dimes, quarters, bobby pins, a comb, gum wrappers, a lipstick case, the cap off a fountain pen, some Kleenex with lipstick marks all over it, and, best of all, a little tin box of Anacin tablets that rattled when you shook it in your beak. More stuff than a crow could bury in a dozen gravel piles had clattered out of that purse.

At first, Sam just stood there with his beak open, his eyelids fluttering and his chest heaving up and down. Then he started to fuss while skipping back and forth and jabbering to himself, trying to decide what to fly off with first. But when he couldn't decide, he stood in the middle of the whole pile and nestled down on it with his wings spread out.

But that wasn't any fun. What good is a million dollars in crow money if it's never spent? Finally, he picked up the Anacin box, lugged it to the edge of the desk, and dropped it on the floor. *Whoooop wow.* He did a little war dance when it clattered apart and all the white bugs inside it skittered across the floor.

"Hey, Sam. Who is this handsome chap?" Miss Andrews opened her compact to show Sam the little mirror inside.

Gaggle ooop. Every feather Sam owned stuck straight out until he looked twice his normal size. *Yerk-yerk.* He screwed his neck around until he was looking at his reflection upside down. Then he straightened up and hopped around to the other side of the mirror. When he lost himself, he gawked all around the room.

"What a handsome crow." With her red fingernail tapping against the mirror, Miss Andrews helped Sam locate his reflection again. *Yuk yuk*, Sam agreed. His spread-out wings glinted bluish black as he stretched his neck and pecked gently at the mirror.

"I think he's in love," Miss Andrews said.

Gloooo. Sam made a soft pigeon-sounding noise, picked up a piece of chalk, and strutted around with it in his beak. It was a present for the mirror crow. But when mirror crow wouldn't take it, Sam dropped the chalk on the floor. *Eeek!* he yelled when it broke in two.

The kids were all pointing at Sam and giggling and talking back and forth over the tricks a smart bird like Sam could do. "He could be in a circus," Corky Meyers said.

What a warm and shiny feeling I had inside. Sam was my crow—mine. He belonged to nobody else.

For his next trick, Sam picked up a gum eraser and carried it over to an empty pint milk bottle Miss Andrews kept her pencils in. Sam had already pulled the pencils out. Now he dropped the eraser inside. *Ooook ooook.* He began ticking his head back and forth and looking at the eraser from all sides like it was a fish in a bowl. He wanted it back again but couldn't see how to get it out.

Heh heh, Sam said after a while, sort of like someone who'd come up with a bright idea all at once. Scratching around on the desk, he found a paper clip and dropped that in the bottle too. Now there were two things he wanted to get out, so he picked up Miss Andrews's car keys and dropped them inside. Another paper clip clinked in . . . a ballpoint pen . . . some thumbtacks . . . a rubber band.

Poor Sam. Maybe he thought he might hit a jackpot and win everything back if he kept dumping more stuff inside the hole. Back and forth he skittered, swearing and scratching and poking through everything Miss Andrews had dumped from her purse, then cramming that milk bottle full of everything that would fit inside. When nothing came out of the bottle, he stood on one leg and then the other for a while.

Geeburblefritz. Letting out one of his German cuss words, he ran at the bottle and tried to screw his head inside. It tipped over and rolled across the desk with Sam dancing on it like a log roller while pecking at everything tumbling around inside.

Czyzk. Now it seemed like he was swearing in Polish as he lost his balance and fell off the bottle when it rolled off the desk and crashed to the floor.

Wow wow wow. There were all kinds of excitement dancing in his black eyes as he bobbed his head like he was counting the glass bits, paper clips, and other stuff spinning and rolling on the floor.

By this time, the room was filled with kids laughing and jumping all over the place. As Dad would have said, it was pandemonium times ten. And Miss Andrews was laughing the loudest of all.

All that noise made Sam kind of scared, so he flew around the room, scattering arithmetic papers and book reports like confetti on New Year's Eve. After a couple of trips around the room, he landed on the guinea pig cage and yelled at the guinea pigs inside. Next stop was the globe in the back of the room. But it spun him off, so he flew around the room again. I was afraid he might hurt himself, but he found the open window and flew outside. Before leaving, he landed on Arvey's desk and went to the bathroom on the report Arvey had written about army ants.

"Well now!" Miss Andrews shouted over all the noise made by a human anthill of kids bouncing up and down in their desks and yelling all at the same time. "Would you all like Sam to come again?"

Everybody cheered, Arvey the loudest of all.

While Arvey and I swept up the broken glass, Miss Andrews went to the blackboard and drew another cartoon picture of a crow. It had a top hat and bow tie, along with a walking stick tucked under one wing.

"What a wonderful experience we have all had." Miss Andrews was smiling and shaking her head at all the stuff scattered all over her desk. "It isn't very often that a wild animal can learn to love people and trust them the way Sam does."

And when she looked at me and smiled, I felt like I had a gold medal pinned on my T-shirt front.

Chapter 26

During the next few days, Sam turned into a mascot around Elmwood School. He flew into some of the rooms and went mining for shiny things on the teachers' desks. The kids gave him paper clips and shiny new pennies and laughed when he hid them all around the school.

"Ya know, we ought to paint his head white." Buddy Leadford was going up and down on the teeter-totter with Arvey and me and Wally on the other end and Sam perched on Buddy's head. "Then we could take him to all the Elmwood Eagle touch football games."

Yaaaa. Sam agreed. He hopped off Buddy's head and dived into one of those big army pants pockets of his, snagged a pretzel, and flapped away. But it was during recess the next day that Sam picked up a bad habit that got us both in Dutch. It all started when a kid named Norman Hackenschmidt showed up wearing a helicopter beanie—the kind with a little wooden propeller on top of it that spins around and around when you're running or riding your bike. I remember hearing Sam carrying on about something but didn't know what it was until Sam attacked.

Norman was playing softball and had just hit a line drive that scooted over third base and rolled between Buddy Leadford's legs. Norman took off for first, and the yellow propeller on his beanie started to spin. Right away, Sam had a fit and nearly tumbled off the schoolhouse roof. He caught his balance, though, dropped the dead mouse he'd been tenderizing by banging against the roof, squawked a war cry, and launched himself.

"Hey!" Norman grabbed for his cap. But it was too late. Sam had the beanie and was flapping toward the roof.

You'd have thought they'd closed down the school by the way everybody was laughing and running around. Old Buddy let out a whoop, flung his baseball mitt in the air, then just stood there laughing and rubbing his hands back and forth across his stomach. June Morris was laughing, too—a honking sound that sort of bleated out of her nose as she followed poor Norman around saying, "Hey, Normie, Where'd your hat go? Huh?"

Meanwhile, Sam was having a real party on the roof. We couldn't see very well, but from all the cawing and hooting, you could figure that the beanie might be sitting in such a way that the wind was spinning its propeller around and around. Sam probably thought he'd caught a dragonfly or something. We could hear him screeching while his head and wingtips bobbed up and down above the edge of the roof.

"Rotten bird." Norman threw a rock at Sam, so I piled on him and we rolled around on the ground, sweating and grunting ferocious comments like "I'm gonna bash yer teeth down yer throat," or "My dad can whip your dad any day." Miss Andrews made us stop. Then she sent Arvey to find Mr. Stubbs, the school janitor, and ask him to go up on the roof and get the beanie back.

I'll never forget our janitor, Mr. Stubbs. He was a big grouchy guy, kind of red-faced, with a neck as big around as a stove pipe and such a monster of a belly it looked like someone else was inside his shirt with him. Every time he got mad, which was kind of often, he'd whip out a red bandana handkerchief and blow his nose like a gun going off: "Honk . . . Pfoot." Then sometimes he'd scowl at whatever was in the handkerchief, fold it over and snort out another blast. The madder he got, the more times he'd blow his nose.

Mr. Stubbs was so mad he must have fired off his nose cannon a dozen times. "Ding blast it. I've been hired to clean floors, not to climb up and down ladders like a dad-gummed monkey." Finally, though, he got a ladder and hauled himself up on the roof.

I wanted to explain to Mr. Stubbs how it wasn't much use trying to get the beanie away from Sam, but he was honking and wheezing so fearsomely that I just kept my trap shut and held on to the ladder like he said.

Sam rang his warning call as soon as Mr. Stubbs went clumping across the roof, and he grabbed the beanie and flew off with it in his beak.

"Dag nab it! Honk-pfoot!" You could tell Mr. Stubbs was in an especially ferocious mood when he came back down the ladder because his ears and the back of his neck were even redder than before. He didn't say anything. But his jaws were clamped shut, and his belly kept pumping in and out like a bellows as he carried the ladder back inside the school. Sam made matters worse by sitting in a tree and flinging crow talk insults down on the back of Mr. Stubbs's sweaty red neck.

The next morning Sam flew off with a green-and-yellow scarf and a Cub Scout hat.

"By gawd, I'm gonna get me a gun! Honk-pfoot!" Mr. Stubbs's neck flared up as red as a sore when he had to haul himself and his big belly up on the roof again. He was able to rescue the Cub Scout hat, but Sam made off with the scarf, which looked real pretty, almost like a kite as it sailed off in the direction of Sharon Park Creek. When Mr. Stubbs lumbered back down the ladder, he was so puffed up and ferocious looking it seemed as if the ground might break open each time he took a step.

After school let out, I peddled home as fast as I could and told Mom what Mr. Stubbs had said about getting a gun. I was scared and mad at the same time—like the time when Richie said he was going to get Sam.

"Well." Mom hugged me, then roller-skated into the kitchen and came back with some vanilla cookies for me and Sam. "Maybe you need to learn that some people don't have a sense of humor about certain things."

"But Sam's just havin' fun."

Yuk yuk. Sam agreed. He was sitting on my shoulder nodding his head up and down. In his mouth was a piece of tin foil. He flew over to where Carson John was lying on the floor. With a screwing motion, sort of like changing a light bulb, he stuck the foil in Carson John's ear.

"Gummm." Carson John took the foil out of his ear and stuck it in his mouth.

Waaaak. Sam jumped on Carson John's stomach and poked his beak between Carson John's lips.

"I know he's only having fun. But he can be a royal pest." Mom picked up Carson John and pinched his nose until his face turned red and he opened his mouth. Then she made him spit out the tinfoil and give it back to Sam. "You've been mad at him yourself."

"Yeah. But I ain't gonna shoot him with no gun."

Mom and I talked some more about Sam and about how some people might not care about somebody's pet crow. I was mad at first because I figured everyone, except Richie, liked Sam. Then I thought about the crow shoot with the breeze ruffling the feathers of those dead and wounded crows. They'd been just like Sam. But I hadn't known it then. I felt kind of gray and rotten inside that night when I went to bed.

The next morning, I caught Sam and put him in the basement before taking off for school. Wally and I could hear him screeching like one of those horror movie banshees—the kind that's made of fog and howls around haunted houses just before someone dies. I felt kind of creepy and started thinking about Mrs. Funk and how she might be in a straight jacket and howling away, and it was all my fault. Then I got mad at Wally, when he kept running over all these big brown-and-black woolly bear caterpillars that were crawling across the road.

"Aw, they're only bugs, fer cripes sake." Wally swerved his bike again and left a yellowish green spot on the road.

"Yeah? Well, howdja like it if some giant went and squashed you every time you wanted to cross the street?"

Wally just laughed and squished another woolly bear. I quit riding with him and picked up some woolly bears and let them crawl across my T-shirt front while I rode the rest of the way to school.

After a couple of hours or so, I guess Mom couldn't stand Sam's complaining and must have turned him loose. He showed up in time for recess and swiped June Morris's scarf.

It was great fun watching old June's pink scarf sail back and forth. Everybody laughed and carried on, especially Norman Hackenschmidt, who followed June around yelling, "Hey, Joooonie, where'd yer scarf go? Huh?"

Boy, was I mad at Sam for getting Mr. Stubbs on the warpath again. "Git on home." I picked up a handful of pea gravel and flung it at Sam. You weren't supposed to throw pea gravel around the school, but I was trying to shoo Sam away. He just shrieked at me and flew back and forth through the elm trees around the school.

When we went in from recess, there was Sam on the window ledge asking to be let in. All the kids except June wanted to open the window, but Miss Andrews said no. She was smiling while trying to be serious as she explained how Mr. Fields, the principal, didn't want Sam in the rooms anymore.

She called me to her desk. "Can you keep that bandit friend of yours from coming to school?"

"I don't know. I put him down in the basement this morning, but I guess my Mom let him out. He doesn't like it when he's cooped up."

Miss Andrews smiled, and I smelled her lilac perfume when she gave me a little hug. "Well, do your best. I think Mr. Fields will understand."

I went back to my desk and got to work in my handwriting book, stringing together a bunch of O's and A's until my fingers started to cramp up. Meanwhile, old Sam kept jabbering and skipping back and forth on the window ledge. When nobody let him in, he flew away and came back a little later with June's scarf.

"My scarf!" June ran to the window and opened it, but Sam only laughed and flew off with it swishing behind. June was boiling-over mad. On her way back to her desk, she stuck her tongue out at me and hit me over the head with my handwriting book. "I'm going to tell my dad to turn your electricity off." June's dad worked for the electric company, and she was always telling us he'd do things like that.

"Aw, go stick that big old tongue of yours in a wall socket," I told her. That really made her mad, so she started twisting her pigtails around and putting them in her mouth, which was what she did when she was all upset. She bit her fingernails too, sometimes until they got all bleedy and stuff. What a nervous wreck.

I spent the morning being nervous myself because there was old horse-faced June Morris eating her pigtails and sticking her three-foot purple tongue out at me every chance she got.

The day sort of limped on to lunch time, and we all went outside. "Hey," Arvey yelled. "We're gonna play marbles. Hurry up an' eat." The place where we played marbles was across the street, only we had to eat our lunches either in the lunchroom or on the steps in front of the school. Arvey was in such a hurry to play marbles he shoved a whole hardboiled egg in his mouth and took off across the street.

I wasn't very hungry, so I ate just half of my liver sausage sandwich and gave the other half to Sam who flew off with it to the roof. With a bunch of marbles jiggling in our pockets, Arvey and I ran across the street to where Buddy Leadford was drawing a circle in the cindery dirt. Buddy was the marble millionaire of Elmwood School because his dad was a furnace repairman who found marbles in furnaces and air vents and places like that.

"Let's play for keeps," Wally undid the draw string on his marble bag.

Buddy frowned while digging around inside the gigantic pocketful of marbles on the front of his army pants. We weren't supposed to play for keeps around the school because some of the kids like Norman Hackenschmidt would go home and whine about being cheated, even when the game was fair.

"Aw, c'mon," Arvey said. "Ya must have fifty million of them at least."

"Yeah," I agreed. Arvey and I needed slingshot ammunition because we were going rat hunting next Saturday with our slingshots at the Twenty-ninth Street dump.

Just as Buddy was sorting through his stash, a police car drove up, slow and kind of sneaky, and parked under the big elm trees in front of the school. "Gosh," Arvey said. "Wonder what they want?"

We scooped up our marbles while watching the policemen get out of their car. All at once, the liver sausage sandwich started getting heavy in my stomach as they stood on the sidewalk looking into the trees. I cupped my hands to my mouth. "Here, Sam. C'mon."

"Keep callin' him." Arvey shoved his marble bag in the pocket of his blue jeans. "I'll shag around to the bike rack and get yer bike. He'll go with you if you start ridin' home."

Buddy didn't say anything. He just hitched up his pants while squinting through those thick glasses of his.

Just then, Mr. Fields hurried out of the school and started craning his neck and looking up too. One of the policemen pointed into the trees, then reached in the cop car and took a funny-looking pistol out. It was an air gun of some kind because he pumped it up six or seven times with a lever before aiming it into the trees.

"Here, Sam!" I yelled.

There was a sound like a cork popping out of a bottle, and Sam swore in the trees.

For a second, I just stood there without knowing what to do—like I was a little kid again and Richie and his brother were tossing my gray-and-white kitten back and forth. Came another hissing, clicking sound as the policeman pumped up the pistol again. Another pop echoed up and down the ravine running along one side of the school.

All at once, I was running and crying at the same time. Behind me clinked the rattle of marbles along with a wheezing sound. Without looking back, I knew Buddy was running too.

"Quit it!" I yelled. "Cut it out!"

Mr. Fields's big hands grabbed my arm. But I fought hard and grabbed his tie and pulled his head down next to my face. He grunted and I smelled tobacco and Sen-sen on his breath.

"All right now. All right." Mr. Fields grabbed my shoulders and pushed me back. He grabbed Buddy and pushed him back too. A big-eyed look popped out on his face when old Buddy tried to kick him in the crotch.

Now the world was full of grown-ups, all staring down at me and watching me cry. The policemen stopped, squinting into the trees and stood with their mouths open, as if they'd never seen kids as fierce as old Buddy and me. Then Mr. Stubbs was there too, with his big belly, his wheezy breath, and his gray shirt puffing in and out like there was a breeze blowing inside. "Ding blast it!" he yelled. "What're you jokers tryin' to do with that kid's pet?" Over in the playground a little girl started to cry.

Now there was a woman's voice. It was Miss Andrews, with her black hair flying and her red shoes clicking as she ran down the front steps of the school. "Please stop it! Just stop it," she said.

One of the other teachers ran over from the playground and grabbed Buddy and me. Talking in a low voice, she sort of herded us across the street. "It's all right. No one is going to hurt your crow."

From where we were standing, I couldn't hear what Miss Andrews was saying. Mostly, she talked to Mr. Fields, whose face flushed kind of red while she pointed into the trees, then nodded her head over to where Buddy and me and the other kids were standing around.

Mr. Stubbs, though—you could hear him. "Ding blast it. Honk-pfoot. Ought ta be ashamed of ya self, shootin' at a kid's pet, even if it is a dad gummed pain in the patoot."

You just can't tell about some people. You really can't.

Anyway, Mr. Fields kept tugging at his tie while Miss Andrews talked and Mr. Stubbs blew his nose. Finally, Mr. Fields said something to the policemen and walked back inside the school. The policemen got in their car and drove away.

Miss Andrews had a kind of fierce, dark look in her eyes when she came across the street. It faded when she saw Buddy and me. I smelled her lilac perfume again when she put her arm around my shoulder and gave me a squeeze. "It's all right now. Do you think Sam will follow you if you go home?"

Still crying, I managed to tell her I didn't know because Sam was scared and kind of mad about what was going on.

"Well, why don't you go home for the rest of the day? I have a feeling Sam will follow you after a while. I'll phone your mother and tell her you have permission to go home."

Wally had been playing softball, and he came and stood next to me with his new Luke Appling bat in his hand. "It's okay, Beaner." He picked up a marble-sized piece of gravel and batted it in the direction of where the police car had been parked. Then Arvey came pumping along like crazy on my bike. We weren't supposed to ride our bikes or hit pea gravel on the playground, but Miss Andrews didn't seem to notice. Even though I was still crying, I managed to smile a little bit as old Wally and Arvey and Buddy gave me a friendly shove as I got on my bike and took off down Thirty-first Street for home.

At first, I had trouble steering because my arms were shaking and my breath heaved in and out. It's tough when you've been crying so hard you can't stop the air from sort of getting caught in your chest.

Meantime, I'd forgotten to roll my pant leg up and got it caught between the sprocket and the bicycle chain. I was always doing that—forgetting to roll my pant leg up.

Wobbling like a tiddly wink, I coasted into a ditch and tipped over into the mud. I lay there, sort of swearing and crying for a while, then yanked my pant leg loose, hauled my bike out of the ditch and took off again.

I was just a couple of blocks from home when Sam dived right past my ear, cawing loud and excited, as if he was telling me about swiping old June's scarf and getting shot at by the police. Then it was almost like he was telling me everything was okay and I shouldn't worry anymore. I sort of knew he could tell how I felt, as if maybe there was an invisible thread attached to us both. You have to have a real good friend or a pet before you know what I mean.

I answered back, cawing loud. Soon his shadow came racing along the road beside my bike, then flicking, skippity-skip along a white picket fence I was riding past. A second later, the windy sound of his wings ruffled the back of my neck, and his claws dug through my T-shirt as he landed on my shoulder.

Brrrook brrroook, he gargled in my ear.

I started crying all over again. And laughing too. Sam cackled as he ran his beak back and forth across the back of my neck.

Chapter 27

"Horse apples!" Dad yelled. "Why in Sam Hill would anyone try to shoot a kid's pet crow?" Dad was pacing around in the kitchen, getting in Mom's way, and puffing like a volcano on a cigarette—about the umpteenth one he'd lit up since getting home. Most of the others were still lit and lying around in ashtrays and saucers. One even smoldered on the edge of the sink.

"Simmer down, Theodore." Mom had given up trying to set the table and was following Dad around, rubbing the back of his neck while he paced back and forth. "It's one of the parents, that's all. Mr. Fields got some phone calls because Sam flew off with some scarves and caps."

"Horse apples!" Dad yelled again, waving the hand his cigarette was in and spilling ashes on the kitchen table. "Well, he's about to get one more call, that's a cinch. I don't give diddley if he flew off with their socks and underwear."

Dad was on the warpath, that's for sure. He'd taken his hat off and put it on again about ten times. Finally, Mom took it away from him and sailed it into the living room. Now he was steaming around and rubbing his bald spot the way he did when he was really mad. When he got that way, Mom would jolly him along by rubbing the back of his neck and telling him if he didn't stop flying off the handle, he'd rub what little hair was left off the top of his head.

Dad stomped into the living room to call Mr. Fields. Of course, I wanted to go listen to Dad give Mr. Fields what for, but Mom said my ears were too tender for that. "Stay in the kitchen and look after your brother while he eats."

I tried my darndest to listen to Dad's half of the conversation but didn't have much luck. Old Carson John kept banging his spoon against the table and blowing mashed beets like spray paint back on to his plate. The only part I did hear was Dad flying off the handle and bellowing, "I'll buy every kid in the school a doggone helicopter beanie if that's the only thing bothering anybody."

Dad put the phone down and grumped back into the kitchen to get in Mom's way while she checked the rib roast in the oven.

"Well, anyway," he said, lighting another cigarette. "At least part of my faith in school principals has been restored. Mr. Fields hadn't called the police.

Someone living near the school rang up the police and said there was a rabid hawk diving at her kids and yanking clothespins off her clothesline."

"A rabid hawk!" I started to laugh.

"Wabbit awk." Carson John was dabbing bits of mashed beets across the high chair top.

"That's right," Dad snorted. "Anyway, Mr. Fields is sorry about the whole mess, and I apologized too. Meanwhile, we're supposed to do all we can to keep old Sam from going to school."

"Suppose we build him a cage," Mom suggested.

"No, sir." Dad stubbed out a cigarette, went to light another one, made a face at it, and stuck it behind his ear. "I'll put old Sam in the car, drive him all the way to Canada, and turn him loose before putting him in a cage."

"Eeeee." Carson John laughed and pointed his spoon at the dining room window. Sam was in the cottonwood tree, hooting and clucking and bobbing his head as if he agreed with everything Dad said.

Finally, we decided that we'd put Sam in the basement or maybe the kitchen every morning just before I left for school. Then Mom would turn him lose after about an hour. Usually, he'd show up at school after getting turned loose, but none of the teachers let him in their rooms. Mr. Fields had asked us not to wear caps and scarves for a while, so hanging around the school wasn't nearly as much fun. While we were all inside the school, Sam visited with Mr. Stubbs when he was out raking leaves. Pretty soon, though, he'd fly off, maybe figuring that visiting with pajama bottoms and rearview mirrors was more fun.

Pretty soon, it got to be October. And lots of times in the morning, frost sprinkled itself like sugar all over the ground. Chickadees and juncos kept fluttering and peeping their way south, and strands of geese made Sam jumpy and excited when they honked overhead. Sometimes it was all I could do to call Sam down from wherever he was overhead. And after landing on my arm, he'd dart his eyes back and forth, then fly off when the wild crows cawed above the woods and fields along the railroad tracks.

"Maybe it's just as well he's going wild. Maybe it's just a sign that he's getting to be a grown-up crow." Mom had stepped out of the house and was standing beside me as I tried to call Sam down from the top of his favorite fir tree. It was a crisp Saturday morning, and you could almost bite chunks out of the frosty air. Mom's breath mixed with steam wisping up from the cup of Maxwell House coffee she held in both hands.

Without saying a word, I just stood there and thought of not having Sam chattering in my ear or riding on my bike handlebars anymore. And when he took off from his fir tree and flew off cawing across Anderson's cornfield, I thought of going wild myself—like maybe being an Indian or a caveman running barefoot through the frosty grass and the dry, crackling leaves.

Chapter 28

Pretty soon, November 10 rolled around, the day before hunting season opened in Illinois. Dad brought home a big cardboard sheet cut from a toilet paper box at the store. The two of us went down in the basement and dug around until we located the rest of the brown paint used on the front and back porches last spring. Sam came with us, stepped on the open paint can lid and tracked his footprints all over the cardboard while we made a sign in big letters that said: Please do not shoot the tame crow.

Then Sam flew back and forth, jabbering and cawing while we walked over to the railroad tracks and nailed the sign up to a wooden power line pole.

"There." Dad took his hat off and rubbed his bald spot with the palm of his hand. "That ought to keep some trigger happy character from screwing up."

He rested one hand on my shoulder and gave it a squeeze. Then we walked home, scuffing our feet through dry leaves while Sam danced and bow-wowed on top of the green station house.

That night, a shivery wind blew out of the north, howling around the house like a ghost, or maybe a banshee of some kind. Trees close to the house swayed and groaned and clawed with their branches at the windowpanes. For the first time since last winter, my feet felt cold for a long time after I crawled into bed. I lay there, all curled up and shivery, listening to the wind and the trees before falling asleep.

Maybe it was for real, or maybe it was a dream, but our old house seemed like it was moaning and creaking all night in the wind. Sparky kept barking next door, and I thought I heard an owl hooting in the dark. I woke up several times, and each time I fell asleep, I dreamed I heard shotguns banging and echoing back and forth.

"Sam? Sam?" The next morning, I thrashed out of some partly remembered dream—about wolves I think it was—and sat up in bed. There was sweat in my hair and on my forehead, and it made me feel cold.

Bleep bleep. Yaw yaw yaw. Then I grinned as I heard Sam up on the roof arguing with the half-tame squirrel that lived part of the time in our backyard.

I hurried in to my clothes, ran downstairs, grabbed a slice of Mom's homemade bread, and went outside. It was going to be a warm day. The north wind was dead, and the sun had already started to melt the frost that sparkled like something good to eat across the ground.

Then Sam landed on my head and started rubbing his beak through my hair. I tore the bread in half, threw part of it on the porch roof for the squirrel, then started feeding the rest to Sam. While he ate, you could hear the bullying sound of shotguns grumbling back and forth down in the woods. I'd never been afraid of those sounds before. Now I was. Juncos and chickadees peeped in the lilac bushes along the edge of the fence, like maybe they were fearful of the shotguns too.

I was thinking about the crow shoot with Wally and his uncle Floyd when this greenish, rusty Ford pickup rattled across the tracks and parked along the edge of Thirty-third Street. Two guys got out of the truck. One of them was wearing an old army jacket, the other a red-and-white mackinaw. Both of them carried shotguns propped sort of carelessly across their shoulders.

"Har-har." The guy in the army jacket laughed and threw a brown bottle way up in the air. The other guy aimed and fired—the echo bouncing back and forth between our house and Anderson's barn.

After the shotgun went off, Sam flew into his fir tree and started screaming, *Caw caw caw.* The man in the red-and-white mackinaw wedged his gun under his arm, cupped his hands to his mouth, and tried to imitate Sam. Even though I was scared, I had to laugh. It was even worse than the stupid calls Richie made.

Laughing and hooting as they went, the men walked off down the tracks, and a little later, an old blue Chevie sputtered to a stop behind the pickup truck. A man in an orange jacket got out and turned loose two big black-and-tan dogs from the backseat. They jumped and frisked all floppy-eared around him, then ran sniffing through the grass below the edge of the railroad tracks.

The man started walking, saw the sign Dad had made, then stopped and looked around. The dogs loped up to him, then ran sniffing through the weeds again.

Sam started yelling, "Caw caw." He'd been on the roof trying to swipe bread from the squirrel. But when he saw the man, he flew toward the railroad tracks with me running after him as fast as I could. "Here, Sam," I yelled. "C'mon back."

I stubbed my toe on one of the railroad ties and almost fell down.

The man in the orange jacket had taken off down the tracks again, but when he heard me yelling, he stopped and turned around. Then Sam made this big, wide-winged swoop and landed on a telephone pole where he perched with his head yo-yoing up and down. *Chig a chig a chig.* It was a new sound he'd learned—like marbles rattling in a tin can.

From off in Anderson's cornfield somewhere, another shotgun blammed.

By now, I was running hard and breathing hard too. But then the man smiled at me and hollered," Hey, don't worry, sonny. I won't hurt your pet."

By this time, the two dogs had gallumphed up to me, all long-legged and friendly, with their tails wagging and their tongues slurping my hands and wrists. The man waved at me, so I waved back.

"Ark-ark," Sam barked.

The man jerked his head and whistled for his dogs until they loped after him down the tracks.

Not quite so scared now, I called for Sam, and we went back in the yard. In my back pocket, I had a red pea shooter I'd bought at the new Ben Franklin Store, and when Carson John toddled out on the back porch, I started shooting him with it—not very hard or anything, but hard enough to make him whine. But then I twanged him a good one on the ear, so he started to cry and went in the house.

Pretty soon, Mom came outside, scowling and looking around with her hands on her hips. By this time, I was hiding in some bushes next to the back fence while Sam was on the roof fighting with the squirrel again. A few seconds later, Mom went back in the house and shut the door. I was going to crawl out from under the bushes, then decided to stay hidden out in case she might see me and make me rake leaves.

Besides, it was nice under the bushes like that. The chickadees and juncos fluttered and peeped, some of them coming real close and perching only about five feet away. Another little bird called a nuthatch fluttered in and hung upside down on a branch until one of the juncos chased it away. Then the juncos sort of played tag in the bushes along the fence, and the chickadees fluttered on the ground and made rustling noises in the dry, curled-up leaves.

While watching those little birds, I started wondering what it was like to fly south, especially if you were so small. I mean, I could see how a Canada goose could migrate, because they were so big and all. But a teeny little bird like a chickadee had to flap its wings a thousand times, just to fly from one tree to the next.

Anyway, I was lying there thinking about flying south when Arvey and Wally came riding their bikes up Thirty-third Street and turned into the alley near to where I was hidden out.

"Remember," Arvey was saying, "we're gonna blast him as soon as he opens the door." When they rode past my hideout, I saw they each had a pea shooter stuck behind one ear.

"Okay." Wally rode one-handed, wobbling back and forth. "But watch out ya don't hit his ma." There was a sticker on the side of his German army helmet that said:

The Grand Canyon
Nature's Wonderland

I had to bite my lower lip to keep from laughing as they rattled by. Then I got out my pea shooter, stuffed half a handful of dried peas in my mouth, and waited while they got off their bikes, leaned them against the fence, and sneaked through the gate. I aimed at Wally's helmet and let fly.

Phooot . . . Ping.

Phooot . . . Ping. I nailed him again with another round.

"Uff. I-I'm hit." Wally grabbed both sides of his helmet and staggered around until he found a pile of raked-up leaves. Then he went stiff and fell over on his back.

"Take cover, men." Arvey tilted his head back and poured a batch of peas into his mouth.

"Dow dow dow!" I jumped from under the bushes and ran toward the back gate. While running, I turned and fired several rounds of peas at Wally and Arvey who were lying on the ground shooting back.

Ducking out the gate, I ran hunched over down the alley toward the weed lot next door. A dry pea tinged against the wire fence. Another zapped my cheek.

"Blast him!"

"Charge!"

I dived into the weeds, then bellied along the ground until I got to the cherry tree at the edge of Mrs. Powel's tomato patch.

Hunched behind the cherry tree, I crammed my mouth with more peas, waited a minute, and then looked. Nothing but high weeds and bent-over goldenrods.

And everything quiet, except for a blue jay screaming in the oak grove by the railroad tracks.

Then some dry goldenrod beside Mrs. McFarlan's shed quivered and waved back and forth. Like a turtle shell, or maybe the turret of a German tiger tank, Wally's helmet eased above the weeds, turning slowly back and forth.

I rolled another pea around my mouth and slid it into place.

Phooot . . . ping.

"Braaaap." Wally jumped out of the weeds and let fly in my direction with a salvo of peas.

"Yer dead," I hollered across the dry goldenrod.

"No, I ain't!"

"Y'are too!"

"Ain't!"

"Are."

"Are not!"

More peas rattled off the cherry tree branches. One of them stung my cheek.

"Gotcha!" Arvey was bellied out on the roof of Mrs. McFarlan's shed.

"No, ya didn't!" I blasted away at Arvey, then took off across Mrs. Powell's tomato patch. There was an old barrel full of shingles. Down behind it I went.

"Dow dow! Dow dow dow!"

"Brrrrraaaap!"

Peas were clattering like bullets off the side of Mrs. Powell's garage.

"Banzai!" I ran again and dived behind a rusty oil drum standing next to the alley.

Then the sound of a shotgun blast sort of slapped my face and made me blink. I felt sick inside.

"Geez! What was that?" Wally stood up, tall and gangly in the weeds.

"Somebody's shootin' over by the tracks!" Arvey came sliding off the top of Mrs. McFarlan's shed.

I was running really hard. But my feet felt slow and heavy in the mushy dirt of the tomato patch. "Sam," I kept yelling. "Sam!"

Wally's mouth gaped open as I ran past. Then I heard him running too.

I fell down. Got up. Ran again. Wally panted beside me as we ran across Galilee and jumped over the ditch on the other side.

"Wait up!" Arvey yelled as we raced through the oak grove and headed toward the tracks. We didn't slow up, and I remember Wally's helmet flying off and clattering past me as I slid on my fanny down the hill toward the tracks. Wally didn't bother to stop and pick it up.

Arvey caught up to us by the time we reached the ditch at the bottom of the slope. The three of us jumped over it, then clawed and heaved ourselves up on the tracks. My breath was pounding against the back of my throat, and I was crying, almost. Something awful had happened, and I kept screaming Sam's name over and over again.

We were maybe two hundred feet from the crossing at Thirty-third Street, and Wally and Arvey were yelling Sam's name too.

Ahead of us along the tracks, some guys were laughing—loud, nasty laughs—with swear words mixed in. It was the two hunters I'd seen earlier, and they were walking toward their pickup truck. One of them held another brown bottle in his fist. He lobbed it like a German hand grenade, the kind with a handle on one end.

"Wooooeeee!" he yelled.

It smashed against the tracks.

The other guy had something in his fist too. It was Sam, my beautiful pet crow. Only he wasn't beautiful anymore—just limp and tattered and hanging down by his skinny legs. With every long-legged step the guy took, Sam bumped dead and limp against his leg. I can hardly talk about it. Not even now.

Then the guy started swinging Sam around and around, like he was nothing but a dirty old rag. Sam's wings opened up like he was still alive, and he twisted back and forth in the guy's fist.

"You dirty guys! You dirty guys!" I'd never felt so little and alone, and I'd never screamed as loud as I did that awful time when I stood on the white rocks of the railroad tracks. He couldn't be dead. Not Sam. Not my bossy little friend.

The guy was swinging Sam so hard his wings made a soft shushing noise. Then he flung Sam so high and far that he was a messy blotch tumbling in the blue sky. I started running hard, stumbling across the white rocks and wanting to catch Sam before he hit the ground. But I knew I could never reach him, even if I lived to be a hundred years old. I heard this nasty clattering thump as Sam bounced and rolled across the white rocks.

I picked Sam up and pressed him against my neck. He was still warm, but his feathers were broken and stiff. Behind me Arvey was screaming, "I'm gonna get my dad!"

The men were walking fast, almost running as they headed for their pickup truck. I charged after them, still holding Sam and wanting to hit them with him so they'd feel his broken feathers and get bloody with his blood. Then I dropped him and picked up a rock. "You killed my crow! You killed my crow!"

"Hey!" the guy with the red mackinaw yelled and stumbled when the rock hit the side of his face. His shotgun clattered on the ground.

"Damnit," he yelled when I threw another rock.

I ran up to him and tried to kick him between the legs.

He pushed me and I went down. But I got up and ran at him, and he pushed me down again. "You killed my crow!" I scrambled up and clawed at him with my fingernails. Only girls are supposed to fight with their fingernails, but I didn't care.

"Aw, hell." He knocked me down again, but I got back up, put my head down, and butted him in the stomach as hard as I could. His muscles felt big and hard, like Richie's. But I wasn't scared. He could have been as big as ten Richies, and he could have killed me even, but I didn't care.

A pair of big hands grabbed me, jerked me around, and made me run across the tracks. I got to the frog ditch and flew out over it, high and far. I sucked in a deep breath, sort of swimming through the air before jolting down in a hard splotch of cold water and mud.

After that, I just laid there crying and hurting with my face pressed against cold mud. Wally was yelling how he was going to get his uncle's twelve gauge and blast them to shreds if they ever came back. And Arvey kept screaming, "I'm gonna get my dad!" Then quietness settled in, like some sort of cold, miserable fog.

After what seemed a long time, a train whistle moaned. I'd thought of just staying in the frog ditch and not getting up, ever again. But the train whistle made me think of Sam just lying there on the tracks. Even if he was dead already, it would be awful if the train howled by while he was flopped out on those white rocks.

I got up, and my pant legs flapped and swished as I climbed out of the ditch. Wally and Arvey were walking toward me along the edge of the ditch. I'd stopped crying, but when I saw them, I started up again. Arvey had his jacket off, and by the way he held it, I knew he had Sam wrapped up inside. I took my jacket off to wrap Sam with too, even though it was wet. Then Wally took his jacket off, and Arvey held Sam while Wally wrapped our jackets around him, folding them over and tucking them underneath.

"Oh jeez, Beaner. Uh-oh jeez." Arvey gave me the bundle, crying. And the bundle was so light it didn't feel like anything at all. Holding it against my stomach, I realized how little Sam really was. It had been the way he'd flown around stealing watches and helicopter beanies and tugging ears that made him so big. A terrible ache tore at my insides as I pressed the bundle against my cheek and walked all doubled over and sobbing toward the house.

Chapter 29

It was early morning just a few days after Sam had been shot. Lying in bed, I heard sparrows and jays, and some distant crow calls too. But no Sam. There were no squirrel sounds either. The day after Sam had been shot, Wally and I found the half-tame squirrel lying dead in the oak grove beside the tracks.

"Just shot him and left him." Wally said. "Didn't bother to skin him and take him home to eat."

I rolled over and faced the wall that was covered with cowboys riding bucking broncos and shooting rifles and pistols in the air. Only there was one place where some of the wallpaper was coming loose, so I started digging at it, like picking a scab. Underneath a bucking bronco, I found this picture of a teddy bear, leftover from the teddy bear wallpaper I'd had when I was a little kid. Wouldn't it be great, I thought, if a guy could go back to when he was little, just by pulling wallpaper off his wall?

I'd uncovered part of a teddy bear when there was the sound of Dad's footsteps coming up the stairs. I rolled over and faced the bedroom door as he came in the room. My pants were wadded up in the middle of the floor. Dad picked them up, grinned, and threw them at my head. "Hi," he said.

I grinned. "Hi, Dad."

When he sat on the edge of the bed, I was afraid he might notice the wallpaper. But he didn't. Instead, he reached down and Dutch rubbed the top of my head. "Hey. How'd you like to play hooky today?"

"Hooky?" I sat up.

"Sure. I was thinking we'd take an all-day hike, you and I. We can hike through Third Park over to the Northwestern railroad tracks, then on through Dunes Park and all the way to the lake."

"Wow!" I grabbed my wadded-up pants and started yanking the legs right side out. I told Dad it was a great idea—especially the hooky part.

Dad laughed. "Hey, an all-day hike just isn't a real all-day hike unless you're playing hooky at the same time."

Downstairs we sat in the kitchen and talked about the all-day hike while Mom fixed bacon and eggs. She was frying an extra slice of bacon, the way she'd done when Sam was alive. She split the extra slice between Dad and me while we ate our bacon and eggs.

"Ever have hamburgers wrapped in tinfoil?" Dad was buttering a slice of toast.

"No."

"Well, that's what we're going to have for lunch. Dad gave half of his toast to Carson John who began eating it upside down. "We'll build a fire, see. And when the coals get good and hot, we'll throw the hamburgers wrapped in foil right in and let them cook in their own juice.

It sounded like a great idea, even though I was full up to my ears with bacon and eggs. "But ain't they gonna burn if you get the fire too hot?"

"Never burned one in my life." Dad was shaking his head at Carson John who had pulled his T-shirt up and was getting ready to stick the toast's buttery side against his bare skin. "Used to cook them that way all the time when your uncle Norm and I'd go hiking in the woods."

"Did you do lots of stuff like that? Hiking in the woods?"

A dreamy expression drifted across Dad's face while he stirred his cup of coffee with a fork. Mom was always forgetting to give Dad a spoon with his coffee, so he'd stir it with anything, even a pencil if he had one behind his ear.

"Hiking in the woods? You bet. Did a lot of that. Trapped mink and muskrat in the swamp along Camp Logan Road. Bought my first bike with money saved up from selling mink and muskrat pelts."

"Wow!" I almost swallowed bacon down the wrong throat. "I've never seen a mink."

"Maybe we'll see one today." The dreamy look wandered across Dad's face again as he stirred his coffee around and around.

Breakfast over, Dad wiped the butter off Carson John's stomach, went to the refrigerator, and got out a big package of hamburger meat. While I sliced an onion, he made four big patties, hefting each one when it was done. Then he wrapped each hamburger in tinfoil with a slice of onion inside. "Cripes, they look good. Let's take one extra for the pot."

After stuffing the hamburgers in our pockets and promising Mom we wouldn't get wet and muddy, Dad and I went outside and walked through the front gate.

"Oh-oh. Make a run for it. Quick." Dad nudged me with his elbow, then took off running hunched over across Thirty-third Street. At the other side, he ducked behind a telephone pole.

I looked all around, not seeing anyone except Wally and his sister Joan riding their bikes away from us down Thirty-third Street. But what the heck. I took off after Dad, zigzagging as if a Jap sniper had me in his sights.

"Careful." Dad reached from behind the telephone pole and pushed me down on my hands and knees. "Can't let the police see you ditching school." He looked up and down Thirty-third Street, then lit out running toward the railroad crossing, cutting left, and heading on down the railroad tracks. Jumping up, I lit out after him, laughing out loud at the way his old Fedora hat was jiggling around and almost falling off his head. The air smelled sweet and crisp.

We ran until we were out of breath, then walked along, laughing and throwing rocks at power line poles. Soon we stopped at a place where a little stream called Rhineer's Creek flowed under the railroad tracks. I showed Dad the pool where this giant snapping turtle was supposed to live. The pool was like a dark mirror with reflected trees shimmering across its top. A purple oak leaf fell in the pool, and the reflections trembled and swam.

"Son of a gun." Dad took off his hat and scratched his head when I made a big circle with my arms to show how gigantic the turtle was. "A turtle that size must weigh at least fifty pounds."

I made the circle smaller. "Well, maybe it ain't quite that big. But it's a really big one just the same."

We stood at the pool's edge looking for the snapper but saw nothing except dead leaves floating around. Finally, Dad picked up a rock and threw it in the creek. "It's pretty late for turtles to be moving around, even as warm as it is. I bet that old whopper is buried in the mud and won't come out until next spring."

We left the turtle pool, walked down the tracks, and crossed the overpass at Wadsworth Road. Over a fence we climbed, then crunched through dry corn stubble to the edge of Third Park Ravine. "Hey, Dad," I said. "Let me show you the tree where Sam was born." We walked along the edge of the ravine until coming to the big white oak. Sam's nest was still there. A squirrel barked at us while I was pointing the nest out to Dad.

He said, "Whew. That's a long way up." Then he laughed while I told him how I nearly set my pants on fire sliding down over all that rough bark. The nest was ragged and empty now. But if you looked extra hard, you could see little puffs of down stuck to the outside of the nest. A kind of sadness drifted over me like a cold wind.

Dad had picked up some bright-colored leaves and was shuffling them back and forth in his hands. "Maybe next spring, you can get another crow."

"Don't think I want another crow." I'd picked up some leaves too and was rubbing them back and forth in my hands. They crumpled into flakes and blew off in the breeze.

"Don't be too sure." Dad smiled and poked some red maple leaves under his hat band. "I had this wonderful dog that got run over when I was a kid. First thing your grandpa Sabine did was crank up the old Ford and drive to the pound to pick up another dog."

I shook my head. "Another dog? Just after the old one had died?"

Dad gave me another Dutch rub on top of my head. "I don't want you to think I forgot about my old dog—Cap was his name. But I felt better right away. Had a new dog named Lucky to take care of. No time to feel sorry for myself. Know what I mean?"

"Yeah, I guess."

"Sometimes people let themselves get too miserable about things they can't change. It's almost as if they enjoy feeling sad."

"Well, I sure don't enjoy it—feeling sad. But maybe it ain't right to take something wild out of the woods."

Dad said, "You're right. Maybe old Sam would be alive if he hadn't been tame and hadn't trusted people so much. Then again, maybe a hawk or an owl would have eaten him. Or he could have been shot flying wild in the woods. There just aren't any sure bets in life."

That bothered me, like a scab, or my loose wallpaper that needed to be picked at sometimes. No sure bets. How awful not to be able to count on anything for sure.

But Dad wouldn't let me keep thinking those cold, miserable thoughts. Every time I got a long face, he'd Dutch rub my head or poke me in the ribs. It's hard to stay gloomy when you're being Dutch rubbed or tickled half to death.

Anyway, we hiked through Third Park, working our way along the creek and sailing twigs and leaves downstream. A little redstart warbler followed us for a while, twittering and darting along like an Indian scout watching us from the underbrush. After about half an hour, we crossed the Northwestern railroad tracks and waded on into the swamp. Wild geese flew up ahead of us. Their wings whooshed, and water sprayed out behind.

We waded to some dry hummocks and sat for a while, hoping to see some muskrats moving around. It didn't take long for our rear ends to get cold, so we went on without seeing one.

While sitting still, I'd thought some more about what Dad had said about no sure bets in life. He was probably right. But it bothered me, not being able to count on anything and having your pet crow killed by a couple of guys who were half-drunk and having fun being mean. And it bothered me some more when I remembered the time Dad had told me it was important to believe in something and have faith. Like old Mr. Marquand who was sure God had blown the awning through Dad's store window last July.

I thought more and more about it, kind of picking away while we hiked to a place where the swamp got narrow, maybe only fifty feet wide. It was called Dead River now. In another mile or so, it would empty into Lake Michigan.

We started following Dead River as it wound through a stand of pines. We threw pine cones in the river and listened to red-winged blackbirds flocking up to fly south. There were crows too—a whole mob of them raising Cain in the top branches of some tall pines.

All at once, I felt ready to cry and said, "If there ain't any sure bets, how is it that a guy can have faith?"

Dad was walking bent over, trying to find mink tracks for me to see. He straightened up. "Faith?"

"Yeah. You know. Like Don Coyote—whatever his name was. And old Mr. Marquand, the funny guy who thought Dowie was still alive."

Dad was kind of mixed up about what I'd said, so I asked him again.

"Well." He shook his head. "I don't know for sure. All I know is that a person should have some kind of faith."

"I used to have lots of faith. Only I ain't going to have it no more. Not after what those guys did to Sam."

Dad kept quiet for a while as the two of us looked for tracks along the riverbank. There were raccoon tracks, like little handprints in the mud. And deer tracks too. The first I'd ever seen.

I was looking at the deer tracks when Dad straightened up. "Maybe it's all the more important to have faith because there are no sure bets in life."

"Well, jeez. Why?"

I felt Dad's arm go around my shoulders. "I'm not quite sure."

Then we got to talking some more about faith, with Dad trying to convince me that even if you had what seemed to be the wrong kind of faith, it was better than having no faith at all. I just couldn't see how anything could be good if it seemed to be wrong.

Dad said, "Well, look. That funny old codger, Mr. Marquand. Didn't we agree that his faith kept him going, even though you and I both thought he was as crazy as a loon? And how about poor Mrs. Funk, that old lady that lived with Grandma for a while?"

I grinned and nodded. "Yeah?"

Dad picked up a rock and skimmed it across Dead River. "Well, maybe she's another example of what can happen when a person loses their faith. For years, she probably convinced herself that God would protect her, no matter what. Maybe she believed that all she had to do was fold her hands and pray. I think God doesn't do things that way. He just doesn't go around protecting people from every bad thing that happens in life. And maybe when the poor old soul discovered God doesn't hand out that kind of insurance policy, she lost her faith and just gave up after that. The way Don Quixote did."

We walked on, skipping rocks and throwing sticks in the river until we came to a place where a little pond was set back from the river about fifty feet or so. It had been connected to the river by a sort of channel. But the channel had dried up because of the funny way Dead River has of changing course when it gets near the lake.

"Look there." Dad pointed to animal tracks in the dried-up mud leading over to the pond.

I was following some raccoon tracks across the mud when all of a sudden, something heaved up and made a big ripple in the middle of the pond.

"A snapping turtle," I yelled.

"Where?"

"Over there. Look."

Something really big and rubbery heaved up and made a loud splat.

Dad laughed. "That's not a snapping turtle. That's a carp. Look. There's another one over by that log."

I looked to where Dad was pointing, and then the log itself moved.

"Cripes," Dad yelled. "That is one big carp."

We stood there and watched that big carp we'd mistaken for a log heave and roll in the middle of the pond. Other carp heaved and rolled too. You could tell they'd been stranded when the channel to the river dried up. Now they were thrashing in water that was only about a foot deep.

"Phew." Dad kicked at a dried-up, half-eaten carp that a raccoon had probably hauled out of the pond. After he turned it over with his foot, several beetles skittered across the dry mud.

"Let's save them," Dad said all at once.

"Huh?" I'd been lobbing chunks of dry mud into the pond.

"Come on. Let's haul those big ugly fish out of this mud hole and put them back in the river where they belong."

I looked at Dad, then at the carp. One was near enough for me to see its mouth gulping and its gill covers panting up and down. Like a big old flash of lightning, Dad's suggestion sounded like the best idea in the world.

First, we took off all our clothes, except for our underwear, although Dad put his hat back on his head. Then we waded in after the big carp we'd mistaken for a log. It flopped all around the pond with us right after it, sliding and falling down and getting really gooey before we pinned it between our knees. It was thick and strong, and I could feel it fighting hard between my legs.

"Come on, old horse." Dad jammed his fingers under the carp's gills and heaved it out of the mud. It was three feet long at least, and its scales gleamed kind of silver-gold in the sun.

"Wow!" Dad shouted, the little kid in him busting out. "I bet that old codger weighs at least thirty pounds." A funny look crinkled his face. "You know what. I bet these carp aren't really carp at all. They're fair maidens who've had a magic spell cast on them by an evil witch. They've been waiting patiently for Don Quixote and his sidekick, Sancho Panza, to show up"

"That's a fair maiden?" I whooped.

"Of course. Look. Look at its lips. It's just waiting to be kissed in order to break the magic spell." Dad was laughing and holding the carp close to his face. Sure enough, its lips made a kind of gurgling, smooching sound.

I thought I might fall in the mud from laughing so hard when Dad made a face, puckered up, and gave that old carp a kiss. Then I skipped around him, trying to help, but mostly getting in the way while he dragged the carp along the dried-up channel and dumped it into Dead River. There was this big King Kong splash, and it swam out of sight.

Well, back in that mucky old pond we slopped, running and belly flopping and laughing when Dad's hat fell off and got squished underfoot. The carp, or fair maidens, were big and slippery; and I had to hug the ones I caught against my chest. "Remember," Dad kept yelling, "you've got to give each one a kiss."

Meanwhile, it seemed like the crows in the pines were cheering us on while we spent the next half hour or so hauling at least three dozen giant carp out of the pond. And we rescued a few suckers and bullheads for good measure after we got done with the carp, sort of like making up for the fish Wally and I couldn't scoop out of the Zion Pond. At first, I didn't care much for the mud. It was slippery and cold, even if it was a really warm day for November—almost hot. But after the mud got smeared on thick enough, it was almost like a celebration every time I flopped after a fair maiden carp. And after what had happened a few days ago, it seemed like Dad and I couldn't have picked anything more important to do that day.

After hauling the last carp, bullhead, and sucker out of the pond and fishing Dad's hat out of the mud, we squished over the dunes and went swimming near the mouth of Dead River. The bottom was sandy there, and the water was fairly clear. It sure was icy, though. We got out and ran gasping up and down the beach. "Wowie," Dad said. "We sure do stink."

Sure enough, that gaggy carp smell followed us around, no matter where we went. So we went and rolled around in the warm sand, then splashed into the river again. After doing that a couple of times, we still smelled a little like fish, but we agreed we'd gotten used to it by now.

"I don't care how bad we stink," I said. "It was worth it—what we did."

"Shoot yes," Dad agreed.

"I'll never forget what Dad looked like when he said that. There he was, still wet and naked, except for his hat and a light coating of sand. He'd just lit a fire to warm us up and cook the hamburgers with. And when the flames licked around the twigs he'd stacked up, he took his hat off and fanned it back and forth. He looked comical but, at the same time, kind of wise.

"Well." He coughed and squinted, turning away from the smoke. "As soon as we dry off, we probably ought to at least put our underpants on, just in case some little old ladies from the birdwatcher's society come hiking over the dunes."

A warm Indian summer breeze had been blowing up from the southwest, and the lake was smooth, almost like glass. We started skipping rocks, and Dad said he'd never seen such beautiful fall weather and such calm water on the lake this time of the year.

While skipping rocks and tending the fire, I kept thinking about the carp and how they'd gasped and flopped around in the mud, fighting really hard to stay alive until Dad and I'd come along. I decided if I ever found another batch of carp or even bullheads and suckers dying like that, I'd try saving them too.

I could tell Dad was thinking too. Maybe about the carp. He kept looking back toward the pond and at the flock of crows on the other side. They were yelling and carrying on in the pines like kids arguing over a softball game.

"Maybe there isn't any right or wrong faith," he said all at once.

"Huh?"

"Well, whatever kind of faith you need to keep going—maybe that's the kind of faith you need."

Now the crows were making an even bigger ruckus in the pines. At least a dozen of them screamed in crow talk as they hopped and flapped back and forth. Then the whole mob of them took off racing toward the swamp, like maybe their softball game was over and now they were playing tag.

"And by golly," said Dad all at once. "You know what kind of faith a couple of muddy, smelly characters like us need to have?" He reached over and gave me another Dutch rub that ground about a ton of sand into the top of my head.

"Ouch." I looked up and laughed at the way his old hat was shriveled up and sort of squatting like a toad on top of his head.

"Well, I'll tell you," he went on. "We need to have faith that there will always be a swamp to hike in, some smelly carp to rescue, and a flock of crows to see cawing overhead." I didn't quite know what Dad meant. But what he said made me feel good anyway. Looking out over the swamp, I saw that the crows had circled over it and were chasing each other back toward the pines. *Caaaaaaw caaaaaaw caaaaaaw* Even though they were far off, their voices sounded close.

While watching them, I started thinking about the old Weed Lot Bum and how he'd gotten into that poison, maybe because I hadn't taken him home. But then there was Sam. He'd been shot because I had taken him home, and he was so tame and trusted everyone. Dad was right. You couldn't tell for sure how things were going to turn out. You just had to have faith.

Like those carp floundering around and hanging on to life, even though their pond was nearly dried up.

By this time, the crows had flown back from the swamp, screaming and circling and playing tag through the pines, as if they never worried about a single thing. I felt happy, but at the same time kind of sad, maybe like dandelion fluff blown off by the wind and forever gone. Cupping my hands around my mouth, I cawed at the crows, the way I used to caw for Sam, only louder than ever before.

Dad was laughing behind me and saying the crows reminded him of noisy innocent kids playing tag. "Innocence," he said. "Maybe it's another word for 'faith.'" Then he started cawing at the crows too. *Caaaaw caaaaw caaaaaw.*

The crows came racing over the pines. Then over the pond where we'd rescued the carp. *Caaaw caaaaaw caaaaaw.*

The skin on the back of my neck really started tingling as they flew right overhead. A couple of them swooped so low you could hear the whoosh of their wings.

Caaaaaw caaaaaw! Now they were this big noisy circle overhead. Sometimes they just hung there on the wind. Then they dipped and swooped, like sliding down a long airy hill.

Caw caaaaw caw.

Circle. Then swoop.

And it was as if Sam was with them up in the sky. *Caw caw caw.*

Dad and I kept answering them, our heads thrown back, cawing loud.

Cawing so loud—it seemed like our lungs and maybe the rest of our insides might bust wide open as we flung our voices and maybe even a part of our souls higher and higher.

Into the clear, autumn sky.

Edwards Brothers Malloy
Thorofare, NJ USA
October 4, 2012